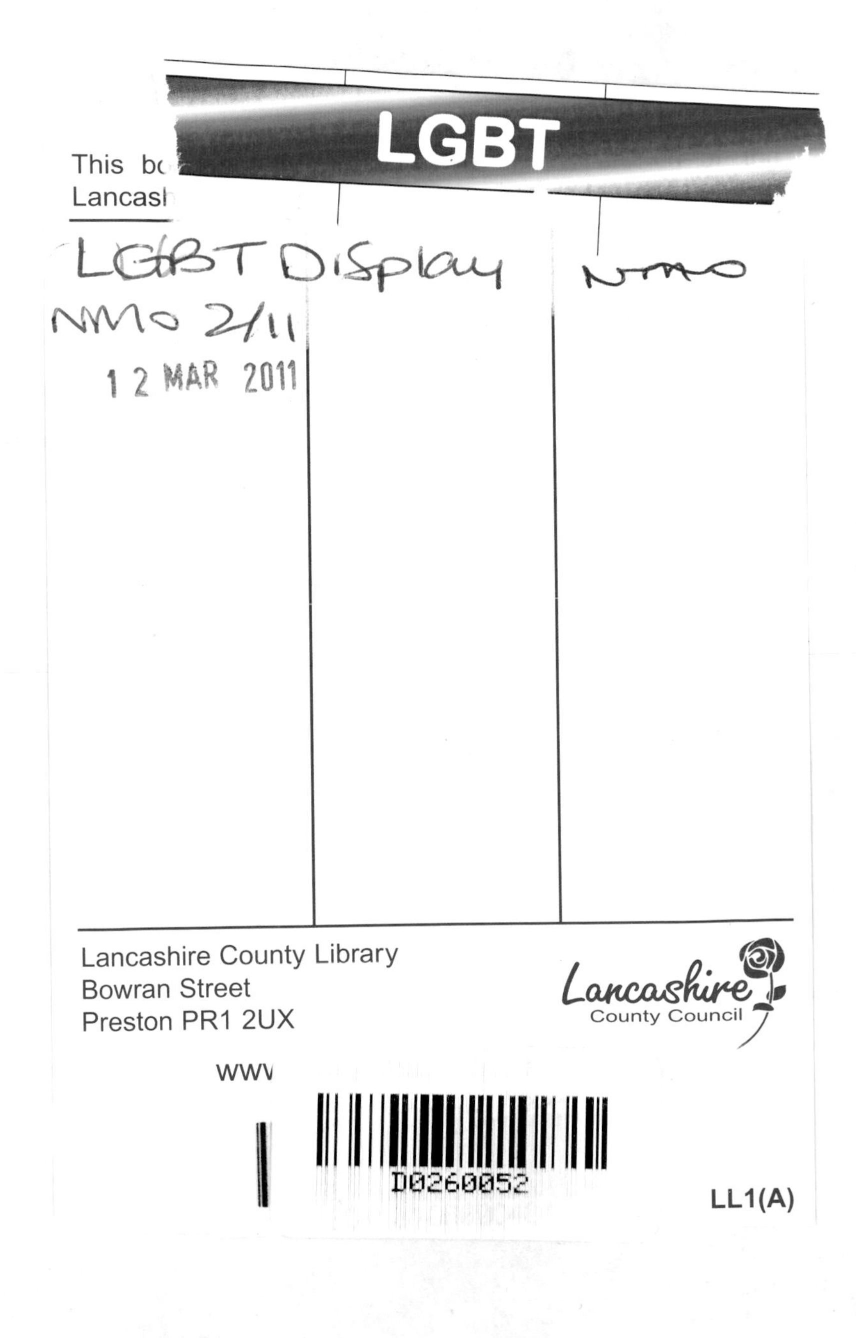
LGBT
This bo
Lancash
LGBT Display
NMO
NMO 2/11
12 MAR 2011
Lancashire County Library
Bowran Street
Preston PR1 2UX
Lancashire County Council
www
D0260052
LL1(A)

What Reviewers Say About The Author

"Fulton has rescued the romance from formulaic complacency by asking universal questions about friendship and love, intimacy and lust. The answers reflect both depth and maturity; this is the romance novel grown up a bit. Girl gets girl is always popular; more inspirational is when the girl gets to know herself."—*The Lesbian Review of Books*

"Fulton takes an age old formula for love and plants it in modern surroundings. The writing is smart and quick, and she portrays innocence with loving, irresistible humor. She delivers flesh-warming, flush-inducing seduction and pages of slippery, richly textured sex. Her knack for depicting current social dilemmas also makes her a compelling contemporary author."—*The Lesbian Review of Books*

"Fulton has penned another wonderfully readable, erotically-charged book…fun, and well worth your time."—*Lambda Book Report*

"Fulton tells a dark and disturbing tale of friendship and betrayal, of love lost before it has a chance to begin. That may sound rather hackneyed but her use of these themes is anything but trite. The writing is outstanding…Fulton creates characters that live on in the memory and in the heart…An extraordinary novel. I could not put it down and days later, I'm still thinking about it."—*Bay Area Reporter*

"Perhaps needless to say, the paths the friendships take are fraught with, among other things, lust, unrequited love, infidelity and dishonesty. Good intentions are trampled in the pursuit of passion. Problems, both past and present, shape the relationships the women share….The writing is sharp…a realistic account of contemporary urban lesbian life."—*Melbourne Star Observer*

"The ending left me grinning to myself for hours and wishing for an immediately available sequel…One of the best writers on the roster….Her books are always entertaining and often thought provoking."—*Dimensions*

"I'm not sure why I found the book so completely erotic. The author knows how to tease and how to deliver."—*Lesbiana*

"One of those books that is hard to put down until you finish it… Whether you're in the perfect relationship or still looking for it, you'll enjoy this story."—*MegaScene*

By the Author

ROMANCES as Jennifer Fulton

Moon Island Series

Passion Bay

Saving Grace

The Sacred Shore

A Guarded Heart

Solace

Heartstoppers Series

Dark Dreamer

Others

True Love

Greener Than Grass

More Than Paradise

CONTEMPORARY FICTION as Grace Lennox

Chance

MYSTERIES as Rose Beecham

Amanda Valentine Series

Introducing Amanda Valentine

Second Guess

Fair Play

Jude Devine Series

Grave Silence

Sleep of Reason

More Than Paradise

by

Jennifer Fulton

2007

MORE THAN PARADISE

ISBN: 10-digit 1-933110-69-4
13-digit 978-1-933110-69-1

This Trade Paperback Original Is Published By
Bold Strokes Books, Inc.,
New York, USA

First Edition: February 2007

Credits
Editors: Stacia Seaman
Production Design: Stacia Seaman
Cover Photo by Sheri
Cover Design By Sheri (GRAPHICARTIST2020@HOTMAIL.COM)

Acknowledgments

Novels cannot be written in a vacuum. I am very fortunate to have led an adventurous life, mostly as a consequence of a common-sense deficiency, and to be surrounded by people who intrigue me. An author could not hope for richer sources of inspiration. I worked on this novel with the support and encouragement of the women who make my life make sense: Fel, Sophie, Wyn—my mother, and JD.

Stacia Seaman has my sincere thanks for her careful editing and willingness to operate a tight timetable. And, as always, Sheri's wonderful cover is a credit to her gifts and skills much more than to any dull-witted suggestions I could ever make—but thank you for asking.

Finally, I thank Radclyffe for being the publisher authors hope to have. Without her encouragement and mentoring, this job would be so much less rewarding.

Dedication

For my sweetheart. Thank you for the orchids.

Visit us at www.boldstrokesbooks.com

Author's Note

I have always wanted to set a passionate romance in the renegade seediness of postcolonial New Guinea, a place unmatched on this planet for its mystery and dangerous enchantment. This novel would not make sense if I didn't touch upon the plunder of this extraordinary land and its indigenous people by the merchants of misery now exploiting it. So if you prefer mostly sweetness and light in your romances, you may like some of my other stories more.

However, I hope those of you who spend your hard-earned money on *More Than Paradise* enjoy reading it as much as I enjoyed writing it. Thank you for buying my books. You are the reason I write them.

CHAPTER ONE

The babe in the pink dress was making eye contact. She had designs, no question. Ash Evans knew every cue in the book, from the slow, sensual application of lipstick to the legs crossed then uncrossed. The exaggerated pout and the occasional head toss to extend a succulent throat. The hand absently caressing the skin where her neckline plunged. Hair tampering. Tip of the tongue teasing. Finally the hot come-hither look that said, *Buy me a drink.*

It took slightly less than three seconds for Ash to signal the barman and order a repeat of whatever girlie cocktail the hottie was sculling. Although this was an upscale club, she didn't wait for one of the sleek staff to carry the *okay, I'm tempted* offering to the table fifteen feet away. Instead she negotiated her way through a smorgasbord of exposed flesh and set the napkin and brimming martini glass in front of the seductive blonde.

Femmes liked to hunt in pairs, Ash had learned that long ago. This one was on the prowl with spare bait, a fetching Rita Hayworth look-alike, complete with chestnut waves to her shoulders and a slinky retro cocktail dress. Normally Ash would have bought her a drink, too, but she seemed intent on nursing the one she had, the designated driver maybe. All the same, Ash offered to flag down a cocktail waiter right after she'd introduced herself.

The brunette, who had *Trust Fund Baby* stamped on her head and said her name was "Carla spelled Karlah," proceeded to ruin her fifties-goddess impersonation by declaring, "No, it's cool. I'm doing lunch with the folks tomorrow, so, like, seriously…two drinks and I'm totally on notice. I mean, you have *no* idea. Rehab. Both of them."

Her companion added, "Omigod, your mom can smell last week's cosmos at, like, a thousand paces." The galpals giggled and the blonde extended her hand daintily to Ash, announcing, "I'm Dani Bush. No relation."

"Well, that's encouraging."

"Sit," Dani commanded, like Ash was a hunky version of a Chihuahua.

Ash deposited her sipping whiskey and recruited a chair from a neighboring table. As she got comfortable, both women surveyed her with blatant sexual interest. Apparently she could take her pick. This, she had to admit, was a relief. She'd been Stateside for seventy-two hours, a record for the usual lag time between hitting the tarmac and getting laid. She'd been busy and the wait had made her even hornier than her vacation norm. No wonder. She hadn't so much as smelled a woman she'd want to fuck in three months.

"You're not from 'round here, are you?" Karlah asked.

Ash checked her out thoroughly. For reasons that baffled her, she often missed the chance to score with an attractive brunette if there was a platinum blonde within fifty feet. But Karlah was very attractive indeed. Her features were more even than Dani's and she had cheekbones. Everything had been fixed, Ash guessed. The nose, the smile, the chin, and although she was probably under thirty, her serene brow suggested she was already well acquainted with that shit women got injected into their faces.

Not that Ash had any complaints. Every time she returned to civilization she was thankful for well-maintained eye candy. To answer Karlah's conversation starter, she said, "I live overseas."

"London, right?" Dani guessed.

"Wrong."

Dani tilted her head and flicked a shimmering strand away from her cheek. "Hmm. The accent. You're American but you haven't lived here for, like, years."

Ash nodded. "You have a good ear."

And excellent breasts. Dani was more successful at starving herself than Karlah, but the breasts made up for the bony shoulders, and amazingly they looked like the real thing. Ash was happy about that. Lately she'd encountered more and more of those weirdly round fakes perching like grapefruit on women's chests. They were never the same and she got nervous handling them, knowing a bag of evil lay just below the surface.

Dani took another stab at the accent. "Australia?"

"Close. Papua New Guinea. I spend a lot of time with the Aussie expats working over there. Maybe the accent has rubbed off."

"I like it," Karlah noted. "It's hot."

"Totally," Dani agreed, cruising Ash some more. "Papua New Guinea..." She frowned, evidently searching some rarely explored recess of her mind. "Oh, shut up! They've only got, like...headhunters there, don't they?"

"A few. In the highlands. No one goes up there unless they're stupid."

Both women squealed.

"No way! Cannibals?" Karlah confirmed with breathless horror.

Dani planted a small hand where her cleavage intersected. "Omigod, can you imagine?"

"Cannibalism is almost unknown now," Ash said curtly.

She needed to change the conversation. Already, she could feel the beginnings of irritation. Westerners who knew nothing about the region or its complex tribal cultures usually flaunted their ignorance by repeating the most titillating stereotypes. No doubt Dani and Karlah pictured a real-life version of that asinine television show *Survivor*.

Ash didn't kid herself that New Guinea would be transforming itself into a contemporary society any time soon. But as far as cannibalism went, the practice had all but disappeared. The Asmat in West Papua were the most dangerous of the cannibals. In their culture anyone who had never taken a head in battle went to his grave feeling like a sad failure who had betrayed the spirits of his ancestors.

The tribe was rumored to have killed and eaten Michael Rockefeller, the son and heir of Nelson Rockefeller. Back in the sixties, he'd been studying Asmat culture and was in their territory with another anthropologist when their canoe capsized. He vanished, and the ensuing search-and-rescue operation was the biggest the country ever saw.

The official conclusion was that he had drowned and been eaten by crocodiles. Ash had heard a very different tale from an old Asmat guide she hired occasionally. He said a white man had been killed in Otsjanep long ago, in revenge for the murder of the village leaders by the Dutch. Many years later another white man visited and paid an impressive bounty for three prized skulls. They were the skulls of the only white people ever killed and eaten by the tribe. Ash had always wondered if Michael Rockefeller's was among them.

The rumor had spread and these days tour companies brought thrill-seeking clients into the region and paid the local tribesmen to display their skull collections. Some day, Ash figured a party of Westerners would insult or double-cross their hosts and end up on the dinner table. The Asmat hadn't forgotten their old ways, they had simply found new ones that paid better.

They were not the only cannibals in the area. Ash was certain human flesh was still eaten upstream of Asmat territory by a couple of tribes in the Jayawijaya Mountains. There were some who had still never seen a white person. A few weeks before she'd caught the plane back to modernity, she had been drinking with a Californian tour guide in a pub in Bougainville. The guy had been making a buck hauling groups of flea-brained tourists on rafting trips in the high country, as only a card-carrying lunatic with a death wish would. He and his party got themselves ambushed one day when a group of tribesmen cut down some trees to slow their passage through a neck of water. At first the guide thought the noisy locals just wanted to sell souvenirs to the tourists. Then they started firing arrows.

He'd quit his job after that narrow escape and seemed astonished that his passengers were happily snapping photos the whole time while he was fighting to keep their asses out of the fire, so to speak. Ash felt like saying, *Wake up, pal.* In her experience, most tourists thought everything was part of a show staged expressly for their entertainment. That's why they made such great targets in a place like PNG. They had no idea how to keep a low profile or why they needed to. Wasn't the world one big fun park for the dumb, happy, and privileged?

Those rafters had been dead lucky that the average New Guinea tribesman was a lousy shot and still hadn't progressed far enough from the Stone Age to put feathers on his arrows. That was one reason the Indonesians had been able to annihilate them so successfully since they took over West Papua. So far about thirty percent of the indigenous population had vanished to make way for the likes of Freeport-McMoRan and their "vital projects." Where would the world be without another gold mine?

Ash steered her mind determinedly away from that track. She was here to kick back and have a good time, not guilt-trip herself into another drunken stupor, thinking about things she had no control over.

"What are you doing over there, anyway?" Dani asked.

"I'm a consultant in local affairs for foreign business interests." It sounded better than *I'm a mercenary soldier turned hired gun and chopper pilot, services for sale to the highest bidder. No questions asked. Specialties—drug lords trying to muscle rivals, mining executives scoping out new places to plunder, military goon squads hired by said mining executives as "security," plus the usual scumbags who show up in Port Moresby looking for a place to hide.* PNG was one of the world's primo destinations if you were on the run from the law. Or anything else.

"Cool," both women said.

"So you're here on vacation?" Dani sipped her cocktail and took a moment to slowly, temptingly lick the excess off her lips.

Ash registered the come-on with a throb between her legs. Automatically she cast a glance around the bar, sizing up the alternatives just in case Dani and Karlah turned out to be nothing but bored housewives taking a walk on the wild side by flirting with a lesbian. The odds of scoring with such women were only slightly better than fifty percent and not worth her time. She was pretty sure Dani was looking for action, but she had been wrong before.

A mature, lushly attractive redhead a few tables away offered up a smile. A brittle blonde at the bar made eye contact. She always got lucky here, Ash reflected. She had no idea why the place was a hang-out for upscale lesbians looking for no-strings sex, but she counted on it whenever she was in Boston. Ash acknowledged each of the women with a warm, flattering sidelong glance. She'd be back here tomorrow, looking for company again. Maybe one of them would show up on the off chance.

Returning her attention to Dani, she said, "I'm in town for family reasons. But that's not going to take up *all* of my time."

How long would the dance continue? Ash hoped no one would have to tell her life story. A friend was always a complication, too, maybe more so tonight since both women seemed interested. Ash would happily settle for either. Her mind latched on to that idea and expanded on it. Picturing both her companions naked, she reached for her whiskey and felt her shirt slide across her tightening nipples. She could go there, she reflected—two babes and her horny self. No problem.

She lowered her gaze to the amber-red liquid in her glass and reminded herself that girl-on-girl threesome action only happened in porn movies when actresses got paid, and it was schmucks like her whose money paid them. She had quite a collection of so-called lesbian porn back in Madang. Occasionally, when she left a DVD in the player by accident, she would come home and find her houseboy and cook watching it in bemusement. None of the PNG locals had ever heard of a lesbian, let alone seen two women getting it on in the sack, while wearing white stilettos the whole time, too, of course.

A hand connected possessively with her arm and Dani informed her, "We're going home soon. Want to come?"

Ash repeated the invitation in her mind and figured she should nail down exactly what was on offer. Women were sometimes just being nice and had visions of serving late-night coffee and talking about politics. Tonight she wasn't in the mood to be disappointed, so she got right to the point.

"Only if you're going to get naked with me."

She said it mildly enough that it could sound like she was kidding. That way things didn't have to get awkward if Dani had something other than bare skin in mind. But the baby blue eyes flirting with Ash got smoky and Dani lowered her hand from Ash's arm to her thigh.

"Sure," she answered the question. "Want to watch?" Her fingers beat a rapid path upward.

For the sake of public decorum Ash arrested their progress just short of her crotch and smothered the groan of desire that tightened her throat. It had been way too long. "That would be a yes."

Dani and Karlah exchanged knowing looks. Karlah didn't seem pissed in any way that her friend was scoring and she wasn't. Ash felt mildly irked by that. Didn't Karlah find her hot? This adolescent reaction amused her. She wasn't used to getting the brush-off in any form and it made her want the unimpressed woman.

"Let's get out of here." Dani eagerly flagged down their cocktail waiter, who returned a few minutes later with a couple of fur coats and handed the check to Ash.

Once the Amex slip was signed and the women had on their status-symbol pelts, Dani started fumbling around in her oversized purse for the valet pass. While this was going on, Ash was surprised to feel a hand on her butt.

"I hope you have lots of energy," Karlah murmured hotly in her ear. "We're both, like…needy."

Ash's pulse accelerated. It hadn't occurred to her that they might all be on the same page in the fantasy department. Now that she thought about it, she could see why these two were hunting together.

"You won't be disappointed," she said.

Karlah appraised her thoroughly. "That's quite a promise."

"I don't make any I can't keep."

"Well, you just got *very* lucky, Ashley Evans," she pronounced and wrapped an arm around Dani's waist.

Both babes offered greedy little smiles.

CHAPTER TWO

How long was it going on?" Charlotte Lascelles handed her best friend, Tamsin, a Kleenex and a compact mirror.

Tamsin wiped her running mascara and blew her nose, which made even more of a mess of her lipstick. "Months," she hiccupped. "I can't believe I could be so stupid. When I think about it now, it was so fucking obvious."

She slapped the tissue down onto a mushy heap cluttering the table. Charlotte hoped the waiter would remove them soon. She didn't like the thought of all that mucus accumulating near her dessert.

"Don't be so hard on yourself." She nudged her barely touched crème brûlée to one side. "It's not your fault you trusted your partner and gave her the benefit of the doubt. You're a decent person."

"She used me. All she really wanted was a part in Dad's new show."

Well, duh! Charlotte kept her mouth shut. She'd known Dani Bush was a gold-digging bimbo the moment they'd met. Since then, she'd been waiting for the other shoe to fall for Tamsin.

"I can't believe the lies." Tamsin snuffled. "It's like I never knew her at all."

"I'm so sorry you're hurt, sweetie." This was not the time to state the obvious—that Tamsin had refused to see what was right under her nose and only had herself to blame.

Tamsin sipped her coffee. Her eyes had the faraway look of a woman mining past events for the clues she should have added together. "I suppose I got suspicious four months ago, but I kept thinking I was being paranoid."

"I know how that is," Charlotte said dryly.

She'd been there herself during her one attempt at a long-term relationship. It had been hard to believe that Britt Conway, the successful attorney who talked all the time about the future they would build, the children they would have, and the importance of open and honest communication, had cheated on her. Worse than that, despite her deep suspicions, Charlotte had allowed herself to be taken in by Britt's denials. She had even felt guilty and stupid when her initial attempts to seek reassurance were met with angry recriminations. Britt's righteous indignation had eventually culminated in physical violence, at first shoves and slaps, then punches and kicks. Then much, much more.

Only when Charlotte found herself in the emergency room at Massachusetts General with a broken collarbone, two broken ribs, and a black eye did she finally accept who her partner really was. Not the woman of her dreams who needed support and understanding because her work was so stressful, but an alcoholic in denial, unable to take responsibility for her behavior. She'd made herself a promise that night. No one would ever lay a hand on her again. Never again would she ignore her instincts.

Every train-wreck relationship she'd witnessed among her circle of friends since had added to her conviction that love was overrated and not worth mutilating heart and soul for. In fact, she'd concluded that love virtually guaranteed bad decision-making. Especially in her case.

Since Britt, her relationships had been few but pleasant because she only dated women who were as sensible and pragmatic about romance as she was. In other words, it was nice in theory, but in practice it did not occupy center stage in their lives. Charlotte supposed there were wonderful soul-mate relationships out there, but she didn't know anyone who had one. Like mice on a treadmill, everyone seemed to endlessly repeat the same futile journey from lust to deluded optimism and commitment, then steadily downhill to disillusion and sorrow. All that misery, yet they still returned yet again to the quicksands of hope. Charlotte knew better. She avoided visiting that risky terrain even for a minute.

Realizing she'd missed part of Tamsin's sad tale, she tuned in again, nodding like her attention hadn't slipped.

Tamsin said, "I thought it sounded like a good idea. You know, everyone wants unique handbags. I told her I would put up the capital, but she said that was maybe not such a good idea for a couple…one owing the other all that money for a business venture. I was proud of her. You know, for wanting to make it on her own."

Charlotte kept a straight face to hide her exasperation. This uncharacteristic embrace of noble scruples should have set off alarm bells in the woman Dani had been bleeding white since day one.

"She said she'd found someone who wanted to invest," Tamsin continued. "Anyway, they kept having these meetings till two in the morning. And whenever they were on the phone, Dani would go in another room and get all weird if I came in."

How many clues did it take for an intelligent woman to piece together a brain teaser a five-year-old could solve? Apparently a truckload.

"Well, there's no point blaming yourself for not being psychic," Charlotte said briskly. "What we have to do now is make sure you're okay. I hate to sound heartless, but have you checked your bank accounts and cancelled all the credit cards you gave her?"

Tamsin's face froze and she was silent for several seconds. With strained defensiveness, she said, "I told my attorney to talk to my accountant."

"When was that?"

"Thursday."

"Thursday as in yesterday? You've been suspicious for months and you broke up with her two weeks ago, but you've only just thought about the financial side?"

Tamsin stared at her wine. "I didn't want to do anything hasty. I thought we might get back together."

"Oh, Tamsin." Charlotte bit down on her lower lip to stop herself from saying things that would only hurt her friend's feelings.

One of these days Tamsin would develop the self-respect that inoculated women against accepting poor treatment from a partner. Meantime it was Charlotte's job to encourage her to gain strength. She'd always tried to build Tamsin up, but she also wanted her to face reality and let go of her blinkered delusions about finding true love. Tamsin stood to inherit an enormous fortune from her TV mogul father, and because she was also desperately insecure, she would always be a target for opportunists like Dani. Their betrayals only made her even more insecure, so it was a vicious cycle.

"Listen to me," Charlotte said seriously. "There's nothing wrong with your instincts and it's time you started paying attention to them.

Remember what you said when you first hooked up with Dani? You wondered if she was trying to use you. That was your gut talking."

"I've been thinking about that," Tamsin conceded with a small frown. "It's like I sensed things weren't right, but then I just…"

"You wanted the fairy tale," Charlotte completed. "So you turned a blind eye. How many times do you need to go through this?"

Tamsin's mouth trembled. "I just want someone to love me. You know…for me."

"*I* love you for you."

"It's not the same."

Charlotte thought about trying to give Tamsin what she really needed and was instantly flooded with relief that they would never go there. It would be a disaster. She loved Tamsin, but they could never have a relationship as equals. Tamsin would be emotionally dependent and need constant reassurance, and Charlotte would struggle against the inevitable loss of personal space.

"Thank God I'm not a romantic," she said, thinking aloud.

Tamsin leapt on this opportunity to change the subject. "That doctor. Are you two still dating?"

"I haven't seen her in months. I thought I told you."

"Maybe you did. I'm sorry, I'm not thinking clearly. What went wrong this time?"

"We're not here to discuss me," Charlotte said firmly. "We're here to make sure you don't get screwed over by yet another gold-digger."

Tamsin winced. "I guess I deserve that."

Charlotte regretted her mean-spirited comment. She had promised herself not to get personal about Dani, even though that grasping little bitch had also hit on *her*. Charlotte wondered who she'd traded Tamsin in for. Was there another lesbian heiress even richer? Or had Dani found someone she was at least hot for and decided she could have it all? Perhaps she thought she could keep Tamsin as a cash cow and have a woman she really wanted on the side.

Charlotte knew for a fact that things hadn't been going too well in their sex life. It had been fireworks for a few months, then Dani lost interest. The pattern was fairly common, Charlotte supposed, although she'd heard the honeymoon period was usually more like two years. In her own case, the rosy spectacles had come off after one. She could still remember the day when everything changed. At the time she didn't understand why Britt got so belligerent over a stupid domestic issue, but she'd added two and two long afterward. That memorable Friday, the day she was first struck across the face by her partner, was the day Britt had fallen off the wagon.

If only she had just walked out then and there, Charlotte reflected. It still confounded her that she'd stayed, that she'd fallen for the apologies and excuses. That she'd believed the promises, time after time. Just thinking about her determination to stay the course made her feel like the most stupid woman to draw breath. But she had loved Britt, and she thought that meant standing by her through good and bad. Britt had milked that naïve loyalty for all it was worth.

Of course, things got really ugly by the end, and when Charlotte packed her bags and left, Britt got hysterical and said she'd kill herself. She blamed everything on alcohol and seemed to think if she checked into rehab, all would be forgiven and they could pick up where they left off. She claimed her affairs didn't mean anything and "just happened," as if voices told her to sleep with other women. She refused to see why Charlotte couldn't trust her to change—that lying about her betrayal and reacting violently when challenged had made trust impossible.

Five years had passed since that dark period, and these days Charlotte had the advantage of perspective. She never quite stopped being angry with herself for staying so long in a violent relationship. But mostly, when she thought about Britt, she felt sorry for her. Anyone who could wantonly destroy the best thing in her life and still not examine her own behavior was a pitiful coward. That she could have given herself wholeheartedly to such a person truly appalled her. *Too naked to be safe.* She hated that.

Unfortunately, Tamsin still hadn't learned what Charlotte now saw as a tenet of happiness. *Never expose yourself.* She had railroaded Tamsin into seeing an attorney when Dani first moved in and, predictably, Dani had put up a fight over signing a legal agreement. But Tamsin's attorneys threatened to freeze payments from her trust fund and when it looked like she might have to live with the woman she "loved" minus the unlimited flow of cash, Dani had signed on the dotted line quick smart.

"Apart from the Beemer, what else is in her name?" Charlotte asked bluntly.

Tamsin fidgeted with her empty wineglass. "You know the new condo in P-town—"

"Are you serious?" Charlotte spotted their waiter and waved him over so she could take a moment to control her temper. After ordering another bottle of Pegasus Bay, she said, "Please tell me you didn't put her name on the title."

In a small, bitter voice, Tamsin replied, "We were fighting. She was always guilt-tripping me about how unequal our situation was and how we'd been together all that time but I didn't act like our relationship was real. Like we were married."

All that time? It hadn't been two years. "So you wanted to prove something to her?"

"I thought if I made a meaningful gesture—"

"Wait. You paid for her plastic surgery. You bought her a fifty thousand dollar sports car and that ridiculous diamond ring. You got her a role in one of your dad's shows and a Hollywood audition. You took her all over Europe and stayed in a palazzo, for crying out loud. And you thought *you* owed *her* a meaningful gesture? What did Dani Bush ever do for you?"

Tamsin studied the table once more. They both retreated into silence as their waiter returned with fresh glasses and performed the wine ritual.

After he departed, Charlotte swirled her pinot noir and said, "Tamsin, why do you do this?"

"Do what?"

"You know what I'm saying."

"Choose bitches with no class for my partners?" She gave a rueful laugh. "Well, you won't have me."

"Be serious." They'd known each other since grade school and had occasionally shared a halfhearted kiss. But there was no chemistry.

"I think I try to rescue them," Tamsin said. "It makes me feel…I don't know."

"Needed?" *Why not rescue small animals?*

"Yes. Like if they need me they won't leave. I know that's all about my mother." She gave a tight, ironic laugh. "Twenty shrinks can't be wrong."

Charlotte sighed. The parent in question was a self-centered socialite who'd eventually been killed when her private plane crashed. She'd walked out on her family when Tamsin was five, leaving her to be reared by a long succession of nannies who also kept leaving for whatever reason. Back at elementary school, Charlotte could remember Tamsin buying expensive presents for these young women and trying to behave like the perfect child so they would stay. She epitomized the poor little rich girl, an only child who had grown up spoiled but emotionally neglected in a huge Connecticut mansion.

Charlotte had no patience with the stereotype, or the way it was served up to excuse bad behavior or stupidity. But Tamsin was a genuinely sweet person who had somehow made it intact through the kind of upbringing that would usually produce an ethically stunted parasite. All the privilege in the world could not guarantee good fortune in love, and sometimes Charlotte wondered if that was the price the Fates exacted from women like Tamsin for the accident of their birth.

By contrast, she considered herself dead lucky. Despite her own relative privilege, she had grown up with two loving parents, a couple of smartass brothers who refused to treat her like a princess, and a ten dollar allowance until she was a high school senior, when her father gave her a mind-blowing raise to fifty. And she had to help him with translation work for those big bucks.

Her parents were philanthropists who made it clear most of their money was destined for charity. There would be no big trust funds for their kids. Charlotte had always known she would have to work for her living and make it on her own merits in whatever field she chose. Although she could have walked into a legacy place at Harvard, she'd chosen to compete for entry to Stanford so she could join her lab-rat older brother there. Whereas Tamsin's father expected nothing more of his daughter than big credit-card bills and eventually marriage to some Hollywood player, Charlotte's parents expected her to shoot for a Nobel Prize.

Feeling sad that her dearest friend was now hurt and disillusioned all over again, Charlotte took Tamsin's hand and said, "I have a great idea."

A shaky smile plucked at the corners of Tamsin's mouth. "I could use a great idea."

"Good. Here's what we're going to do. You can come home with me and watch a DVD while I finish some work I need to do tonight. Then we'll go over to your place and pack your bags."

Tamsin gave her a blank stare. "Did I miss something?"

"You're coming to Australia with me for a vacation. I'm leaving in four days."

"Australia?" Tamsin toyed dazedly with a honey-kissed wave that had strayed onto her face. "For real?"

"Kangaroos. Boomerangs. You name it."

"Kangaroos. Oh! I'd love that." A puzzled frown drew Tamsin's fine eyebrows together. "I thought you couldn't take any more vacation this year. You're not just doing this for me, are you?"

"Not exactly, although I would. Actually, I have some news." Charlotte gathered herself. She didn't want to sound too gleeful in the face of Tamsin's unhappiness. "Remember that job I applied for with the Sealy-Weiss Institute?"

Tamsin's small heart-shaped face lit up and she bounced in her chair. "You got it? Oh, my God."

Charlotte could only nod. She'd flown to Chicago for her final interview the previous week and had received the call soon after. She was now a research biologist assigned to one of the most prestigious teams in the country. And, as if that were not enough, one of the Sealy-Weiss Institute's major donors, Belton Pharmaceuticals, was funding a multidisciplinary scientific expedition to the Foja Mountains. Charlotte had been invited to participate.

"I've been asked to go to this amazing place in New Guinea, kind of a lost world." She could hardly believe it even as she said it. "That's my first assignment. It's the chance of a lifetime."

"A lost world..." Steadying her wineglass, Tamsin gasped out, "I'm so proud of you. I always knew you'd do something amazing one day. Like invent a cure doing that bizarre stuff with plants. You're such a genius." Tears began rolling down her cheeks and she wiped them against the backs of her hands and lifted her glass. "To you, Charlotte. Congratulations. You're my hero."

Touched, Charlotte thanked her and took a quick sip of wine. "So, you see, I figured I could have a vacation in Australia first. I've been wanting to talk to you about it, but so much was happening and you've been hard to get ahold of."

"I know."

"I was worried when you didn't return my calls." Charlotte had finally left a message yesterday telling Tamsin she urgently needed to see her and giving her a place and time. She had almost expected her not to show up.

"I'm sorry," Tamsin said. "I needed some time to think, so I guess I've been avoiding people."

"I'm not *people*," Charlotte chided gently. She wasn't going to say any more than that. Tamsin was already battling tears. "Now, where were we? Oh, yes. organizing for you to come Down Under with me." She located her BlackBerry and consulted her travel file, looking for the e-mail addy for her agent. "I'm going to buy your ticket right now. We'll go to Melbourne first, then we'll Jeep across the desert to Ayers Rock."

The despondency fled Tamsin's face and her tear-drenched hazel eyes suddenly sparkled. "I've always wanted to go to Australia. I can't believe you're asking me."

Charlotte smiled. "Just say yes."

"Yes!" Tamsin beamed, then a flash of apprehension seemed to cloud her delight. In a strained voice, she said, "I'll have to pack."

Charlotte understood her anxiety. At the best of times the impractical Tamsin couldn't decide between Prada and Chloe, and she had no idea what a baggage allowance meant. "I'll help. I know more than you do about what's in your closet."

Tamsin shook her head. "It's okay. I can buy new stuff. I'll be ready in time, I promise."

"Don't be silly. You bought all that safari gear for the Tsavo trip last year. I'll come over and get you organized and then you can stay at my place till we leave."

"No." Tamsin gulped some wine and started chattering like she always did when she was dissembling. "I mean, thanks. But actually, I wasn't planning to go home for a while tonight. I thought I might hit a movie or whatever."

Since when did Tamsin Powell do late-night movies by herself? A germ of suspicion took root in Charlotte's mind. Tamsin had been very evasive about seeing her since the breakup, and there was always some half-baked reason why Charlotte couldn't just drop by her house in Brookline.

She lost her temper. "No! Surely not."

Tamsin was the picture of shame. A miserable whine gurgled from her throat.

"She's still in your house!" Conversation at the tables around them ceased like someone had just fired a gun in the air. Into the pregnant hush, Charlotte said, "You are coming with me right now and we are throwing that cheating skank out on the street. Along with her crack-whore clothes."

An older woman at the next table remarked, "You go, girl."

As Charlotte dealt with the check, Tamsin pleaded, "I can't face her. Please, Charlie. Don't make me do it. She twists everything I say. She makes me feel bad about myself."

Charlotte terminated this litany with an impatient snort. "So she calls you names and makes you cry. For Christ's sake, it's your home." Another thought occurred to her. "And on that subject, where exactly have you been living for the past two weeks?"

"The Four Seasons."

Appalled, Charlotte took her cell phone from her purse and handed it to her fretful companion. "Phone them right now and tell them you're checking out."

CHAPTER THREE

Lose the dress," Ash said.

She could not take her eyes off the deepening vee of creamy flesh as Dani inched the zipper down the concave arch of Karlah's spine. The skin exposed had to be prickling in anticipation but Ash didn't touch. She wanted the elegant brunette to beg first. Dani pushed the thin straps aside and dragged the dress down, her eyes locked to Ash's. Karlah wasn't wearing a bra. She didn't need to. Her breasts were taut and high.

Dani had already stripped to her panties, if that's what you could call the scrap of lace glued to her crotch. Ash ran a caressing hand back and forth over the firm round ass exposed before her, then hooked a finger inside the panties and twisted upward. She could smell sweet salty arousal from the flood of Dani's juices as the fabric strained against her clit.

"Let's get rid of this." She snapped the flimsy thong away. Twisting Dani's pale hair in her fingers, she forced her head back, exposing her slender throat. "You're really, really wet," she said, sliding the tip of her tongue down the life pulse just beneath the taut skin. "Maybe I'll let you get yourself off."

A shudder altered Dani's breathing. "And maybe I'll let you fuck me afterward."

"Would you like that?" Ash lifted her head to glance at Karlah. "Want to watch me do your girlfriend?"

Karlah uttered a small "Yes," and Ash steered them farther into the bedroom.

A huge king bed with a noisy floral comforter stood near the windows. Ash pulled the cover aside and pushed her two companions down onto the pale sheets. Karlah's dark waves spilled over the pillows and her raspberry-tipped breasts scalloped like pale half-moons against the fading tan of her torso.

Dani crawled up the bed and knelt next to her, sweeping her platinum hair back so Ash could watch as she bent in for a kiss. Ash's throat felt tight and her breathing shallow. The walls of her chest squeezed her heart, making every beat reverberate through her body.

The tension at her core increased when Dani looked up and said, "I know what you want."

"Really?"

"Uh-huh." She rocked back onto her heels and pinched her peach-toned nipples between thumb and forefinger, one hand cradling each full breast. "You want these. And this." She opened her legs and tilted her hips just enough to display a compact blond mound and a neat rosy seam of flesh.

"Looks like you got my number," Ash conceded thickly.

"Come on," Dani said.

"I can wait."

"What if I can't?"

Ash played along. "You better figure out how to get me interested."

Dani squirmed and giggled. She and Karlah started touching themselves, eyes closed, mouths parted, like they watched the same movies Ash did. Slightly disconcerted, but still turned on, Ash removed her jacket and slung it over the back of a shabby leather club chair. Like everything else in the room, it seemed out of step with the owner.

Ash would never have picked this bedroom, in this sedate Brookline home, for the private retreat of a woman like Dani Bush. Large, with an ornate plaster ceiling, the room was crammed with a random collection of antique furniture, threadbare Persian rugs, gilt-framed paintings of flowers and country scenes, an old rocking horse, a dollhouse, and a scary quantity of lavender velvet drapery. Every surface was ankle deep in trinkets and mementos.

Ash sat down in the club chair and tried not to be distracted. She had the eerie sense that she was seeing the history of someone's life played out in a private code that took the form of inanimate objects. The dressing table looked like a flea-market stall, the kind Ash would associate with old people, not sexy lesbians into threesomes.

It just goes to show, she thought as Dani began caressing Karlah's breasts, first impressions could be misleading. Who, for example, would guess that Karlah had a tattoo of a small pig tucked in the shadow of her pelvic bone? Ash got a flash of her drunk as shit on a spring break and waking up the next morning wondering how the souvenir body art had ended up on her person.

Dani had a nipple in her mouth, sucking and teasing. Karlah moaned softly and opened her legs a little more. Dani gazed back at Ash. Slowly, deliberately, she slid a couple of fingers between her own thighs and worked them provocatively.

Holding her gaze, Ash unbuttoned her shirt and let it hang open. She trailed her hand down the white cotton of her tank, unbuckled her belt, and flicked open the top button of her pants. Both Dani and Karlah stared, transfixed, as she slid her hand idly down over her pants to rest on her crotch.

Dani seemed to gulp a breath, her breasts rising and falling so sharply they wobbled. She lifted a couple of glistening fingers to Karlah's mouth, tracing them across her lips before slipping them inside. Droopy-eyed with desire, Karlah sucked intently, then pulled Dani down onto her and the two women squirmed against one another, kissing and stroking and sighing. Dani's golden tan glowed against Karlah's creamier coloring. Her voluptuous breasts crowded Karlah's. She worked her way upright until she was sitting astride Karlah's belly, then leaned forward so her nipples swung low enough for Karlah to fondle and kiss.

Between gasps of pleasure, she twisted to stare at Ash. Almost solemnly, she wet her lips and asked, "Want to fuck?"

Ash eyed the flare of her narrow waist and the pearish perfection of her ass but stayed where she was, legs stretched indolently in front of her. "Soon."

With a knowing smile, Dani turned away again and tangled her hand in Karlah's hair. Head back, eyes closed, she surrendered herself to sensation for several minutes before sliding off and rolling onto her side. Face-to-face, breathing hard, and almost as one, the lovers reached between each other's thighs, their long, slender legs scissored.

A tight lump in Ash's throat began to melt, flushing liquid desire down into her chest and belly. Her tank felt like sandpaper against her nipples. They were always unbearably sensitive as she got hotter, never letting her forget for a minute that she needed to come, and soon. She could smell the brackish musk of her own arousal and the subtle scent her skin emitted when she craved release.

Her hosts writhed and ground against one another, their mouths locked, their breathing torn. Ash opened her zipper and shoved her hand between her thighs, clamping down, needing to slow her own response. She wanted to remain in the grip of this urgent aching need a while longer. Nothing made her feel alive like this did, every nerve end screaming, every hair bristling.

"I'm so close," Karlah whined softly to her partner. "I want your mouth."

Her breasts heaving, her face taut with concentration, Dani sought Ash's approval.

"Do her," Ash said. Unable to wait any longer, she got to her feet, stepped out of her pants, and got rid of her shirt and tank as she stalked over to the bed.

Both women drank her in for a few startled seconds, the usual response. Ash knew it wasn't about her spare, muscular physique or the breasts so closely molded to her chest that a few sexual partners found them inadequate. When women with fancy lifestyles stared at her, openmouthed, it was always about the scars. She'd added quite a collection since the jagged hole in her gut that had ended her military career.

Thankfully, her accomplices in tonight's distraction refrained from killing the mood with awkward questions. With a purposeful air, Dani pushed Karlah onto her back once more and knelt between her legs. Parting the soaked mat of her hair, she exposed cabled folds of pink and red.

"That's right." Ash released a breath, firmly in the moment once more. "Let me see her."

Karlah bit down on her lip as a finger circled over her clit, drawing the hood back slightly. Whimpering, she lifted imploring eyes to Ash and whispered, "Please."

"Very pretty." Ash meant that for the both of them. She drew closer and trailed the palm of her hand up and down Dani's back, pausing between her shoulder blades. "Now show me that cute ass of yours."

She applied firm downward pressure and Dani complied, getting busy with her tongue, making sure Ash knew exactly how good everything tasted. The sound of her sucking and slurping, the sight of her ass in the air, and the feel of her damp, pliant flesh made Ash's pulse jerk within her clit. A pounding, flooding pressure in her head seemed to compress thought, jamming her senses at a primal pitch. The smell of sex, and the soft cries and moans crowded her airwaves.

She dipped into Dani's gleaming core and trailed a wet finger up and down along her crack until Dani bucked against her and briefly turned her head, fixing her with a wild, intent look. With her other hand, Ash gave her what she wanted, burying several fingers deep inside her pussy. A little rough, a little short on finesse, but nothing tonight's plaything couldn't handle.

"Is this what you want?" she asked hoarsely.

Dani made a noise but she had her mouth full again and it looked like Karlah was lost in bliss, about to get off. Ash's clit thrummed unbearably and she squeezed her thighs together, applying just enough pressure to contain the inevitable. It felt so good to be inside a woman again that she almost keeled over.

The slippery warmth, the sight of her fingers disappearing into a body, the way the flesh she invaded stretched and molded to take her deeper, only made her greedy for more. She withdrew slightly, rolled her thumb over her wet palm, and transferred moisture to the wrinkled entrance she wanted to explore. Dani responded to the implicit request by reaching around and parting the cheeks of her ass.

Ash circled intently until all the reflexive resistance dissolved and her thumb was welcomed inside. Dani's ass clenched tightly around her, and through the thin walls that separated them, her thumb found her fingers and she kissed them gently together.

Dani made muffled sounds and frantically jerked her hips. Ash obliged, easing back, then sliding in again. It wasn't enough. Dani pushed sharply against her, signaling how she wanted it. Ash pumped faster, fucking her with deep, hard strokes. She couldn't hold on much longer. Her briefs were dripping wet. Her clit wanted what it wanted.

With her free hand, she pinched the tiny, throbbing head between her index and middle fingers just in time to hear Karlah lose it, rocking the bed with her shudders.

Dani gasped, "Yes. Fuck me. Come on."

"Like this?" Ash drove deeper. Crudely. Ramming into her.

She was so close, she was shaking, every muscle tensing and pulsing. Her legs quivered from the strain of staying upright when they needed to fold. Blood raced through her limbs too fast to carry the oxygen needed and her head spun. She leaned her knees against the bed so she wouldn't sink down in a heap. All she wanted was to surrender, to let it all wash over her, to lose herself completely.

The final shock of orgasm tore through her body, wrenching the breath from her chest and blossoming from her core to her extremities. Her low animal cries merged with Dani's small scream of release and sweat broke across her skin. She slumped down over the body beneath hers, gasping and shaking as she caught her breath. When Karlah began struggling at the bottom of the body heap, Ash carefully withdrew her hand from its warm wet sheath in Dani. Ignoring the weak cry of protest, she rolled off and fell flat on her back against the cool sheets, unable to think, let alone move.

For a while all three women lay in silence, their breathing gradually slowing down, then Karlah crawled off the bed and Ash heard bathroom sounds followed by a metallic rattle. She forced her eyes open as the bed sagged next to her. Karlah was sitting on the edge with a black doctor's bag on her lap. From this, she pulled a strap and dildo and dropped them a few inches from Ash's face.

"My turn," she said brightly.

❖

A couple of hours later, Ash extricated herself from a tangle of limbs.

"I should get going," she said, sliding off the bed. It was almost two a.m.

Smiling through the mumbles of dissent, she gathered her clothes and boots and headed for the bathroom. Her legs felt like rubber and her head spun from hours of nonstop exertion. Strange, she thought as she stood beneath the jets of hot water, normally she couldn't get away fast enough after an encounter and held off showering until she was back in her hotel. But knowing she wasn't guilty of leaving a woman alone in bed after sex made her more at ease. Dani and Karlah had each other. They were lovers, she'd discovered as the night wore on, not just friends with benefits. She didn't have to feel bad.

She was drying off when she became aware of a female voice she hadn't heard before. Someone was angry. Ash couldn't make out what was being said but she reached instinctively beneath the clothing she'd piled on a chair by the vanity. She always carried a handgun, even when she felt safe. Unclipping the Sig's safety catch, she padded to the door and cracked it open just enough so she could see what was going on.

"Get the fuck out of here," Dani shrilled. "You can't order me around in my own home."

"This is Tamsin Powell's house and you are trespassing." The reply flowed like husky caramel. Ash craned to see who the startling voice belonged to—someone who should seriously consider phone sex as an occupation.

"Where's Tamsin?" Dani snapped.

"Downstairs. She doesn't want to see you."

Ash's neck prickled and her nipples tightened. Trying to fathom how any voice could affect her so much when she was this exhausted, she replayed it in her mind. Wry smokiness tempered with a sexy girlish lilt. The result—an awesome combination of Anne Bancroft and Marilyn Monroe. This woman could say anything and it would sound like verbal foreplay. Unfortunately she was out of sight, obscured by the open bedroom door. Ash imagined a Kim Basinger look-alike. Tall. Classy. Unattainable. A real woman.

"I don't know who you think you are." Dani's nasal whine seemed more pronounced all of a sudden, grating across Ash's nerves. "But if Tamsin wants me out of here, she can tell me herself."

"Listen carefully, both of you." Softly spoken. Sexy as all hell. *Talk dirty,* Ash prayed. *Just once, please.* "Henry Powell is sending some of his security guys over. He got agitated when I explained the situation. And here's the thing. Those guys, they're not hired for their brains. Do you understand?"

A threat had never sounded so good.

Dani got louder. "What are you saying?"

"Put it this way. You have ten minutes to pack your things and get out. Tamsin doesn't want blood on her carpet. The steam-cleaning chemicals bother her."

Ash hovered indecisively in the doorway. She knew she ought to be gallant and rush to Dani's defense, but from the sound of things Dani had created her own problems. Besides, life held so few surprises she wanted to make the most of this one. It didn't sound like the woman calling the shots was armed with anything but her delicious arrogance and extraordinary vocal cords. Ash wanted to meet her. As in, yesterday.

Karlah belatedly piped up. “Can someone please tell me what’s going on?”

“Dani,” the voice sensually invited, “perhaps you’d like to explain why you’re still living in the home of the partner you’ve been cheating on. Is this the other woman, or are you just slutting around with whoever?”

“Dani? What’s she talking about?” Karlah sounded genuinely shocked.

Dani was silent.

The unwelcome visitor knew she had won. Ash could tell from the silky satisfaction that entered her tone. “Shall I call the police and have you both arrested? Or do you want to take your chances with Henry’s boys? Dani, you know a good plastic surgeon, I’m sure.” A sigh. “Facial reconstruction…ouch.”

Whoever this sultry-spoken hardass was, Ash would pay to be intimidated by her. At the risk of making a poor first impression, she wished she could hang around for an introduction, but she didn’t like the way things seemed headed. *The police.* She pictured herself downtown trying to explain why she was on an Interpol watch list. Bad idea.

Silently she closed and locked the door, then headed for a bay of double-hung windows at the far end of the room. Cold air rushed at her face as she lifted one and peered down into the floodlit gardens below. It was maybe a twenty-foot drop. She’d handled worse without breaking an ankle.

Determined to get out before she could be sucked into someone else’s drama, she hurriedly finished dressing and double-checked that she hadn’t left anything crucial behind. Like her car keys and wallet.

Someone thumped on the door and Karlah’s muffled voice begged, “Ashley! Come out here!”

Ash thought she could make out the stranger’s response. “Oh, tell me this isn’t happening. There are *three* of you? No wonder this place smells like last week’s crotch stains. Someone hand me a sanitary wipe.”

Ash had to cover her mouth so she wouldn’t laugh out loud. An object crashed against a wall. Dani was throwing stuff, she surmised.

“Tell her to get up here right now,” the outraged blonde yelled. “She can’t just throw me out.”

“Oh, but I can.”

Ash could not believe how wet every word made her. *Get a grip on yourself,* she thought and lifted the window all the way up, thankful that it was high enough and awkward enough to access that it didn't have security locks. Hauling herself onto the ledge, she twisted and got her legs out, then scanned the grounds for the softest place to land. A strip of lush lawn looked promising. Even better, a huge pile of wood chips and leaf mold had been dumped near a flower bed, obviously part of some fall landscaping project before the snows came. Ash wasn't sure if she could hurl herself far enough to hit the mound dead center, but it was worth a shot.

As the door-thumping grew more insistent and the handle started to rattle, she reflected that this had been quite a night. Then she jumped.

Chapter Four

The Grove Nursing Home in Millbury, south of Worcester, was a converted mansion surrounded by charming gardens. Residents could happily roam the manicured grounds within the safe confines of ten foot stone walls and 24/7 video monitoring.

Ash had chosen the place because anyone who could keep psychiatric patients inside as successfully as these people had the kind of security that also kept unwanted visitors out. At one time she'd been plagued by nightmares of her father breaking in and killing her younger sister. Her fears had not been completely baseless, but in hindsight, she could see they were a consequence of her own trauma more than a reflection of reality.

Emma had witnessed the murder of their mother and had testified at their father's trial for the killing. Cartwright Evans had also been charged with attempted murder for his attack on Emma. These days he was serving a life term at MCI Cedar Junction. The last time Ash saw him, he was being led away after the judge had handed down her sentence.

His parting words were, "Your mother was a problem."

Hers were, "Die slowly and rot in hell," a prophetic sentiment given all she'd heard about conditions at Cedar Junction.

Occasionally letters from the maximum-security facility found their way, via mail redelivery, to her home in Madang. Requests for money. Complaints about brutal prison guards. Claims of life-threatening illness. Ash took pleasure in these self-serving communications because she liked to know her father was suffering. She shredded every last one without replying. The only time she ever planned to see him was if he appeared before a parole board. She would be there to make sure he stayed where he belonged. In a cage.

She slowed her rental Buick to a crawl and turned in to the parking lot behind the main building. It was pouring and she didn't have an umbrella, so she looked for a spot near the entrance. An elderly couple was attempting to reverse out of the ideal location. After they'd almost backed under a Hummer, Ash got out of her car and stood in the torrential rain to guide them. Her shoulder ached as she waved her hand, and pain shot through the ankle she'd sprained leaping from the bathroom window. The injury made driving a problem so she'd skipped two of her daily visits out here.

After she parked, she dragged a box of chocolates out of the backseat, locked the car, and made a run for the entrance. The security guard on the door checked her ID and waved her into an elegant parlor redolent with the aroma of coffee and fresh-baked cookies. A couple of well-dressed city people sat awkwardly in tapestry-covered Victorian chairs. Ash suspected from their hushed conversation and darting glances that they were applying for an admission.

She knew exactly how they felt. After Emma's neurologist at the McLean Hospital had recommended she remain in long-term care, Ash had been desperate to find the right environment. The Grove was affiliated with McLean and had a warm, old-fashioned feel. But its olde worlde façade disguised a state-of-the-art facility. There, Emma received the medical care she needed as well as long-term rehabilitation.

For a long while this had been paid for by the large insurance policy their mother left. Ash had often wondered if, knowing the man she had married, she'd also known how much she was at risk. The money had enabled the finest care for Emma, and by the time it ran out Ash had left the military and was earning a salary that usually arrived bundled in suitcases. She had no problem paying the bills.

She gave her name to the receptionist and a few minutes later she was shown to an office that looked nothing like the front parlor. It was modern and functional, with art on the walls alongside backlit panels where X-rays could be displayed. At one end of the room an internal window provided a view of the room next door.

"You've redecorated," she noted after shaking hands with Dr. Winterton.

"Yes, and you have no idea how I've mourned that love seat."

Ash grinned, a little surprised that such a busy man would have remembered their previous banter about the awful peach upholstery with the Cupid pattern. The sofa had been a legacy of his predecessor, whose tastes ran to pastels and sentimentality. Ash glanced around again. The walls were now a quiet shade of dove that looked good with the art and a new chrome and glass desk.

With a quick look at her bandaged ankle, Dr. Winterton said, "How is the world treating you, Ms. Evans?"

"With the contempt I deserve," she answered lightly. "You look rested."

"Blame my wife. She finally divorced me."

"Hell, I'm sorry." Ash was startled by this lapse into the personal. Normally Dr. Winterton was a closed book. She supposed people who had to hide unhappiness cut loose a little once the charade was over.

"Don't be. We're friends now." He pinned up the usual diagrams and X-rays, signaling an end to their introductory pleasantries.

"I got your report," Ash said. "Thank you for making time to see me during your week off."

"There've been some developments," he said. "That's why I'm here today."

Ash's lungs froze against her heart. "I see."

He came to the point by degrees. "Emma's grand mal seizures have become more frequent and about an hour ago we believe she suffered a stroke. I'm sorry to be telling you this now. We tried your cell phone number as soon as we stabilized her."

"I keep it off when I'm driving." Ash felt dazed. "She's only twenty-eight. How can she have a stroke?"

"Unfortunately her brain is not that of an average healthy person her age. As you know, the TBI left her with permanent frontal lobe damage and while we have achieved progress with her cognitive deficits and behavioral issues, we are seeing a deterioration of her physical condition."

"You're saying she's getting worse, not better?"

"In some important areas, yes. And the stroke is a serious concern."

"What about decompression?" Ash felt embarrassed as soon as she'd asked. It wasn't like Dr. Winterton and his team were sitting on their hands wondering what to try next and just hanging out for advice from a helicopter pilot. To spare him the need for a diplomatic reply, she said. "Dumb question. I'm sorry."

"There are no dumb questions, Ms. Evans. I'm here to explain Emma's condition and to talk with you about the options."

"So…the deterioration. Does that have to do with the aneurysm from the original injuries?"

"I don't think they're directly related."

"Then what's happening?"

"Let me first say this." He spoke gently. "Neurology is not a perfect science. The brain remains a mystery even to those of us who have devoted a lifetime to its study. In Emma's case, some things are known, some things we can only guess at."

Ash's eyes flooded and she stared down at her hands. She had always envisioned a time when Emma would be well enough to leave the Grove and come live with her. She now had enough money invested that she could hire a full-time nursing team from New Zealand or Australia, semiretire, and work in the tourist sector somewhere like Thailand or Sri Lanka. Pilots were always in demand, especially those who weren't fussy about the quality of their clientele.

"We've adjusted her medication," Dr. Winterton said. "But I'm not going to beat around the bush. At this time we can only be cautiously optimistic."

"What are you saying?"

"She may not regain consciousness. And if she has another stroke…"

Ash tried to clear the fog swirling in her mind so she could interpret the doctor's face and tone. He was trying to reduce the shock of bad news, circling around the naked truth while he prepared her for it. "You're saying my sister might die?"

"I'm saying it would be wise to prepare yourself for the worst, but hope for the best. It's too soon to make precise determinations. However, there has been additional brain damage. Emma is in a coma."

"Tell me what the options are." Ash knew she sounded frantic, but she couldn't hide her distress. "I don't care if it's a long shot. If there are trial drugs and the side effects aren't terrible, I'll sign off on that. Anything."

"We're doing all we can, Ms. Evans. Maybe one day, a long time from now, new treatments will emerge from fields like stem cell research and we won't use the word 'irreversible' anymore."

"She's been through so much." Ash spoke her thoughts aloud. "She doesn't deserve this."

The doctor's calm brown eyes met hers. "You know, a lot of people discard a family member like Emma. They give up. Your sister may not be able to show you how much you matter, but trust me, she always responds to you. Even unconscious, she may still do so."

"I'll never give up on her," Ash said emphatically. "I love her and I know who she was…is…inside."

Dr. Winterton rose. "We'll talk some more about her condition, but first let's take a walk so you can see how she's doing."

❖

The sign on the terminal said *Port Moresby. Jackson International Air ort.* Out on the tarmac, Charlotte waited in the stifling heat with the other unfortunates who'd disembarked from the bumpy flight across the Coral Sea. She wasn't sure why the gantries weren't being used, or why everyone was being forced to stand out in the blazing sun, but she knew enough about her destination to understand that the mores of Western civilization did not apply in Papua New Guinea.

Thank goodness Tamsin had decided to stay in Australia for two more weeks instead of coming with her to explore a little of this remarkable land before the expedition was due to depart. To Charlotte's surprise, her best friend seemed to be thriving among the laid-back, unpretentious Australians. They'd met a lesbian couple at Ayers Rock who had invited them to visit and really meant it. So, after their travels in the outback, they'd headed for Sydney and soon found themselves enjoying poolside barbecues with some of the friendliest people Charlotte had ever met.

No one there knew who Tamsin or her father were, and Charlotte told her to just be herself. When she was asked what she did for a living, she said she was a professional shopper, which, as Charlotte pointed out, was almost the truth. She was always shopping for her father and various pals of his in television. Last year she'd even house-hunted for one couple. And every time Charlotte wanted to buy a gift for someone difficult, she always asked Tamsin's help.

The Australians seemed to find the whole idea hilarious, and this put Tamsin at ease. She could tell stories about stores she knew well and show-business people she'd met without having to explain how she really came to be rubbing shoulders with the rich and famous. Charlotte had left her planning a beach party with their hosts, excited that a woman she'd met at a neighbor's potluck was going to come.

Charlotte had also met Tamsin's lust object, a no-nonsense equine veterinarian who made beautiful blown-glass pieces as a hobby. Rowena Knox struck her instantly as the kind of person who would never have materialistic motives for anything. And she was hot. Tamsin had been completely giddy after they met and Charlotte found it hard not to be carried away herself. The last thing she'd expected to happen on their vacation was that Tamsin might meet someone. But as they'd lain awake on Charlotte's last night in Sydney, Tamsin couldn't talk about anything else.

"You just don't know what's around the corner," she sighed. "This was meant to happen. I just know it."

Wanting to keep her best friend's feet on the ground, Charlotte said, "It's early days. You'll have a chance to get to know her better while I'm in New Guinea."

"I feel like I've known her my whole life already," Tamsin gushed.

Charlotte thought *Oh, God*, but she couldn't be entirely dismissive. She'd seen how they hit it off. There was something quite uncanny about the way Rowena related to Tamsin. She seemed to sense she was dealing with someone who was emotionally fragile, and the instant connection between them was obvious.

"Just take it slowly," Charlotte cautioned.

"I will," Tamsin said. "But I'm not going to run away just because things haven't worked out for me before. I made bad choices. It doesn't mean I can't make a good one."

Charlotte had thought about that comment a few times over the hours since, and she had to admire Tamsin's persistence. She would never be the kind of person Charlotte was, able to compartmentalize her emotions and abide by self-imposed rules. She would always fall prey to her romantic dreams. Maybe the odds were finally in her favor and she would find what she was looking for. Charlotte hoped so.

As for herself, she didn't need what Tamsin needed. She'd gotten over all that and her life was exactly the way she wanted it to be. Free of drama. Entirely within her own control. And, most importantly, professionally satisfying.

Smearing beads of moisture back into her hairline, she scanned her surroundings. A couple of security guards loitered nearby. They carried bows and arrows instead of guns. A team of sweat-soaked men shoved push-mowers back and forth along the wide belts of lawn that separated the runways, fighting a losing battle to keep the grass down. In this hot wet climate, vegetation grew like it was on crack.

About a hundred yards away, a burned-out DC10 was parked in front of a hanger. Its body was stripped of parts and under each shelled-out wing locals had set up makeshift stalls selling drinks and souvenirs. Their children swarmed toward the droopy passengers, hawking coconut water and fruits Charlotte recognized only because she was a botanist.

She purchased a small bag of guavas for five dollars, which, according to the weathered man standing next to her, was "daylight bloody robbery." In a broad Australian twang, he added, "Welcome to the shithole of planet Earth. Whatever they're paying you to come here, it's not enough."

Charlotte said with level dignity, "I'm with an international research expedition to the Foja Mountains."

Dubiously, the Aussie looked her up and down. "You don't say."

Charlotte swatted at an insect trying to land on her mouth. She had a feeling anything she shared about the significance of the expedition and what it meant to her would be lost on this dog-eared traveler, so she asked, "What about you—what brings you here?"

"It was this or ten years in an Aussie jail." At her faint start, he added, "I'm not one of the bad guys. I just made a dumb mistake."

Charlotte didn't ask.

"The Fojas," he mused. "Yeah. I heard about that. The lost world, right?"

"Yes. A completely undisturbed ecosystem. No human impact at all. We're being dropped in by helicopter."

"Good luck. How long are you planning on staying up there?"

"Two months."

He gave a low, expressive whistle. "You know that TV show *Survivor*?"

Charlotte usually refrained from assaulting her intellect with the dross that passed for television entertainment, but she didn't want to sound condescending, so she said, "Yes, of course."

"They were out here scouting a location a couple of years back, but they figured no one would *survive* long enough to finish the show."

Charlotte guessed he was trying to be funny and offered a smile. "I gather it's very difficult terrain."

"Yeah. And that's not counting the cannibals or the Indonesian army."

"The Fojas are not inhabited." Charlotte tried to sound confident about that. "And we'll be going in with local guides and a security team, so I think we'll be fine."

He looked unimpressed. "A friendly word of advice...the genocide. Just ignore it. You don't want to end up in an Indonesian jail for the next twenty years because you acted like a bleeding-heart do-gooder."

Charlotte felt herself blanch. "Genocide—what genocide?"

"Exactly. Keep that up and no worries. One more thing—don't use the ladies' loo inside the terminal unless you want to catch cholera." He tipped his yellowing Panama hat and strolled off into the crowd.

Charlotte considered scuttling after him to ask some more questions, but before she could assemble her wits, a small boy seized her shirt sleeve and tried to sell her a mango. He was painfully thin and appeared to be almost blind, so she bargained half-heartedly and finally purchased the fruit for a crazy amount. As she peeled the mottled skin away with her pocket knife, she craned to see the Australian. He was standing twenty yards away, handing money to a guard. He then strolled off toward the terminal.

Obviously a bribe had just changed hands. Charlotte wondered what the going rate was. Right now, she'd pay most of her salary to escape the merciless sun. As soon as she had consumed the mango she was going to pay up so she wouldn't have to die of heat exhaustion before her trip had even begun. She supposed she could have flown into Jakarta and stayed in a decent hotel like most of the team. Instead, she'd decided to arrive early on the Papua New Guinea side of the border, to do some sight-seeing and walk the Kokoda Trail. In hindsight, she could see this was a mistake.

She finished eating and cleaned the sticky juice from her hands with a Wet Wipe. It seemed the arrivals had now been fleeced of sufficient cash—the vendors were busy counting a cut of the proceeds into the hands of the security guards. A moment later she and the other passengers were herded into the open-sided hangar that passed for the airport terminal and she was assailed with a cacophony of sights and smells unlike any she'd ever experienced in a foreign country. Which wasn't surprising, since she'd only traveled in Europe and Great Britain.

The arrival hall was a clamor of women carrying their babies in string sacks, Polynesian islanders with hibiscus flowers in their hair, loud Australian men in shorts and knee socks, tall blueish black locals from the city, and short sturdy tribesmen with grass and leaves covering their butts. These indigenous people carried umbrellas—a smart idea, Charlotte thought. Their country routinely saw brilliant sun and drenching rain within the same half hour, according to all the travel guides.

There was no air-conditioning inside the grubby, foul-smelling terminal and the crowd waiting to clear passport control was a haphazard melee. A single official sat at a desk, casually issuing entry visas. A couple of his buddies were accepting bribes to allow people to the front of the line. American dollars were the currency du jour and after a few moments of determined disdain for corruption, and flea bites from an aggressive species that infested the filthy carpet, Charlotte overcame her reservations and waved a twenty. This secured a berth behind a group of businessmen who gallantly offered her a spare place in their rental cars so she wouldn't have to take one of the notorious "public motor vehicles" or PMVs, as they were known. They told her cheerfully that these were involved in fatal accidents most days of the week.

A short while later, they escaped the airport and a sign on the highway to Port Moresby bade them "Welcome to Paradise." When the howls of laughter subsided, her fellow travelers instructed her never to go out at night, never to travel alone in the highlands, and to beware of "rascals." Eventually they pulled up outside the Crowne Plaza, hauled her luggage into the lobby, and wished her luck. As a whoosh of air-conditioning greeted her, Charlotte almost got down on her hands and knees in thanks. All she could think about was washing. She was only twenty-eight hours away from Boston, but she might as well have landed on another planet.

CHAPTER FIVE

Where was the perfect pick-up line when you needed one? Ash contemplated the woman nursing a drink at the bar. Alone. Gorgeous. The one beddable female in this sweltering, roach-infested dive in Port Moresby.

Are you out of your mind? or *What the fuck are you doing here?* were the only conversation starters that sprang to mind. Ash thought this was probably a consequence of her distraction level. All she'd been able to think about since returning to PNG was Emma, alone in her big white hospital bed, surrounded by machines. After the meeting with Dr. Winterton, Ash had extended her stay and spent every waking hour with her sister, desperate for the smallest sign of improvement. There was nothing, and knowing she could be stuck in the same limbo indefinitely, she had decided to return to PNG and wind up her affairs, completing only the assignments she could not wriggle out of.

Ash hadn't been in town for a day when Tubby Nagle, her biggest customer, chased her down for a lousy gig rescuing a copper mining executive who'd been taken hostage by a small band of so-called resistance fighters. This label was applied to West Papuan landowners who got upset when their homes were destroyed, their wives and daughters raped by goon squads, and their animals killed in a process known as "resettlement"—at least by the Indonesians, who'd invaded the country back in the sixties.

Once the villagers were forced off their land and intimidated into signing timber and mining concessions, the big overseas companies moved in—BP. Rio Tinto. Freeport-McMoRan—along with them, a fleet of Western executives who made attractive targets for the few tribal activists who weren't already rotting in Indonesian prisons. This all made for a profitable service niche for the private security firms in the region—providing guards, extracting hostages, and capturing kidnappers they could sell dead or alive to the Indonesians, who thought it was important to set an example by torturing them to death.

Ash had handled some of Nagle's most successful extraction operations, her subtle approach proving more effective than the Rambo tactics favored by most of her colleagues. It helped that she spoke some of the more widely used languages in New Guinea. There were about eight hundred, more in one small land mass than anywhere else on earth. Of course, this was rapidly changing with the transmigration from Indonesia and the quiet extermination of the indigenous tribes. Unluckily for her, Ash spoke the kidnappers' language, which, as far as Tubby Nagle was concerned, made her indispensable for the latest assignment.

It wasn't as if she could explain why she needed out. No one knew she had any family other than her father, and Ash preferred to keep it that way. After ascertaining that there was no change in Emma's condition, she'd accepted the job because it would be easy money and she'd be out in a couple of days. She went into the kidnap area on foot with one local guide, carrying an array of gifts and a pitiful ransom.

The fighters wanted their land back and their lives to return to normal. It was never going to happen. They had grown up in a place barely touched by foreigners until recent times. Ash carried a set of photographs the tribesmen would understand, images that showed them how much worse things could be. In their own language, she explained the new world order and how they would only be able to survive the changes if they laid down their spears and found much better weapons, such as legal representation.

She usually advised kidnappers to demand more than the paltry ransom on offer so they'd have money for a lawyer. In this instance, they saw the sense in that suggestion and asked her to talk to the boss man. So she made the call to Tubby, letting him know the good news and the bad news. She'd located the prisoner but, as was lately the case, the men holding him had a regrettable knowledge of Western ideas. They wanted real money and, worst of all, they had a certain Australian go-between advising them. This was not quite true, but invoking the name of Bruce the Roo by inference meant she would get instant results.

An Aussie lawyer turned environmental activist and local hero, the

Roo was linked to countless highly sophisticated sabotage operations against mining and timber interests. He had a big reputation among the private security forces who worked the PNG region and struck fear into the hearts of mining management. Ash wasn't sure if Tubby saw him as a blessing or a curse. On the one hand, his involvement in a situation meant a fat check. On the other, the guy was a faceless loose cannon with no affiliation who seemed to enjoy sticking it to the man.

Predictably, Tubby foamed at the mouth this time round, ranting about how Bruce the Roo was on his list and no one got away with pissing him off this many times. But he made the deal and Ash knew the client would have to produce extra hazard money for her services because the handover supposedly involved their nemesis. She could sleep okay on that count. Screwing a mining company was a public service.

Amazingly, by the time she was ready to make the switch, Bruce the Roo had caught wind of the affair and actually showed up to play the role assigned to him. Ash was cool with that; they'd done business before. He thanked her for the gig, and she handed over the ransom, photographing the proceedings with a few strange camera angles so it would seem like a hidden device was used. The Roo was cooperative about that and flashed an AK-47 for effect. It was in both their interests to have the mining company and Tubby Nagle think the peril factor was high.

The Australian troublemaker then told the tribesmen to remove the blindfold from their captive and hand him over. The poor, soft Seattlean immediately went into hysterics at the sight of seminaked, paint-smeared tribesmen with bones through their noses and a white man wearing a fake kangaroo head. While Ash examined him for injury and slapped his face a few times to calm him down, the kidnappers vanished into the jungle richer by a few hundred large.

Her back still ached from having to half carry the guy out with her scrawny guide claiming lumbago so he didn't have to help. The victim wasn't hurt. She'd had to sedate him in the end so he'd stop blubbering. Being an American, he'd insisted on personally tipping her two large for the rescue once they got back to the city. When Ash told him that would buy helpful goodwill and she'd do her best to make sure he wasn't targeted again, he increased it to five. She didn't say no. She put such bonuses to work, buying eyes and information all over PNG.

Right now, two of the men on her payroll were in the seedy bar in downtown Port Moresby, watching her back. Later in the day, there would be women here, hookers and pickpockets. But for now the occupants were male, a mix of betel-chewing locals minding their own business, hard-drinking expats who knew the drill and had armed body guards, plus the usual array of predators—rascal gang members who raped, robbed, and murdered at will.

Everyone was watching the one woman in the room. Some with dismay, some with delight, and some with sorrowful hunger. Ash recognized the condition. It had its roots in what was lost when you lived in a place like this—the nobler self. Somehow this unsullied visitor to their realm had called up long-forgotten feelings and ideals, tapping a tenderness no one here could afford if they wanted to survive. In this netherworld neglected by God, such a woman was a miracle. Only the dull of soul could fail to feel more human, more complete, just looking at her.

At least that was how Ash saw it after three double Jacks, a quantity of whiskey that usually took the edge off reason. She indulged herself in a long look at the one beautiful thing in this disgusting fleapit. Her face was that of a serious child, pensive and hopelessly innocent. Her black hair was parted at one side and had a narrow wave that spilled in ripples across her smooth forehead. Ash guessed she tried for a more mature look by drawing the chin-length mop into a little bunch at her nape. The curve of her neck, the red bow of her mouth, and the fine-boned fragility of her hands complicated her beauty with such vulnerability Ash wanted instantly to shield her.

She imagined standing close enough to do just that and wondered what she smelled like. Guerlain, she decided, one of the haunting classics like Jicky. She looked too clean to have walked here, and so completely unaware of the attention she was getting that Ash felt like shaking her. But something else lay behind that urge. In the worst way, she wanted to touch the ravishing stranger.

Dry-mouthed, she watched the woman trail a hand absently back and forth along her thigh as if in sensual invitation. Ash wasn't usually wrong about women's body language. Or men's. But on this occasion she thought she was kidding herself. Feeling crass for having a sexual response to someone who looked like religious art, Ash inspected her more closely, seeking out the person behind the persona.

She was conservatively dressed and wore no jewelry. Someone had told her to keep her passport and cash in a money belt. Beneath her shirt its outline rested lumpily above a slender waist. She was a good six inches shorter than Ash, so probably around five-four. Her face was a study in concentration as she read a book lying open on the bar counter in front of her. It probably wasn't a guide to self-defense, which was what would have made sense. Flipping a page, she tilted her head and stared dreamy-eyed at nothing, a tiny smile hovering. In that second Ash glimpsed the woman within. Warm. Human. Seductive.

The stranger cupped her chin in her hand and Ash found the mundane movement so profoundly erotic, she was awestruck. This was what countless years without true love did to anyone who still had a soul, she concluded. Even the regular vacations she took from her PNG diet of celibacy and porn didn't change a thing in that regard. She tried to look away but couldn't and in that split second, the woman shifted her inward gaze to her surroundings and her eyes met Ash's.

For what seemed liked an eternity, they stared at one another, and in those few heartbeats of connection, Ash felt like she'd been knocked unconscious and transported to a magical dimension she would never remember except in her dreams. Her heart pounded and her skin tingled. She felt dazed and helpless to do anything but stare across the room, wanting to be seen, yearning for a smile that would bestow permission to approach. She was sweating even more than the climate warranted. Was this a panic attack? Was she finally losing her mind? It happened with monotonous regularity in PNG. Ash had long believed that any Westerner who chose to live here was not quite sane to begin with.

The woman blushed and looked away. She was waiting for some lucky bastard, Ash decided; no other explanation made any sense. A sane white woman would never set foot in a place like this unless she was hooked up with the kind of moron who still slept with his skateboard. At any moment, an unworthy nerd in a Greenpeace T-shirt would roll in, Lonely Planet guidebook in one hand, camera in the other, full of lame excuses for keeping her waiting. Ash would have to resist the overwhelming temptation to beat some common sense into him. How was it that the tofu-eating dweebs always had the most astonishing luck with women?

As she chewed over this harsh reality, she kept tabs on several figures gliding ever closer to the woman, working their way past tables and along walls, surreptitiously signaling one another. She measured the odds. They were armed. Knives and maybe a pistol or two. Chances were they wouldn't try anything in the bar. There were too many patrons paying too much attention. Instead they would find a way to get her out the door. She would be lucky if they settled for taking her cash and credit cards.

Ash signaled her own watchdogs to pay attention, then cast a look toward the narrow entrance of the bar. Still no sign of the dipshit boyfriend who had placed this goddess in a viper's nest. With a groan of resignation, she headed for the bar and positioned herself behind the woman. Yes, she smelled good. Just the faintest hint of an oriental fragrance competing with the smoke and sweat of the bar.

Placing a possessive hand on the small of her back, Ash said, "Do us both a favor and pretend you know me."

Startled gray eyes swung up to hers. Breathless with indignation, the woman demanded, "Take your hand off my…er…"

"Ass?" Ash suggested.

She colored fetchingly. "Just do it."

"That's not a wise idea." Ash bent close to her ear and resisted the urge to brush her lips past the downy cheek just a breath away. "Here's the thing. You're about to be mugged by three guys. Don't turn around."

The woman considered this statement, looked Ash over with flagrant doubt, then said, "Why should I believe you?"

Ash's spine tingled. Her ears insisted she'd heard that hypnotic intonation before but her brain refused to accept the possibility. The voice couldn't possibly be the one she'd heard from her hiding place in that Brookline bedroom a month ago. What were the odds that its owner would be here in Port Moresby, of all places? Sheer wishful thinking. And she was nothing like the woman Ash had imagined. She was not a statuesque suicide blonde in a torch singer's gown. She was an ebony-haired sylph in neatly pressed khaki cargo pants and a crisp beige linen shirt with pockets that hid the outline of her nipples. Her eyes were not sapphire pools, they were an odd hazy shade somewhere between gray and purple. All the same, how often did you hear a voice like that?

Ash collected herself. If she was the kind of flake who believed in destiny, she would probably be chanting a mantra by now, convinced that this whole string of events was somehow connected. But she cringed every time she heard a cop-out statement about situations being "meant to happen" or "God" having a plan. If there was one thing her life had taught her, it was that nothing made any sense and trying to find meaning in the crap that happened was a fool's errand.

Ash never blamed God, fate, karmic debt, or other people for anything she had control over. The buck stopped with her. Period. Right now that meant she had a decision to make. She could walk away because she didn't owe this woman a thing, or she could do a good deed. She generally opted for the latter because she liked herself better when she did. Also, if she was wrong about God and karma, there was no harm in putting some points on the board.

"Listen, do you want to get out of here in one piece?" she asked the soon-to-be damsel in distress. "Or would you rather I just butt out because I smell of booze and look like I spent the past year in a jungle without a change of clothes?"

The reply, a softly murmured "Oh," made Ash want to kiss her senseless, and there was something else, too. Staring down at this stranger from another dimension, the land-of-all-things-beautiful, she yearned irrationally to go back in time and make some different decisions. She wanted the woman staring at her to see a nobler, finer person than the one she'd become. But that was a futile train of thought. Her life was what she'd made of it. There was no going back.

Maybe she really *was* losing it. People did down here on the equator. If the shitty climate didn't fry every brain cell you had, if you didn't catch a sexually transmitted disease or get clipped in a random act of violence, you could go quietly nuts just figuring out how to exist in a city where a guy who jumped off a bus without paying his twenty cent fare was beaten to death by the driver and the other passengers. That had happened just after she got back from her sojourn in the land of the free, reminding her why she'd needed a vacation in the first place.

Ash allowed her gaze to drift by the rascals again. She was being paranoid, but that didn't mean she was wrong. "Act like you're happy to see me," she said.

"That's quite a challenge."

"I can imagine." She gave a self-effacing grin. "But consider this—my teeth are clean and I washed my hands before I came here."

Ash found the response to her mild humor devastatingly sexy. A sparkle lit the visitor's eyes and her mouth tugged wickedly in each corner, parting to reveal small even white teeth. Weak for a split second, Ash could only ogle the full, kissable lips.

"That certainly is convincing," she said hoarsely. "Are you an actress? Obviously you have the looks."

"That's an interesting compliment. But no, I'm a research biologist."

Ash wondered what could be worse than staring at disease cells magnified five hundred times. As sincerely as she could, she said, "Fascinating."

This counterfeit awe earned her a flinty stare. Brains, upper-class sex appeal, and an imperviousness to flattery. It all added up to one thing: certain disappointment. Zero likelihood of first base. Probably a slap across the face if she tried her luck. The alluring smile hovered but the biologist's eyes had lost their sparkle and she was suddenly all business.

"I see one of the men you're talking about. Clearly he'd sell his grandmother for five cents. I have a pocket knife. Should I get it out?"

Ash didn't laugh noisily and roll her eyes. "It's okay. I have two semiautomatics and a compact. If I go down, you'll find that one strapped to my ankle. Ever fired a gun?"

"My dad taught me how to use his .347 magnum."

"Good to know."

The beauty frowned, that is, if her narrowed gaze and sexy nibbling on the bottom lip constituted a frown. "Do you really think they might attack us right here, with all these people around?"

"There were seven killed in a rascal shootout at the airport terminal not so long ago."

"In other words we're not in Kansas anymore."

"More like Kandahar."

"What do you want me to do?"

Ash was full of bright ideas, most of which involved getting a room. She settled for a consolation prize that would pass for a brilliant plan. With a show of professional disinterest, she said, "I'm going to kiss you like we're an item, then we'll walk out of here together."

The reaction was predictably lukewarm. "Would you mind explaining why the liplock is necessary?"

"It sends the signal that we're not just friends and that I'll probably protect you. That's a deterrent. The gangs here would rather avoid a fight if they can roll someone without it."

"What if they follow us?"

"They won't if they have any sense." Rascals weren't stupid.

When they picked their mark, they chose someone who didn't know the ropes. Already they'd probably spotted Ash's lookouts. Angling her body so she could observe the rest of the room, she slid her hand behind the stranger's neck. "Look at me like you want it," she said. *Fat chance. But what a fantasy.*

At first the woman was hesitant, then her dismay gave way to resignation. With an impatient sigh, she linked her hands behind Ash's neck and gazed up at her in a languorous invitation that made her stomach curdle. "Let's get this over with."

Ash's pulse leapt and she cradled the dark head, tilting it back a little. She intended to make the kiss convincing but impersonal, just protracted enough to send a message to the lurking predators. Instead, at the first brush of their lips, she kissed her reluctant accomplice hard on the mouth. It was bliss. Plain and simple. She backed off just enough so she wouldn't be at the wrong end of a roundhouse, then lingered, parting the trembling lips with her tongue.

The deep, sensuous kiss that followed had not been included in their tacit accord. Neither had the response—a muffled gasp and a shiver that told Ash her companion's nipples had just gotten hard. A raw surge of desire almost made her pass out. In danger of losing herself completely and touching body parts she shouldn't, she pulled back in the nick of time, and they stared at one another, neither saying a word. Both drew breath erratically.

Ash was aware of noise and movement around them, but she couldn't concentrate on anything but the woman she was holding. The stranger looked just as stunned. Goose bumps had lifted the down of hairs along her smooth forearms. Wild color infused her cheeks and darkness consumed her eyes. Ash found herself transfixed by the play of emotions across her features, the flash of yearning followed by a strange haunted sorrow, then a fretful restlessness that transferred itself to her body.

Throwing caution to the wind, she didn't back off but dared to do the unthinkable. She slipped both arms around her and held her close, stroking her soft hair and breathing her in. "Everything's okay," she said, kissing the cheek that tempted her lips. "That was perfect. Now pick up your book and let's get out of here."

With surprising compliance, the woman slid from her bar stool, bringing her body into brief contact with Ash's. The brush of her breasts and thighs almost made Ash whine. Disconcerted, she tried to rationalize her response. The memory of her exciting threesome in Brookline had faded like the drive-through fantasy fodder it was. Her libido was alive and well, never entirely satisfied. Also, she inhabited an amatory desert devoid of tender affection. Chemistry was therefore bound to occur with any passably attractive female. And this particular female had a voice that made Ash feel like she was drowning in warm honey, and *hard-to-get* stamped all over her. Ash was a sucker for women who wouldn't give her the time of day.

"What's your name?" this one asked as they headed out the door.

"Ashley Evans."

"Ashley," she repeated with an odd frown of concentration. "I'm Charlotte Lascelles. Thank you for helping me, Mr. Evans."

Mister. Ash deliberated over whether to correct the assumption. She had counted on the likelihood that her companion had initially mistaken her for a man. Most people did. She was tall, built, and had a deep voice and nondescript features that could belong to either gender. In the traditional European uniform of the tropics—loose cargo pants and a four-pocket bush shirt over a tank—her body looked even less shapely than it was. Most of the time, it suited her to let wrong assumptions about her gender stand. In this neck of the woods looking like a man, and one who knew how to use a gun, was an asset.

On this occasion, she thought it was probably the gallant choice to keep her mouth shut. Why make this stranger feel uncomfortable, realizing she'd returned the kiss of a woman? They were never going to see each other again.

Ash hailed a red cab, usually the safest, and checked that the driver matched his ID. Opening the door for Charlotte, she said, "I'll take you back to your hotel."

Charlotte raised no objections. "I'm at the Crowne Plaza."

"I know it." Ash slid in beside her and locked their doors.

The Plaza was Pom's "safe" hotel, all things being relative. They drove toward the waterfront in silence. Ash could feel Charlotte eyeing her.

"What line of work are you in, Mr. Evans?"

"Please, call me Ash. And I'm a pilot in the private security industry."

"You take tourists on scenic flights?"

"No. My work is in cargo mostly." The term disguised a multitude of sins. Illegal arms. Drugs. Espionage. Human tragedy.

"Do you ever spend time in Irian Jaya?"

"We call it West Papua 'round here," Ash said. "Irian Jaya is an Indonesian invention. When you steal someone else's country, you need to give it a new name so no one notices the original inhabitants vanishing."

Charlotte blinked. "So, it's true then? The genocide?"

"That's a word we avoid—those of us who have to work with the Indonesians. I can suggest some coy euphemisms. Transmigration. Resettlement. And a special favorite...vital projects commitment."

"I see."

Ash doubted it. She changed the subject. "Gangs are a problem in Port Moresby. It's better if you stay in your hotel at night. Actually, it's better if you stay there all the time."

Charlotte looked embarrassed. "I only went to that bar because I was supposed to meet a man with some rare plants to sell."

"Plants," Ash repeated.

"For my research."

Brains but no smarts. Tunnel vision. *A man has rare plants—wonderful. Why not get killed trying to buy them?* Ash felt gloomy. She had already pigeonholed Charlotte Lascelles as too brainy and too classy to sleep with anyone just for the hell of it. Even if she was open to experimenting with a woman, she was the type who had to be wooed. That breed of woman expected emotional engagement and intellectual compatibility. They thought sex was about love. Ash was out of her mind if she read anything but expediency into the kiss they'd shared.

She contemplated showing up at the Crowne Plaza later in the evening, looking much more appealing than she did now on the off chance Charlotte would allow herself to be seduced. The likeliest scenario played across her mind: she takes Charlotte into her arms and kisses her. Charlotte gets interested and wants to find out what she's packing. Shock. Disappointment. Ash tries to explain herself and attempts to sell Charlotte on the idea that she won't miss out on anything, in fact Ash will take such good care of her she'll wonder what she ever saw in males. Charlotte doesn't want to know. She is outraged to have been fooled by a liar who only wants to get into her pants.

Ash stole a sideways glance at her companion's profile. Charlotte, she decided, was a straight woman who thought she was talking to a moderately viable man. She probably had no idea of the nonverbal signals she kept sending. Ash was enjoying these, even if they were unconscious and rooted in a false impression. Every now and then, she could feel Charlotte's eyes prowling her body and when they spoke Charlotte looked at her mouth.

She couldn't help but wonder how far she could get by continuing with the deception. What if Charlotte was interested enough in *Mister* Evans and far enough from civilization that she would willingly get drunk and do something out of character? It could happen, and often did in faraway places. The idea was tempting, and since they would never see each other again there was no reason why she shouldn't pursue. Except that it was dishonest and even she had some standards. Besides, Ash knew exactly what would happen if, by some blunder of the Fates, she made it to second base with this woman. There was no way she would want to stop and the truth would be out.

Gloomily she resigned herself to doing the right thing. If she intended to continue their acquaintanceship beyond this taxi ride, she would have to come clean and accept the consequences. The thought of trading the tingle of mutual awareness they now had for an evening of polite companionship was unappealing. And there would be no chance of making out in an elevator, let alone anything more satisfying. But that was the only real option she had. It was a lose/lose.

They pulled up outside of the hotel and Charlotte started thanking her some more.

Ash made her decision and politely cut her off. "There's something I should tell you."

"Oh?" Her mouth parted like she was about to lick her lips. Ash got the chills.

"I'm not Mr. Evans."

Eyes the periwinkle hue of storybook mountains met hers. Charlotte's expression was mildly puzzled, then something seemed to dawn on her and she said, "I'm sure half the people I'm going to meet here are going by different identities. You don't owe me any explanations."

There was a tease underlying her tone, the faintest suggestion of flirtation in the downward sweep of her eyelashes. Ash decided immediately to delay the plunge into candor and instead explain the situation over dinner, assuming Charlotte would accept an invitation. Meantime, she wanted to know if what she'd just heard was Charlotte's way of letting her off the hook, and that she had finally guessed. She thought again about the mystery woman she'd heard in Dani's bedroom that night. She seemed to be a lesbian. If Charlotte was that woman, then Ash was in luck. But there was only one way to find out.

She paid the driver and quickly bailed out of the cab so she could open the other door. Because Charlotte was a lady and clearly accustomed to being treated like one, she accepted the small courtesy with grace. Ash appreciated that. There was nothing worse than trying to get a door only to find the woman on the other side pushing it open in her face.

She walked Charlotte into the lobby and was immediately conscious of her own appearance. Thanks to the weather, her last assignment, and the bar, she reeked of sweat, alcohol, and other people's cigarettes. Her clothes were filthy and one leg of her pants had a tear flapping at the knee. Her Gucci loafers belonged in the trash and she needed a shower two days ago. Oh yeah, any desirable woman would leap at the chance to have dinner with her. Ash cursed beneath her breath and decided it wasn't flirtatiousness she'd detected back in the cab. Charlotte's sidelong glances were probably signs of embarrassment.

The guard near the elevators gave her a long, hard look as they approached. Ash met his gaze unflinchingly. "Personal security," she said. "Rough day."

His eyes prowled her body for the telltale evidence of hired muscle. Concealed weapons, deep tan, expensive footwear. He gave her a nod.

Ash drew Charlotte toward some potted palms. "Listen, there's something else I wanted to ask you." She felt bashful, which had not occurred in living memory.

Charlotte gave her an understanding smile. "I didn't intend for you to pay for the cab." She started unbuttoning her shirt at the waist, reaching for the conspicuous money belt.

"No." Ash caught her wrist. Embarrassed, she instantly let go. "I don't need your money. And you should never open that belt in public."

She stared at their warped reflections in a brass panel that capped a nearby pillar. The brief burn of Charlotte's skin against her own was like a maddening crumb thrown to a beggar. How could this be happening to her? Was she finally losing it before her next big assignment? Was it time to punch out and spend the rest of her days converting her property holdings into a real estate fortune? She knew guys who'd made a killing in Somalia or Iraq and were now kicking back. Maybe she'd tell Tubby Nagle to go fuck himself. There were plenty more wild geese where she came from. He could burn down a village without her help. She didn't want to be there guarding the inhabitants after they'd gathered their few pitiful possessions and accepted their "compensation" before being trucked away like cattle.

"Ash?" Skin again, the tantalizing brush of her fingers. "Are you okay?"

Barely able to breathe, Ash said a shade too quickly, "I'd like to take you to dinner. I have other clothes." She braced herself for the brush-off.

Charlotte laughed. It was better than an outright no. "Dinner?" she repeated, like she was pleasantly surprised.

"Why not?" Ash slowed down, trying for a smooth and confident demeanor. "We both speak English and unless you already have a date, you're going to be eating alone. It's the wrong signal to send around here."

Something flashed across Charlotte's features. Disappointment? Ash could have kicked herself. She'd made it sound like she was doing her a favor.

An edge of stiffness confirmed the faux pas. "I suppose you have a point."

"Listen, I'm an ass," Ash backpedaled swiftly. "Do me a favor and blame malaria or something. I'm asking you to waste a couple of hours of your life with me because you seem like an intelligent, interesting woman and I think we could enjoy each other's company while we eat what passes for a decent meal here."

"So, this is a date?"

"Would you like it to be?"

Charlotte did something to her hair, a sexual cue instantly called into question by her next declaration. "The kiss…back there. It was just an act. You know that, don't you? I mean, I'm not going to sleep with you."

Ash composed her features. "I'm crushed, but can we still have dinner?"

This time, little puckers transformed Charlotte's face to one of schoolgirl mischief. Ash ruthlessly suppressed an image of her perched on a desk in white knee socks and one of those black British schoolgirl uniforms she'd seen working security in the expat community. The thought of corrupting Charlotte in such attire did nothing for her concentration.

"Okay, let's have dinner," Charlotte said.

"There's a decent restaurant right here in the hotel. I'll reserve a table. How's seven thirty?"

"Perfect. Where will I find you?"

Ash gestured toward a waiter weaving between tables, a tray of cocktails balanced on one hand. "Over there in the bar." *Drowning my sorrows because it really doesn't matter if I'm Mr. or Ms. It's never going to happen.*

CHAPTER SIX

Everything she'd packed made her look like a librarian, Charlotte thought.

She dragged the few non-work clothes she'd brought along out of the hotel closet and posed in front of her mirror, holding each outfit up against her. It seemed silly to be peeved that she didn't have anything more sophisticated. She was dining with a man who looked like he could sleepwalk to any bar in the entire of this seedy tropical port. It wasn't like she needed to impress him. And he was barking up the wrong tree if he thought he was going to get lucky. She'd spelled that out in words of one syllable.

She wasn't entirely sure why she'd agreed to meet him, except that she felt she owed him something, and he was unlike anyone she knew. When you traveled to places like this, new experiences and new people were part of the deal. Ashley Evans probably had some fascinating tales to tell over dinner and he also knew the region. Charlotte had a few questions that her manager hadn't been able, or willing, to answer.

There was something else, too. If she were completely honest, she had been shocked by her response during their phony kiss in the bar. She hadn't experienced a jolt to the senses like that one since she'd fallen for Britt, and she'd more or less accepted that she would never feel so alive again. Yet that numb part of her was suddenly reacting. To a man. How was that possible?

Charlotte could almost hear her therapist. Men were safe. She wasn't attracted to them. She didn't have to worry about getting involved with one or being hurt. Whereas with women, she protected herself by choosing partners she felt neutral about at best. The theory made sense intellectually, but Charlotte still didn't see how a lesbian could react sexually to a man. Was she so screwed up that this was the result—a grubby slob paws her in a bar on the wrong side of town and she gets turned on?

Another possibility presented itself. Ash was a gay man, and that's why she felt an affinity of sorts with him. He certainly had an androgynous look if you could get past the Indiana Jones exterior. Charlotte noticed detail. That was one of the reasons she excelled in her field. Very little about Ash Evans had escaped her. He was not the tallest of men, maybe five-ten, but he had a physical presence that compensated for the average stature and he'd obviously worked hard to add muscle to a frame that was naturally lithe and athletic.

If she had to take a bet, Charlotte would guess he knew a martial art in addition to carrying the three guns he had mentioned. He walked with the self-aware grace of someone who possessed those highly trained reflexes, and there was a quiet menace about him, revealed in his carriage and his narrowed watchful gaze. No doubt such skills were an advantage in this lawless part of the world.

For a man who spent a lot of his time in the jungle, he was also surprisingly well manicured and clean shaven, which, now that she thought about it, just screamed "gay man." During their kiss, she'd noticed how soft his skin felt, not a trace of beard. Being blond probably meant he had less regrowth to contend with than men with dark hair. She thought about her brother, Brody. Like her, he had inherited their father's French coloring. Their older brother, Justin, was copper haired and fair skinned like their mother. Brody had to shave twice a day and Charlotte always teased that he got a two o'clock shadow and by five he'd have a beard.

Thankfully, she wasn't cursed with the excessive female body hair that sometimes went with Mediterranean coloring, unlike some of her friends. They were forever bemoaning their wax treatments. She also liked her skin tone. It was somewhere between her mother's extreme milky white and her father's olive, a blend that looked good with a dark crimson stretch knit top she'd packed. Charlotte had been unsure about bringing it because it drew attention to her breasts and if there was an evening event with the other scientists before or after the expedition, she didn't want to be seen to play on her femininity.

She held the top to her body and considered her reflection. It went well with the narrow knee-length black silk skirt she'd purchased in anticipation of the tropical heat. And she had a lipstick that worked with it. Normally she didn't wear a dark red on her lips or nails. Her mouth was small but full-lipped and she worried that it appeared too prominent for her face if she applied anything but quiet, natural tones.

Britt had once told her that in full make-up she looked like a whore. Charlotte had never been able to shake the suspicion that her ex might have a point. After all, Britt was a trial lawyer. She knew how people were perceived. So most of the time she didn't wear make-up at all. And besides, it was a hazard in a laboratory setting where mascara could blot the lens of a microscope and skin products could corrupt anything they accidentally came in contact with.

She laid the crimson top down on the bed, found her make-up bag, and applied a few discreet dabs of Shalimar at her throat, elbows, and wrists. Real perfume extracts were an indulgence of hers. She was sure that her fascination for plants had something to do with it. She never wasted her time with eau de toilette sprays. In those rip-off colognes, the true notes of the various flower oils faded before they were even fully developed. None of her favorite scents—Shalimar, Jicky, and Must de Cartier—smelled like the same fragrance an hour after applying the watered-down version.

As she drew the top over her head, it struck her that she'd just put on the wrong perfume. She'd automatically selected Shalimar because she thought of it as an evening scent. However, it was the most seductive of the fragrances she had with her and she should probably have chosen something more everyday, like the innocuous Chamade. Not that it really mattered. Her dinner companion didn't seem the type who would notice a scent.

Zipping her skirt, Charlotte reflected that she would have been a bundle of nerves if she'd been planning to have dinner with a woman who could kiss the way Ash Evans had kissed her that afternoon. In fact, she would not have been getting dressed up at all. She would never have agreed to the outing in the first place, let alone be putting on make-up and wearing a top that showed cleavage. But Ash was only a man, even if he had evoked a disconcerting physical response from her. She knew how to give males the brush-off without having to announce her sexuality. There was nothing to worry about. She could just relax and enjoy the local nightlife with an escort who was the next best thing to her own personal bodyguard. It was better than being alone and ordering room service.

After combing her hair out loose and flattening her natural waves with some mousse, she blotted her lipstick and applied a fine line of violet kohl to each eyelid, just enough to make her lashes look heavier and her eyes less nondescript than their usual gray. She didn't need to pencil her eyebrows. They were black and she kept them tidily plucked without going overboard. It annoyed her that they wanted to be straight instead of curved. They made her look so serious that people sometimes thought she was frowning. To compensate, she smiled more than she might otherwise.

Charlotte checked the time and realized she was several minutes late, unheard of. Hastily, she slid her feet into the one pair of feminine sandals she'd brought with her, black high heels with a simple band across the toes. She hoped she wouldn't fall over trying to walk in them. A sprained ankle was all she needed before setting off into the rainforest for two months.

She transferred her passport, cash, and credit cards into a small satchel, dropped this over her shoulder, and made a quick turn in front of the mirror to ensure nothing was out of place. She looked attractive but not shameless, and certainly not like a woman in search of a "good time." That was one signal she didn't want to send inadvertently. Her dinner companion would have something nice to look at across the table, and she would make a point of being pleasant. That was the least she could do for the man who had probably saved her from a fate worse than death.

❖

Ash had been in the bar for twenty minutes drinking a club soda when she really wanted a whiskey. She could not shake this feeling of restless anticipation, and it bugged the crap out of her. Charlotte was late. Maybe she'd had second thoughts and was not going to show. By now Ash would normally be checking out the talent around the room so she'd have a Plan B. But no. She was looking at her watch like a moonstruck high schooler.

When she finally caught sight of Charlotte stepping away from the elevator, she almost had a heart attack. The last time she'd seen anything so sexy was…never. She dismissed the thought instantly as her libido talking. She saw sexy women every time she hit a city outside of PNG and if she wanted to hang out around hotels like this one, she could see plenty right here. Or she could hit the Royal Yacht Club and hook up with some of the lonely, bored bi-curious housewives that abounded in the expat community. The reason she steered clear of that occupational hazard was that she had to live here and didn't need a jealous husband putting a price on her head. Five hundred bucks could buy a bullet between the eyes in Pom.

As Charlotte approached, Ash stumbled to her feet and almost knocked over the potted palm behind her chair. Off balance in more ways than one, she propped her hand against one of the hefty white pillars that studded the room and stared down at the beige and burgundy pattern in the carpet, collecting herself. She was only thirty-six. Was it possible that she was entering her midlife crisis fifteen years early? Or had she finally contracted malaria? Swelling of the brain could account for temporary insanity.

She forced herself to look directly at her dinner date and wave with what she hoped was casual panache. She wasn't the only one gawking. A couple of businessmen a few tables away were virtually drooling into their beer glasses. She wanted to slug them. It wasn't like Charlotte was hanging out of her dress or anything. In fact, if anything her outfit was conservative, except that it clung all over in places her pants and shirt had concealed. Ash had noticed her compact body in the bar, but she had underestimated the curves.

"You clean up well," Charlotte informed her and extended a hand the way women did when they wanted to preempt an unwelcome male hug.

Ash obliged with a polite handshake. "You, too."

"I like my martinis dry and a little dirty," Charlotte announced, ahead of the game already.

Ash pried her attention away from the teasing bounce of her date's breasts beneath the clinging red top to flag down a passing waiter. Her brain felt scrambled and foggy, and her heart was galloping. Under the circumstances, she figured whiskey was a bad idea, but she ordered one anyway and pulled a chair out for the cause of her disquiet.

Her plan had been to get the misunderstanding about her gender out of the way right off the bat just in case Charlotte actually hadn't figured it out. Instead she said, like she was a channel for the world's twenty worst pick-up lines, "So, tell me. What brings you to PNG, Charlotte?"

"Well, I can't be explicit, since I've signed all kinds of

nondisclosure agreements. But I work for an organization helping develop a new generation of pharmaceuticals. I'm here to gather samples of certain plant species."

"You've come to the right place. There's nothing that can't grow here. And if you want bugs, we've got a shitload. Cockroaches the size of rats, for starters."

"I noticed." An elegant shudder. "There was one walking along the counter at that bar. I'd swear it was drunk."

"It was. They crawl inside the glasses. You have to watch out if you put your drink down for more than five minutes."

"Yeech." She glanced around in dismay. "Surely they don't have them in a place like this."

Ash didn't want to think about walking into the hotel kitchens in the dead of night and hitting the lights. In a place this size the usual scramble of gleaming beetle bodies would be something to see. She offered a more comforting image. "Not a chance. I'm guessing they have the exterminators in here every week."

"It could be cleaner," Charlotte confided after the waiter had set their drinks down on frilly white bar napkins. "I mean, it's supposed to be the best hotel in the city, but you should see my bathroom. I had to scrub it myself after I checked in."

Ash chuckled. "Something you need to get used to here is lowering your expectations."

"You've been in PNG a while?"

"Ten years in paradise," she replied cynically. "I don't live in Pom anymore. I just keep an apartment here for when I have business in town. My home is in Madang."

She promptly did what she never did and took out a couple of the photos she carried in her wallet. Looking at her house was the only thing that kept her grounded sometimes. That and Emma. But she didn't get her sister's picture out. She only wanted to cry when she saw it, and tonight she was trying to get her mind off that unhappy subject.

"It's stunning." Charlotte examined the closer shot of the house at length. "I love it. The wooden porticos and that long balcony with the white pillars. Those huge palm trees. It's like something from a novel." She pointed to a figure standing on the balcony, leaning against the railing. "Is that you?"

"Yes." Ash had bought her houseboy, Ramon, a Polaroid camera a while back and he'd lost his mind and taken pictures of everything. "You can see the ocean from up there."

"Amazing. Do you have land?"

"Sixty acres. It's a coffee plantation. Kind of run down, but it provides the locals with some work. We just had our main harvest back in September."

"Coffee. I had no idea."

"It's one of PNG's biggest exports. Most of it ends up in Germany."

"Not in Starbucks?"

"Funny thing. We actually prefer to sell our crop for more than thirty cents a pound. It's hard to pay wages when you're giving the stuff away."

"I thought Starbucks had programs supporting small producers."

"Don't tell me you've been reading their propaganda over your morning hit?" Ash teased gently.

"God, no. They'd have to pay me serious money to drink a latte in any place that uses rBGH milk. I can't believe we're the last country on the planet to ban that crap."

"I think they still serve it in Kazakhstan."

"What an endorsement." Her face grew earnest. "You know what's happening back home? Our bought and paid for senate is about to pass the Monsanto laws. That means no more state regulations about food labeling. By all means, avoid telling the consumer about toxins and growth hormones. They know people are getting cancer from their Frankenfoods. That's why they want to hide the information for as long as they can. Just like the cigarette companies."

Ash didn't think she'd ever been so idealistic that hard truths could disillusion her. She said, "Down here we're so undeveloped no one can afford pesticides and antibiotics, so we only have organic foods."

"Lucky you." Charlotte's grave little face took on a brooding cast. "Maybe it's because of my work, but this really bothers me. I mean, genetic modification is in its infancy as a science. No one has any idea of the impact of these foods. But they're putting them on our tables and releasing GE crops into our environment like it's nothing." She fell silent. "Okay, gag me. I'm talking like a crazy person."

A mental snapshot of a fetchingly gagged Charlotte played havoc with Ash's senses. Nothing hard-core, just one of those playful satin accessories. She wrestled the image away and tried for the pensive response that was called for.

"You're talking like someone who knows depressing facts, that's all." She could relate. There were topics she never allowed herself to discuss because she knew how she would sound.

"I can get overly opinionated." Charlotte's tone suggested this characteristic sometimes exasperated her. "I grew up with two older brothers. It was competitive."

Ash didn't think any woman should apologize for being strong-minded. Wanting to put her at ease, she said, "I don't have a problem with people showing they care about something. But tell me, don't you find it a dilemma, working in your field?"

"Not at all. I believe what I'm doing will help people and if I have an ethical problem with anything, I won't do it."

Ash smiled inwardly. She made such rationalizations herself, drawing lines in the sand that made it possible for her to look at herself in the mirror every morning. She did not carry out political executions and she refused to provide operational support for the Indonesian rape and death squads that cleared the path for foreign investment and Javanese transmigration. She would only work on resettlement projects where the New Guineans were not physically harmed.

In the dirty business she was in, making those choices had cost her a lot of money and some powerful friends. But she never kidded herself that she was doing anything noble. She was just clinging to some flimsy moral high ground on a slippery slope that was no place for any truly decent person. A woman like Charlotte would never have to choose the lesser of evils that were truly evil, and that was a good thing.

Ash's thoughts veered to the small truth she still hadn't mentioned. Hiding her gender wasn't a matter of safety anymore, so it wasn't right to keep up the pretense, and if Charlotte had guessed, the least Ash should do was acknowledge it. As soon as the opportunity arose, she was going to do just that.

Charlotte had taken refuge in her cocktail, clearly embarrassed. They'd broken the first rule of pleasant socializing—don't talk about issues. "Maybe we should head over to the restaurant," she suggested, apparently determined to rein herself in. "Didn't you say our reservation is for seven thirty?"

"I sure did." Ash signaled the waiter to collect their drinks and they crossed the lobby. She caught a whiff of Charlotte's perfume as they walked. Shalimar. Ash would know it anywhere. Utterly delicious. The perfume of the classy woman who liked to get physical. Was that Charlotte?

As they settled at their table, Ash said, "How about this? I won't talk politics if you won't talk environment."

"I can live with that. And, between you and me," Charlotte's smile hinted at mischief, "if one more foreigner asks me when we're going to invade North Korea, I'm going to be arrested for doing grievous bodily harm."

"We're invading countries?" Ash marveled with mock innocence. "I don't get out enough."

This raised a giggle that made Charlotte's breasts bounce slightly. She sipped her cocktail and asked, "Do you have family back home?"

Ash hesitated. She was cautious with personal questions. "Just my sister. I get back home to visit her several times a year." That was all she could say without her throat closing up.

"Where are you from, originally?"

The trouble with inane social chitchat was that it meant talking about family and job, topics Ash preferred not to get into. She said, "I was born and raised in Boston. You?"

"Greenwich, Connecticut, but I've been living in Boston since I graduated. Where did you go to school?"

"BU." Ash didn't explain that she'd dropped out in favor of West Point. Smart women like Charlotte always wanted to talk about sexual harassment in the military, and that conversation was old. "Harvard, right?"

Charlotte's dark hair bobbed slightly as she shook her head. "Stanford."

Their waiter arrived to explain the menu. Thankful for the diversion, Ash said, "I've had the barramundi here. It's decent if you like freshwater fish."

"I always worry about eating fish when I'm overseas. Refrigeration is such an issue. And the salad is a concern, too, don't you think? I hate to imagine the bacteria count given the water they must wash their lettuce in here."

Ash normally had no patience with fussiness, but it seemed germ-phobia was one of Charlotte's personal quirks. Worryingly, she found this cute. "You spend too much time looking through a microscope," she said with a grin.

As soon as they'd ordered, she was going to come right out and just say what she should have said in the first place. Pretending to read her menu, she framed the words. *There's something I've been meaning to tell you. I didn't say anything earlier because I didn't want you to feel embarrassed about what happened in the bar. But I'm a woman, not a man. I wasn't sure if you'd noticed.*

"It's weird." Charlotte observed suddenly. "I haven't done anything like this for ages."

The intimate lull of her voice made Ash lean forward to catch every word. Shalimar flooded her nostrils again, reminding her how much she liked to smell it on a lover. "Like what?"

Charlotte pondered for a moment, her head fetchingly angled. "Said yes to having an adventure, I suppose."

"That stunt wasn't an adventure. It was an act of madness."

"I'm not just talking about that. I mean everything." Charlotte swept a hand around. "I'm sitting in a restaurant with white linen and candelabras on the tables, and scary tribal masks all around the walls. I haven't read a newspaper in days. I'm in a place where people speak eight hundred languages, mostly not English. I don't do impulsive things, normally, but here I am having dinner with a stranger who carries three guns and I'm feeling completely comfortable. It's weird. It's like I've been cut adrift and all the rules have changed."

Ash had to prod herself mentally to come up with a reply. She'd lost herself so completely in the sensual melody of Charlotte's voice that she had barely heard the words. "Well, that's not surprising. Nothing you do here has any social consequences. The people who matter to you are five thousand miles away."

"Exactly." Charlotte's eyes were pansy purple in the candlelight. They looked like windows to a soul. Ash knew her own were shuttered, by contrast. "It's like there's a whole new paradigm, a conspiracy you join without even knowing it. Just because you're a stranger in a strange land."

"I think most travelers experience what you're describing. It's part of escaping."

Charlotte rested an elbow on the table and cupped her cheek in her hand. "Does it happen to you, too, when you come back here?"

That voice. It simply had to belong to her. Charlotte was from Boston and obviously hadn't been in PNG for more than a few days. The bizarre coincidence was unlikely but not impossible. Ash contemplated asking her if she knew Dani Bush, then realized how stupid that would be. Did she really want this woman finding out she was about to dine with the third person in the bedroom that night?

"Actually it's the other way 'round," she said, answering Charlotte's question. "As soon as the plane touches down back home all bets are off."

"I can't imagine you doing crazy stuff. You seem so... controlled."

I'm doing crazy stuff right now. She was sitting opposite a woman she knew spelled trouble, trying to persuade herself that she only wanted to sleep with her, yet knowing there was already more to it than that. She was actually indulging in fantasies about having a future with a woman she'd only just met and who didn't even know her gender. As she'd driven to the hotel for their dinner date, she'd tried to see herself in a relationship. Then, when Charlotte was looking at the photos of the plantation house, Ash was picturing her on the balcony late at night, the two of them wallowing in the sunset, then going inside to make love.

Her stomach churned at the thought. That body, this woman, naked in her arms, belonging to her. An aching hunger clawed at her, making its familiar, restless claim on her senses. But there was something else, too, a yearning so profound, Ash was shaken by it. Comprehension flashed across her mind. *Love at first sight.* She instantly rejected the idea. There was no such thing. People who felt guilty about no-strings sex laid claim to that sentiment to justify their urges.

She sipped her whiskey and gathered herself. She was a disgrace to players all over the globe and a walking cliché. She should get up right now, burble some lame excuse, and get the hell out of here. How many warning signs did she need? She didn't *make love* with women. She didn't *fall in love*. Normally at this point in a dinner assignation, her entire train of thought revolved around scoring as quickly as possible and planning an exit strategy that would avoid complications. Angry husbands and messy lesbian divorce dramas like the one in Brookline could ruin even the warmest afterglow.

Ash stared bleakly at the menu. Nothing sounded appetizing and the descriptions of the dishes seemed weirdly sexual. Chicken bathed in a velvet merlot sauce. Succulent oysters clinging to the half shell. Ash didn't want to dip crusty French bread into a warm artichoke spread, she wanted to dip her tongue into Charlotte. And, shockingly, she wanted to wake up to her the next morning.

There had to be a reasonable explanation for her disturbing mind-set. Was she having some kind of reaction to the stressful situation with Emma? The thought of possibly losing the one person left in the world who knew her and loved her no matter what, the person her universe had revolved around for so long, was unbearable. Had it driven her into a panic state?

Charlotte possessed something Ash also saw in Emma, an innocence and tenderness that brought out the best in her. When she was with Emma, she tried to be the person her sister thought she was. A good person. Someone who led a blameless existence and could always be depended upon. And she actually felt like that person. She needed that and she was afraid that if she lost Emma, the feeling would be lost with her.

"I'm sorry, did I say something to offend you?" Charlotte studied her with a trace of alarm.

Ash shook her head, realizing it had been her turn to speak but she was too busy navel-gazing. "No. Just having a menu dilemma." *Leave now,* she thought. "Listen, I need to make a call before we eat."

"Would you like me to order for you?"

"Sure, thanks. The ginger chicken skewers." Ash made a show of fishing her cell phone from her jacket. She could feel Charlotte's eyes on her as she rose and walked away.

She headed out into the stifling night air and stood a few yards from the doorman, wondering why she'd imagined that standing out here in this tropical soup would help clear her head. Having dinner with Charlotte Lascelles was the dumbest decision she'd made in years. Did she crave self-punishment? Did she want to spend a whole evening staring down the barrels of the life she might have had, the kind of woman she could have come home to every day, if things were very different? Ash paced up and down and puffed on a cigar, thinking through her options.

The pragmatic, sensible choice was to write a quick note claiming she'd been called away, pay for the meal, depart, and never look back. The next option was to play the game she knew—get Charlotte into bed, have a good time, and say good-bye. Yet even supposing Charlotte wasn't pissed when Ash finally owned up to being a woman, and even if she was both a lesbian and willing to be seduced by someone she barely knew, Ash was strangely uneasy about the idea of a one-night stand with her.

So what was the point in being here? What did she think was going to happen? She already knew they would never have a relationship. Apart from the small matter that they lived in two different countries and probably had nothing in common, Ash had chosen a life that could only be complicated by the existence of loved ones. She did business with ugly people who used ugly methods to get what they wanted, and one thing she would never give them was an emotional lever. She had to be able to say no, or hold out for her price, without placing someone she cared about at risk. It was that simple.

No one over here knew her sister existed. Ash had made sure to circulate a flawed newspaper report from her past in which Emma was reported bludgeoned to death along with their mother. The fact that her father was serving a life sentence was, however, widely known among her business associates, as was the fact that Ash wouldn't lose any sleep if someone shanked him. She hadn't stayed in touch with friends from her past and avoided making new ones when she moved here. She knew Tubby had figured out she was queer, but he was the kind of guy who got worked up about "faggots" but thought lesbianism was hot. They never talked about it.

By tomorrow he would know Ash had rescued a woman from local thugs and then had dinner with her. He had sources all over town and a couple of his hirelings had entered the bar just as Ash did. There was bound to be someone at the hotel who would pass on the information if she slept with Charlotte. Then they could never be seen together again.

She paced resolutely for a few more seconds, then dialed. "Tubby. You got something for me?"

"Yeah. A new customer. So don't piss me off with any more of that shit about needing time out and business back home."

"You have my complete attention and I'm ready to get back to work." If nothing else, she needed the distraction while she got everything arranged so she could leave PNG for a long period.

"Security detail," he said. "Morons going native. The usual caper."

"Tourists looking for thrills?"

"Even dumber. Scientists."

Another geological research team surveying for new mining sites, Ash assumed. "Who's the customer?"

"It's not important."

Ash groaned inwardly. Since the Sandline scandal, Tubby had become the biggest private-security middleman in PNG, providing operational support for the likes of Rio Tinto and Freeport-McMoRan. He didn't need any more mining clients, but he couldn't resist helping out competing interests for the right price. It created bad feelings, but the local chopper pilot shortage meant the big boys didn't have a whole lot of leverage. They were all deeply paranoid, all competing for the government's favor, and all trying to spy on one another. Tubby made a pile of money serving many masters and having loyalty to none.

"How much?"

Tubby sucked his lips. Ash would recognize that sound in her sleep. "Your end is fifty."

"Fifty large? Just for flying them?"

"Fuck, no. You'll be setting up their campsite. Running the close-protection team. Meeting them at pick-up points. The whole nine yards."

It still sounded like a cakewalk. "How many on the NGD team?"

"Four."

The standard team for a high-risk Iraqi gig was eight, so four seemed heavy duty for a few guys picking up rock samples. On the other hand, Tubby took advantage if he thought he could. He'd probably sold this new customer on a high-priced package, scaring executives with espionage horror stories. Mining companies still shuddered over the Bougainville fiasco. It had been a huge embarrassment to have one of their own caught hand in glove with a corrupt government, funding a private army to attack the entire population of an island. All because the Bougainvilleans had dared to shut down the mining that was destroying their environment and poisoning their children.

Tubby had discovered he only had to mention that weeping public-relations scab and his clients opened their checkbooks. They wanted to do business discreetly and with as little collateral damage as possible. If a problem happened, they liked everything cleaned up ASAP so they could disclaim all knowledge. Sweetheart close-protection assignments like the one Ash was hearing about did not pay fifty thousand bucks unless there was a serious fly in the ointment.

"I'm in," she said. "What's the catch?"

"We can discuss that. Come by after you're done entertaining the broad."

Ash's pulse jumped. "News travels fast."

"Who is she?" More lip sucking.

"No one you know. Call it a favor to a friend. I'm baby-sitting till she hightails it back to her nice life."

Tubby wheezed, his version of laughter. "Hey, if she's stacked and lonely, you know where to find me."

Ash ignored the remark and kept her tone even. "I'll see you later, Tubby. And chain those damn dogs up before I get there. Okay?"

"They're just being friendly."

"Yeah, it's not your throat they want to rip out."

She hung up and carefully tapped out her cigar against the sole of her boot. There was plenty left to smoke, so the doorman would be able to sell it. She wrapped it in a twenty instead of the less desirable local currency and handed it to him.

"Anyone comes asking for me," she said. "I'm in a card game."

The doorman palmed the tip impassively. "They already asked, mister."

"I had a feeling about that." Ash swatted a mosquito and headed back inside the refrigerated sanctuary of the lobby.

She waited there for a few, chewing a breath mint and letting the cigar smell dissipate. She had only one evening to enjoy with Charlotte and they weren't going to sleep together. Instead, she'd decided they were going to have fun the way people did in Port Moresby, drinking and dancing the night away at the Pongo. They could head over there after dinner and Charlotte would get the chance to check out the PNG version of a nightclub. She'd have a blast, talk to some locals, and end up with a few stories to tell her girlfriends back home. Then Ash would walk her back to her door and say good night. No drama. No regrets.

She was relieved. And the plan also meant she wouldn't have to set Charlotte straight about the gender issue. They weren't going to sleep together, so it didn't matter what she believed. If the right moment presented itself, Ash would tell her the truth. If it didn't, so what? No harm done.

CHAPTER SEVEN

I don't normally do this kind of thing." Charlotte left a shoe behind as she lurched into her room. A hand caught her arm, steadying her.

Ash asked, "What kind of thing?"

"Get really drunk and go dancing." She allowed Ash to guide her toward the bed, then flopped onto the pillows, her head swimming. "Thanks for helping me up here."

Ash scooped up the discarded shoe and removed the other one from Charlotte's foot. "Are you okay?"

"You mean other than setting myself up for a splitting headache tomorrow morning?"

"I'll tell housekeeping to send you up some aspirin."

"You know something." Charlotte wanted to sit up straight and speak clearly, but she stayed where she was and slurred like a lush, "You're a real gentleman."

Ash gave her an odd look. "Just on that...there's something I've been meaning to say."

"What?"

Charlotte collected her wits. Was this the moment she'd hoped to avoid, when she'd have to explain her sexual orientation to a man hoping for more than a farewell kiss on the cheek? Things had been going so nicely, she'd started to think it wasn't going to happen. At some point during their after-dinner partying in the Pongo Tavern, she'd decided for certain that Ash was gay. It was the only plausible reason he hadn't hit on her. And it would also explain the odd mix of feelings she had around him. She felt safe and unself-conscious, like she could just be herself. She never felt that way with any of the perfectly nice lesbians she dated.

Then there was that odd feeling of connection. If she hadn't understood what it was about, all kinds of warning bells would have been ringing. But she and Ash shared the bond of strangers who'd colluded in a dangerous experience, and the flickers of attraction she kept noticing obviously stemmed from that bond. Also, in a purely cerebral sense, she could appreciate Ash's looks. Scrubbed up, with his scruffy charm ditched in favor of a distinctly urban sophistication, he seemed neither masculine nor feminine; in fact, she'd barely recognized him when she entered the bar earlier that evening.

The wavy hair she'd thought was dull mouse was actually sun-streaked dark corn blond. His face was not as creased as she'd thought, probably because it was now clean. But the same assessing cobalt eyes stared out from beneath a wave that drooped across his forehead and the same straight but sensuous mouth made him seem very serious until he smiled. The smile was roguish and infectious, flashing teeth that seemed extra white against his tan complexion. He looked like a tough guy with an artistic side. The artistic side had obviously chosen the clothes he was wearing tonight.

Most of the men dancing at the Pongo wore Hawaiian shirts and long, baggy shorts. Ash stuck out as the one who could fit in strolling down any street in Milan. Even when he took off his fine dark weave jacket, he still looked like Mr. GQ in black pants and a charcoal shirt with the sleeves rolled up. Yes, she concluded, he had to be gay. The alternative, one of those "metrosexual" males, would never choose to live in a place like PNG.

"I should have filled you in sooner." Ash dropped the jacket she was carrying onto an armchair and extracted a bottle of Evian from the minibar. "But I didn't want to make you uncomfortable."

Charlotte chewed her lip. Apparently she had missed something he'd just said because she was too busy contemplating how attractive he was. So much for her rock-solid lesbian credentials. In case she was wrong about the gay thing, she took a stab at the information she hadn't heard.

"Are you married?" With those looks, women would be breaking down his door if he were straight. "I mean, if you are there's no reason to feel guilty. We haven't *done* anything."

"I'm not married." She took the cap off the Evian and said, "Here, drink some of this."

"I knew it." Charlotte reached for the bottle but it slid from her hand, spraying water in all directions.

Ash found a towel to put on the floor, then got another bottle and passed it to her.

"You're gay, aren't you?" Charlotte announced. "It's okay to tell me. I'm not homophobic. Drunk, yes. But definitely not a homophobe."

Ash waited till she'd finished rambling, then said, "Yes, I'm gay."

"I guessed that! Even though you're all tough, I could tell."

Ash blinked. "I don't think you understand."

Charlotte didn't blurt out, *Oh, my God. You're transsexual?* How did one tactfully inquire? "Are you…um…"

Ash's wry expression spoke volumes. "Charlotte, I'm a woman, not a gay man."

"A woman?" The cogs of her mind slowly ground to a conclusion. "Are you saying you're FTM?"

"No, just a regular card-carrying butch."

Charlotte let go of Ash's hand and flopped back into her pillows once more. Fuzzily, she stared up at the ceiling.

"I'm sorry." Ash perched on the edge of the bed. "I didn't set out to deceive you. It just seemed like a good idea not to say anything at the bar because I thought you'd be upset about the kiss."

Charlotte touched her lips. *The kiss.* Horrified, she blurted, "I'd never have done that if I knew."

"I figured."

"How can you be so casual about it!" She elbowed her way up the bed so she could prop her back against the headboard. "You should have told me."

"Yes, I should have said something in the taxi afterward. I apologize."

Charlotte snorted, lost for words and bewildered by her own blindness. How could she not have seen that Ash was a woman? Now that she knew, it was so obvious she had no idea how she could have missed every sign. No facial hair. A neck and throat that belonged to a woman. Shoulders and wrists slightly too narrow. Strong smooth hands, somewhat finely boned for a man's. Not much of a waist or butt, but still enough shape that Charlotte should have figured it out, even though the cut of her pants wasn't feminine.

A woman could be quietly spoken, physically powerful, and carry weapons. A woman could be a pilot. Ash had never said she was a man. Charlotte had assumed it, and even if she had failed to notice all the clues that had stared her in the face, the kiss was a neon sign. She'd never had a sexual feeling for a man in her life. Why start now? That, if nothing else, should have made her stop and think.

"I am so stupid," she concluded, stunned by what now seemed like willful self-deception. Apparently she had believed what she wanted to believe. And she called herself a scientist!

"It's really no big deal." Ash seemed serenely unflustered. "People mistake me for a man all the time. And I have to tell you, it makes my life easier."

Charlotte could see how that would be true for someone living in a crime-torn city on the fringes of civilization. She could also see why Ash might not have told her in the bar. They'd walked out of there unscathed, which meant the het-couple conduct had been a good plan. Only they both knew that phony kiss had turned out to be a whole lot more.

"You kissed me like…" Charlotte got stuck on the semantics.

"Like you're a desirable woman?" Ash supplied. "Yes, and you didn't seem to mind."

"Because I thought you were a man!"

"Exactly. And you reacted like any normal heterosexual woman would."

Heterosexual! Charlotte knew she was blushing, but she couldn't do a thing to arrest the pounding flow of blood to her cheeks. If she got up now to splash water on her face, she would only fall over. Summoning all the dignity she could muster, she said, "I think you should leave."

"I think so, too." Emotion smoldered beneath the level blue gaze.

Charlotte wasn't sure how to read what she was seeing. If Ash was angry, it didn't show in her tone or her face. In fact, she seemed infuriatingly calm. Charlotte did exactly the same thing herself when she was in danger of losing her temper. She wished she could pull off her usual arrogant disdain now, but she'd blown her chances with that last champagne cocktail.

Normally she drank very little, at risk of losing control and because drunkenness disgusted her. Tonight she'd made an exception because she was feeling at ease. Ash Evans had fooled her into lowering her guard. Angrily she searched her muddled mind for something to throw at the first woman who'd gotten under her skin since Britt.

"Guess what," she said, wishing she could stop the wavering of her voice. "I'm not as heterosexual as you think. I happen to be a lesbian and I kiss women all the time. For the record, you're nothing special in that department."

Ash's mouth moved a fraction, its taut line quirking like she found something comical in Charlotte's jibe. "You know something? I'm truly happy you feel that way."

Charlotte waited for the punch line, but Ash got to her feet and slid a hand into the pocket of her elegant pants. She was so effortlessly hot, Charlotte could only return her dispassionate regard with helpless fascination, reliving the kiss through a whole different frame of reference. Desire wrenched at her belly. Her mouth dried and her senses quivered.

"Why?" she croaked. "Why are you happy I said that?"

For a fleeting instant, raw emotion wiped all sign of detachment from Ash's face and she almost seemed to be talking to herself. "Because if you felt any other way, I would not be able to walk out of here."

Before Charlotte could convert her surprise to intelligible speech, Ash swung her jacket from the chair and hooked it over her shoulder. She paused as she opened the door, casting a long look back.

"Good-bye, Charlotte," she said with disquieting tenderness. "I'll think of you."

❖

Ash's most important customer had once lived the Spartan life of a British SAS officer. He was making up for it now in an opulent fortress perched above the hillside mansions of Pom's elite. A couple of gilt lions guarded the massive security gates, along with a security detachment Colonel Tobias Nagle, as he was known on the company Web site, claimed made a good advertisement for his services.

Like the rest of his private army, the detail had their own special sand-colored uniforms with the Nagle Global Diligence emblem on the epaulettes, belt buckles, and berets. Tubby paid a starting salary of $120K for his full-timers, recruiting former military from all over the world. He'd been in the business for thirty years, starting out as a mercenary in Africa and gradually working his way up to the pinnacle of his profession—legitimate government contracts.

Rebel wars and covert ops were always a lucrative source of revenue for soldiers of fortune, but they lacked the respectability Tubby seemed to crave. If he couldn't have genuine military credentials, he wanted at least to sit at the same table as those who did, to dine with generals and have regular troops call him "sir" like they used to. He wanted his own men to wear the NGD uniform with pride and to see themselves as elite forces, just like any other.

Consequently, he was still reeling that his archrival Tim Spicer had nailed the $300 million Pentagon contract for Iraq. This was the same loser responsible for the Sandline disaster and the Arms-to-Africa scandal, debacles apparently seen by the White House as compelling evidence of his competence for the job at hand. And if you wanted to believe Tubby's jaundiced opinion, Spicer was a trigger-happy opportunist without a strategic-planning bone in his body.

Ash only knew the guy by reputation and it seemed like things had panned out pretty well for him. She got regular offers from his company, Aegis. Every boss in the private military services sector was desperate for chopper pilots with special ops experience. And with the Bush Administration ignoring overbilling and bleeding a river of money into the coffers of war profiteers, Spicer and competitors like Blackwater were all cashed up and willing to pay top dollar.

Ash knew this was why Tubby watched her every move and tried to keep her on a short leash by piling on the work. He needed to beat out potential rivals if he wanted to keep her on the payroll. She supposed this could be the motivation for his latest fat offer. Fifty large for hand-holding a few scientists. She'd be laughing all the way to the bank if that was as demanding as it got.

To make her happy, Tubby had his slavering guard dogs penned up when she arrived and he waved a bottle of the finest Kentucky sipping whiskey money could buy. He was a single malt drinker himself and tried to convert her every time they shot the breeze. This week, as an additional temptation to visitors, he had procured the services of a couple of Australian escorts, flown in from Brisbane. They were predictably named Bambi and Misty and their job involved lounging around the pool and providing any other services guests required. Tubby thought this type of hospitality made the right impression when he entertained mining executives.

He had a wife stashed somewhere spending his money, and a couple of sons attending a fancy school in England. He liked to show Ash videos of them playing cricket and rowing boats, footage taken by their bodyguards. Tonight he had a snapshot of them standing in the grounds of a castle with a group of their schoolmates, all wearing top hats and tails.

"They met Her Majesty," he said, and in case Ash didn't know who he was talking about, "I mean Queen Elizabeth of England. A garden party at Windsor Castle, this was."

Ash said, "You must be very proud."

Tubby directed her attention to the floodlit terraces beyond a wall of bulletproof glass. Bambi and Misty were frolicking topless in the pool. That had to get old, Ash thought, spending a week at a time in and out of chlorinated water, pretending all you wanted to do was sip cocktails and toss a beach ball around while listening to Bryan Ferry turned up loud on the outdoor speakers. And in between times fucking a corpulent sixty-year-old who kept a doctor on call in case the Viagra gave him a heart attack.

Tubby caught her looking at the women and mistook her quizzical disinterest for something else. With a pointed wink, he said, "Just say the word. Anything you want, my love. You name it."

"This isn't a social call," Ash responded coolly. "But thanks for the mammaries."

Tubby chuckled and sipped his scotch with the gravity of a man about to dazzle those around him. "Okay, here's the deal." In the most formal version of his British accent, he confided, "NGD is breaking into a whole new arena. Take a look at this."

He hit a remote and the flat screen on the opposite wall came alive. The scene was a laboratory, everything white and glassy. People in white coats and masks hung over microscopes and glided robotically around, holding test tubes. Ash wondered if Charlotte was working in a facility like that. No wonder she was germ-phobic.

She asked Tubby, "We're going to be providing chemical hazard zone security?"

"Fuck, no." He dismissed that idea like the small potatoes it was. "That's only part of it. We're moving into multilevel diligence for the drug companies. Not as big as oil and commodities, but it's a low-risk niche. Something for the career mobile leatherneck who doesn't want his head cut off by heathen. See those glass tubes? That could be the cure for cancer."

"Well," Ash conceded, "they fixed impotence."

Tubby nodded cheerfully. "I can go at it all night now."

Ash took a pass on congratulating him and watched the video. A professor droned on about nature's bounty and the quest for the holy grail of cancer research, the pill that's going to persuade the body to kill the bad cells, not the good ones. Finally, emerging from a glossy pool of computer-generated ocean, a range of misty mountains filled the screen and a dove swooped down into a lush jungle teeming with exotic animals and plants.

As this visual feast unfolded, a mellifluous voice intoned, "The Sealy-Weiss Institute. Bringing the knowledge of yesterday to the frontiers of tomorrow. Are you ready for the unexpected? Will you accept the challenge?"

"Is this their recruitment video?" Ash asked.

"Yeah, that's all they could give me."

Tubby sounded chagrined. He liked to receive glossy promotional DVDs from his clients. Since these were mostly oil and mining companies, the footage always showed pristine environments, mother animals romping with their babies, and caring executives talking about all the money they spent on protecting the planet for generations to come. Tubby would show a couple of these whenever he was conducting orientation sessions for new recruits so the guys understood they could hold their heads up. Nagle Global Diligence provided vital services to quality clients who were doing their bit to help the world. They were not mercenaries. They were military professionals providing advice and assistance to private business.

"And this Sealy-Weiss Institute is the client?" Ash asked.

"In partnership with Belton Pharmaceuticals. You've heard of them, right?"

"Sure. Big players. Up there with Pfizer and Merck."

"Ka-ching, ka-ching." Tubby rubbed his fat fingers together. "I'm thinking ahead, my darling. The Iraq war is today's big game but morale is getting to be an issue. The smart talent out there is looking to make a move into something safer and cleaner. I'm about providing an alternative."

Ash read between the lines. "You're getting too much heat from the mining crowd, so it's time to diversify the client base?"

"In a word, yes."

"Sounds reasonable." Now that Ash had established the source of her paycheck, she asked, "When? Where? And who?"

"Next week. Irian Jaya. Sixteen scientists looking for who the bloody hell knows what in the Foja Mountains. They'll be up there for a couple of months, so we need supply drops, flyovers, communications support. The usual."

"You want me to chopper these bozos into Kwerba, then find the lake bed up west." She paused before musing aloud, "How many birds have gone down there? Double digits, isn't it?"

"Yeah, but none of those pilots could fly like you." Tubby looked pleased with this silver-tongued accolade.

"Kiss my ass," Ash said. "So, let's say we make it, and fight our way up the mountains for Christ knows how many miles in the pouring rain to build whatever observation platforms and crap these crazies want. Then what? My copilot heads back to the one-star luxury of Kwerba and gets shitfaced for the duration while my ride is disassembled by the *kotekas* and sold in parts to the fucking Indonesians?"

"That about sums it up." Tubby snickered.

"My end is fifty?" Even a pain in the butt part-time gig like this one would normally only net half of that. Ash gave Tubby a suspicious look.

He beamed sickly, like he'd just won a hot dog eating competition. "I'm being generous."

"Don't bullshit me."

"Okay, there's some fine print." He peered longingly at the women by the pool.

They had finally squeezed the air out of the beach ball and were reclining on loungers. Around them a squadron of mosquito zappers crackled. The women looked young, like only a few years ago they would have been in bed by now after drinking the hot chocolate their moms made. Ash wondered how they'd ended up doing what they did.

"What's the real deal?" she asked.

Tubby gave a theatrical sigh. "Well, see, we got a lead on the Roo. Motherfucking sonofabitch is in there scaring the natives with the usual crapola about resettlement and there's some talk about an attack on the scientists."

"Which makes the client unhappy," Ash concluded.

"They want him taken care of."

"I'm not an assassin," Ash reminded him. There was no way she would take the Roo out. She half liked the guy and he was good for business.

"No one's asking you to pull the bloody trigger. Just find this idiot and bring him in. He's been yanking too many chains for too long and they've voted him off the fucking island, if you take my meaning."

"Jesus, Tubby. You're not going to clip the guy, are you?" She appealed to his baser instincts. "He's money in the bank. You mightn't give a shit about that, but I do."

He gave it a moment. Ash could see him processing the idea that one of his best pilots might not be happy missing out on the Roo bonus hereafter. What if that was the final straw that sent her to Spicer's side of the fence?

"Okay, point taken," he said magnanimously. "We'll have a conversation."

Ash finished her whiskey. "Activists don't usually sell out. They have that conscience thing going on."

"Every man has his price."

"Here's the deal," Ash said. "If I bring him in, he walks out of here alive."

Tubby rolled his eyes. "If he signs on the dotted line, he'll walk out of here a rich man. The Indonesians want him gone. No questions asked. And as for our clients, I can write my own fucking check. He'll take the money."

"Like I said. No accidents, no faked suicide."

"Bloody hell. All right. He walks. But if he shows his fucking kangaroo teeth around here again, I'm not responsible."

Ash stretched out her hand. "Fifty for the job and fifty for bringing him in."

Tubby went through the motions of sucking his plump lips as if he hadn't anticipated the significant counteroffer. Finally he shook hands. "Like I said, every man has his price."

"I'm a woman."

Tubby grinned. "Balls are balls. I don't care who's wearing them."

Chapter Eight

"Dr. Lascelles, I presume."

Charlotte spun around at the sound of a deep soft voice she knew immediately. "You!" She glared at the pilot they'd been waiting for since nine that morning.

"As luck would have it." Her one-time rescuer flashed some identification around the field party. She looked like she'd slept in her clothes. "Good morning, folks. Ash Evans. Nagle Global Diligence."

The guys shook Ash's hand eagerly, as if they didn't notice anything wrong with her crumpled appearance and wandering speech.

Ash consulted the brooding sky. "Foja expedition, huh? You picked the right day for it."

She and the team proceeded to exchange comments on the weather and the importance of bug repellent for when the rain stopped and the mosquitoes smelled blood. She didn't look Charlotte's way once.

Simon Flight, a baby-faced British entomologist on the team to catalog butterflies, was the only one willing to draw attention to the pervasive aura of alcohol. "I say, old thing," he remarked with polite consternation. "A little early, isn't it?"

Ash slapped him on the shoulder. "No worries, pal. Round here, whiskey's a navigation aid."

Appalled, Charlotte said, "We are not flying anywhere with a drunk pilot."

"The lady makes an important point." Ash waved a hand in the direction of a lanky blond man loading supplies onto the helicopter parked nearby. "Which is why you will all be happy to know Klaus over there is flying us today. He needs to learn the West Papua routes."

"Wonderful, a newbie," Charlotte replied tartly.

Their team leader, Harvard professor Miles Hogan, touched her arm as if to reassure her. Addressing Ash, he said dryly, "Your pal is sober, right?"

"Klaus only does hallucinogens, and never on the job. He's South African. They're reliable about that type of thing." To prove her point, Ash called out, "Hey, Klaus. Are you straight, man?"

The South African yelled back, "I thought you'd never ask."

At least half the team found that hilarious. Apparently, *they* had been able to figure out right away that Ash was both female and probably a lesbian.

When they were done with their frat-house hooting, Miles gave Charlotte a patronizing smile and said, "You have nothing to worry about, Charlotte. Nagle are the best in the business. If you'd be more comfortable, we can delay the shuttle for an hour or two."

And have the entire field party kicking their heels in the long, leaky shack that passed for a hangar, because she was having a girly flutter. Charlotte could tell her feminine presence was already a focus for some of the team. Delaying their travel would cement her unpopularity.

"There's no need for that," she said. "If you're satisfied, let's get going."

Ash was apparently sober enough to have noticed this exchange, because she immediately started sorting the field party into smaller groups for the shuttle trips into Kwerba, the foothill village that was to be their staging area in the Sarmi regency. Today they would travel in with some five hundred pounds of supplies. Tomorrow, they would begin their long trek into the uplands, assuming they had a guide who could find the way to their target zone. So far Charlotte was not impressed. She'd been told their logistical support was being handled by highly paid experts. If this was it, they were in trouble.

"Want to fly with the first group?" Miles offered. "Give you a chance to get yourself settled properly at base camp."

Like she would need any more time than a man. Irritated, Charlotte said, "I have a few notes to sort, so I don't mind waiting my turn."

"That's the spirit." He said it like he coached the special team and she was the one who would never hit the ball.

Charlotte produced a saccharine smile and he excused himself, claiming he needed to go check on the supplies being loaded.

Once he was out of earshot, Ash strolled over and said, with one of her shameless grins, "What an unexpected pleasure."

"It's not mutual."

"I'm wounded."

Charlotte lowered her voice. "Look, I know you think this is funny. But I consider it highly unprofessional for you to have shown up here when you've been drinking."

"I tried to dump the job on someone else."

"Not on my account, I trust?"

"Your presence was not a factor. For the record, I had no idea the Dr. Zelda Lascelles on my documentation was you."

"Zelda is my first name. I assume they took that off my passport when they did the paperwork. It happens all the time."

"And there I was, thinking you were getting the hang of things in PNG, using a fake name among strangers."

"Charlotte is my middle name. I've been using it since I was seven." She had no idea why she felt the need to explain herself. She wasn't sure if she felt chagrin or disappointment that Ash hadn't been expecting her. Did she want to think Ash had chosen the job after recognizing her name on the passenger list? How absurd.

Ash stepped farther inside the hangar and sat down on one of several rickety deck chairs arranged in a line beneath the tin roof. Charlotte took the seat a couple down from her and they both stared out at the increasing rain. The other members of the team milled about as Klaus briefed passengers for the first shuttle.

"How was the Kokoda Trail?" Ash asked after a few moments of taut silence.

"Hard work. How was your week?"

"My sister died, so I had to go back home for a few days."

Shocked by the toneless reply and the horrible fact of her loss, Charlotte said, "I'm very sorry."

"Shit happens."

The response would have seemed flippant but for the bitter edge. Charlotte recalled Ash mentioning that she flew back to see her sister several times a year. They were close, she suspected, more so than Ash wanted to let on.

Gently, she said, "I'm really surprised you're here. Maybe you should be taking some time out."

Ash read between the lines. "So I can drown my sorrows on my own dime?"

"That isn't what I meant."

"Yes, it is." Ash finally met her eyes. "Try not to worry that pretty head of yours. I can fly a Huey in my sleep, but I'm not taking her up today. Isn't that enough for you?"

"I don't know why you need to be here at all if you're not flying," Charlotte said. "Under the circumstances, surely your boss would give you time off."

"Someone has to walk you beetle hunters into the highlands," Ash informed her laconically. "The pay is good and apart from the local tribes, no one knows this area like I do."

"Once you take us in there, what then?"

"We have a security roster. I'll be with you for a week until you're settled into the campsite, then Klaus will fly my bird in with extra supplies and my replacement."

Charlotte cast a glance toward a Jeep that bounced across the uneven tarmac and jerked to halt a few yards from the helicopter. Four men jumped out and hauled large backpacks after them. They were wearing beige uniforms, complete with black berets. To Charlotte's astonishment, after throwing their gear into the helicopter, they went back to the Jeep and began unloading an arsenal of weapons.

"Are we fighting a war or something?" she asked. "The Fojas are uninhabited. Who do they think they're going to be shooting at?"

"It's a deterrent. News travels in this place. You never know who might think a team of scientists would be worth robbing."

Charlotte pictured a group of Rambos blundering around in a world untouched by humans, trampling important specimens and scaring shy animals. "I think it's ridiculous. I wonder if the expedition organizers knew it was going to be like this."

Ash shrugged. "They hired us."

Charlotte looked her over a little more intently. She was a mess. Her eyes were shadowed with sorrow, the crinkles that fanned from each corner more pronounced. Her frown seemed perpetual and her corn blond hair needed a cut. The waves were more like curls across her brow and the back of her neck. Even her body language spelled weariness. She was slouched in the deck chair, her legs extended carelessly in front of her. Her arms were loosely draped over the rests, and she looked like she could fall asleep in short order if Charlotte wasn't talking to her.

Bothered by what had transpired in her hotel bedroom ten days earlier, she said, "Well, since we're going to be stuck with each other for the next week, there's something I'd like to clear up. What you said in my hotel room when—"

"There's nothing to clear up," Ash cut across her blandly. "We both had a lot to drink that night."

"You know, alcohol isn't an excuse for everything a person does and says. I happen to take responsibility for myself when I drink."

Ash's expression altered. "Sounds like you're saying I don't."

"I can't speak for you. I don't know you. But I think it's fairly obvious from your appearance today that you have a problem."

"A drinking problem?"

Charlotte rolled her eyes. "Let me see. When you're drinking you say things you later want to retract. You show up for work unable to fly your plane. You had such a hard night you didn't even change your clothes this morning."

"I'm unclear why this is any of your business."

"I don't like alcoholics."

"I'm not an alcoholic."

"Oh, please. I know the signs. Just listen to yourself. You're totally in denial."

"You know the signs," Ash repeated thoughtfully. "Who was it? An ex? A parent?"

"That's not relevant."

"It is when it impairs your judgment."

"My judgment isn't impaired. I know your type at a hundred paces."

"My type?" Ash's expression shifted from annoyance to incredulity. "Why am I sitting here listening to my character being assassinated?"

"Because you're too hungover to get up and walk away?" Charlotte suggested.

"Well, this has been educational." Ash brushed her clothes off. "For the record, I haven't slept in fifty hours. I've had a rough week and I came straight here from another assignment."

"Oh, right. A date with a whiskey bottle."

Ash studied her with aggravating calm. "What's your problem with me, Charlotte?"

"I don't have a problem."

This earned a lazy, maddening smile. "You're behaving like a woman scorned. Are you pissed that I didn't stay with you that night?"

"Don't be ridiculous. That's some ego you have."

"I've seen the symptoms often enough to recognize them."

"Well, don't give up your day job to become a shrink. You're way off base."

"That's a relief," Ash said glibly. "Because I'd sure hate to disappoint a woman as pretty, and charming, as you."

Charlotte choked. "Oh, please. Where do you get lines like that? The loser's guide to chatting up women?"

"You can't blame a butch for trying."

Charlotte couldn't tell if she was being mocked or if Ash was serious and just happened to be a throwback to the Brylcreem era. She glanced around, hoping their conversation wasn't audible to her colleagues in the hangar. No one seemed to be paying any attention and the rain pounding on the tin roof was loud enough that it had probably drowned out their voices. Charlotte shuffled along to the seat right next to Ash's and lowered her voice just in case.

"Don't waste your time. I'd never be interested in someone like you."

Ash's eyes wandered with sensual deliberation from Charlotte's mouth to her throat and down to her breasts, leaving her skin prickling as if invisible fingers had trailed across it. "You've thought about it," she concluded with a knowing look that infuriated Charlotte.

"Oh, now you're psychic?" Charlotte was aware of a tender tension in her nipples. She tried hard to keep her expression immobile so she gave nothing away.

She'd never been a good liar, and the galling truth was she had thought far too often about having sex with Ash Evans ever since their awkward farewell. She'd even tried to find a phone number for her before heading off on the Kokoda trek. Fortunately, Ash had been impossible to track down and Charlotte had come to her senses after a week. Seeing Ash now only confirmed what she already knew—that she was exactly the kind of person she could not allow into her life. A drinker.

Of course she was attracted to Ash. It was her pattern, a special form of self-sabotage whereby she desired the women most likely to hurt her and least likely to be reliable, committed partners. The lesson she'd learned from Britt was that when it came to romance, she could not trust her own judgment. If she was strongly attracted to a woman it spelled only one thing—the woman was trouble.

Ash's candid stare and her own tingling reaction was all the warning she needed. There was no way on earth she could afford to reveal any sign of interest. Ash was the type who wouldn't need much encouragement. Charlotte was stunned by her bad luck. This expedition was the opportunity of a lifetime, and dealing with Ash Evans was one big hassle she didn't need. Perhaps Miles could have her replaced immediately. Obviously Ash didn't want the job. She would probably be pleased if her boss found someone else.

Charlotte cast a glance toward the helicopter where Miles was stroking his goatee and looking very serious as he discussed something with the men in uniform. Most males were susceptible to flattery, and Miles had already shown he would grant her special treatment as the only woman on the team. Charlotte was reluctant to play on her gender, but if things got difficult she would do whatever was necessary to get what she wanted. And what she wanted was results.

After she'd returned from the Kokoda Trail, she'd spent a day carefully studying the Sealy-Weiss briefing papers her new boss had presented her with as she departed. The focus of her research in the Fojas was intriguing. Sealy-Weiss had been conducting a phytochemical research project for the past two years, backed by Belton Pharmaceuticals. Recently, the research team had made a small but significant breakthrough, isolating a powerful antifungal molecule found in the leaves of a fig species previously unknown. The specimens had been supplied by a couple of botanists who had been cataloguing flora in Papua New Guinea. The pair had purchased the leaves from West Papuan tribesmen who appeared to use them to treat leukemia.

Charlotte had been tasked with locating the species, most likely a hemiepiphytic strangler vine. She was to take samples, identify host tree species, estimate numerical abundance distribution, and identify potential seed dispersers. Sealy-Weiss had presented their initial findings to Belton, who had become the expedition's major sponsor in order to have the Sealy-Weiss representative obtain a larger sample and the necessary data. Early findings suggested that the molecule was even more potent than the resveratrol found in grapes and mulberries.

In the body, an enzyme known as CYP1B1 had been found to convert resveratrol into a toxin that selectively destroyed cancer cells.

No one was pretending they'd found a magic bullet in any of the various phytochemical therapeutics already in use, but the field was seen by many as the one most likely to produce a wonder drug in the next decade and it was highly competitive. Although no credible scientist seriously believed that one plant compound would deliver the ultimate cancer cure the public dreamed of, Charlotte knew it remained a secret hope.

Researchers now envisioned the phasing out of traditional radiotherapy and chemotherapy and their replacement with a new generation of treatments that destroyed only the cancer cells. Everyone's worst fear was that the world's most promising biological resources would be destroyed by the timber industry before the holy grail plant could be identified. The race to discover that plant was urgent and serious, and Charlotte was overwhelmed to have been chosen for a key role in that quest.

Her new employers were very clear that if she brought home a winner, billions of dollars and the well-being of countless people could be the eventual reward. The coup wouldn't do her career any harm either. Sealy-Weiss's ultimate aim would be to develop and patent a cell culture production technology that would yield high quantities and be more efficient than harvesting from the original source. But in the meantime, they would need to figure out how the species could be grown commercially. That meant replicating the critical environmental factors that created its unique biology. Charlotte's observations as a botanist would be critical.

She allowed herself a small sigh of satisfaction. Thinking about the ramifications of her work put everything into perspective. She had more important things to worry about than a fleeting attraction to a woman she would never see again once this assignment was completed. Meantime, since they were going to be stuck with each other, a professional relationship was necessary. So far, she had not helped this cause by getting personal.

She shifted in her seat and forced herself to relax. Ash had just said something, a reply to the facetious remark about being psychic, no doubt. Charlotte had been so abstracted, she hadn't listened.

"I'm sorry," she said. "The rain's very noisy. I didn't hear you."

"I said I don't need to be psychic. People give themselves away and you're no exception."

Charlotte wasn't going to be goaded into tit for tat. Trying for a conciliatory tone, she said, "I'm not going to argue with you anymore, Ash. You're right. It's none of my business what you do in your spare time and I apologize for my comments about your drinking."

Ash's eyes narrowed and her gaze sharpened. Doubt infiltrated her expression.

"I was just thinking how silly I'm being," Charlotte plunged on, hoping she came across as a distracted scientist muddling her way through an embarrassing situation. "I guess I was taken aback when you arrived. I had no idea our security arrangements were going to be so elaborate. The organizers never said anything about us being at risk."

She wished she could read Ash's thoughts, but her face gave nothing away and the cool intensity of her stare made Charlotte self-conscious.

"As I said before, it's a good idea to hire security in this part of the world," Ash reiterated tonelessly. "We're not expecting any trouble, but if it happens, you'll want us there."

Charlotte nodded like she was accepting the wisdom of these pronouncements. "Well, I guess that means we're going to be seeing quite a lot of each other. So I was thinking, perhaps we can agree to set our feelings aside and behave like grown-ups."

"What feelings?"

Charlotte considered the comment. "Let's be honest. I think it's obvious that there's some kind of transient chemical attraction going on between us. And since we both have jobs to do and that kind of thing can make working together awkward, I suggest we avoid getting personal with each other."

Ash regarded her thoughtfully. "You're saying you're attracted to me and that makes you uncomfortable, so we should pretend it's not happening?"

For some reason this placid rewording bothered her much more than it should have. Charlotte could feel her cheeks changing color. Aggravated, she hissed, "It's not just one-sided."

"No. But only one of us seems to be concerned about it. Why is that, Charlotte?"

"I have no idea what you mean. I am simply trying to preempt a problem. I think the next few days are going to be hard enough without some kind of…agenda."

"I'm not sure what you have in your mind, but my only agenda is to get your team into the required zone, make sure you can survive, then get the hell out."

"Then we have a common goal," Charlotte said. "All I'm doing is making sure nothing gets in the way of it."

"I see." Ash studied her for a moment. "Answer me something. The kind of attraction you're talking about—how often does it happen for you?"

Never. Charlotte immediately rejected the answer that popped into her head and considered the question rationally. She wasn't normally intensely attracted to anyone, but her feelings for Ash had emerged out of an unusual set of circumstances. Somehow Ash had tripped a switch that connected with a part of herself buried since Britt.

Charlotte hated that inner self, with her unsafe cravings and unreliable instincts. Her life was successful and drama free because she kept that traitorous side of her personality under control. Hell would freeze over before she allowed a few wayward impulses to destroy everything she'd worked for, and that was exactly what could happen here. It didn't help that Ash seemed able to look straight past the person she tried to be, and see the being she wanted to hide.

Disconcerted, she said stiffly, "You know what it's like. There are always women one looks at twice. It passes."

"I've found that acting on a sexual attraction pretty well guarantees it won't last," Ash said softly. "Just a thought."

"Are you suggesting we sleep together so we can…I don't know… move beyond it?"

"Well, getting beyond it does seem to be your main aim."

Suspicious of her velvety tone and the glitter in her stark blue eyes, Charlotte asked, "Do you think this is funny?"

"No." Ash's mouth twitched. "Maybe just a little. Jesus, Charlotte. Chill. So, we're attracted. Big deal. We're two adults. No one can make us do anything we don't want to do."

Charlotte wished she'd kept her mouth shut. Ash obviously had an easy-come, easy-go approach that meant none of this was an issue for her. And maybe she had a point. Maybe Charlotte was taking it all way too seriously.

Angry that she'd revealed herself more than she wanted to, she said, "I'm glad you see things that way. I had a different impression that night in my hotel room, but perhaps I misunderstood."

"What do you want me to say—that I desired you and if you'd felt the same way, we'd have spent the night together? What does it matter now? We're here. We dodged that bullet, and if you're worried that I'm going to hit on you when you're supposed to be looking at spores or whatever, don't be. You're not my type."

A hot little spear of anger embedded itself in Charlotte's chest, constricting her breathing. "Really? What is your type?"

She could have kicked herself for asking. What did she care? She wished Ash wouldn't even answer, but that was too much to hope for.

After chewing it over briefly, she replied, "I was in Boston a month ago and I picked up two women. They weren't brain surgeons but the three of us had some fun. So, I guess that's my type. Dumb blondes who want to party."

"The three of you?" Charlotte caught a flash of Dani Bush. Then she thought about Dani's lover banging on the bathroom door that sordid night in Tamsin's bedroom. She'd called a name. At the time Charlotte hadn't paid much attention, but it came back to her now with a sickening thud. *Ashley.*

Ash met her eyes unflinchingly. "I appreciate variety."

Charlotte's voice froze in her throat. There was something very deliberate in the way Ash was telling her about this threesome. *Surely not.* The coincidence was completely improbable.

Ash seemed to read something into her silence. Without inflection, she said, "Was it you that night, throwing Dani out of the house?"

Charlotte's blood swamped her eardrums, drowning out the sound of the rain and the hum of voices elsewhere in the hangar. Ash had slept with that horrible little slut and her girlfriend?

"You were the Ashley in the bathroom?" she asked numbly.

"Yep."

As Charlotte tried to gather herself, one of the security guards ran across the wet tarmac and dropped a backpack at Ash's feet.

"This what you were waiting for, Major?"

"Yes, thanks, Tanner. Are you all set?"

"Fully loaded and ready to roll."

"I'll change and be with you in five."

The guard saluted her and jogged back to the helicopter.

Charlotte blinked, momentarily distracted by the interruption. Since when did hired security staff get to dignify their work with military rank and salutes? "Major?" she queried sarcastically.

Ignoring her, Ash opened the pack and extracted a small pile of neatly folded clothing. Paying no attention to the men sheltering in the hangar, she stripped off her shirt and dropped it onto the chair next to Charlotte. Unable to stop herself, Charlotte stared at the beautifully formed body in front of her. Ash wore a black tank that made her shoulders seem even more muscular, if that were possible. She wasn't weirdly bulky, just powerfully built and carrying no excess.

As she pulled on a clean shirt, the play of muscles across her chest and belly was visible through the skintight tank, a glimpse of her strength that made Charlotte's mouth dry. She had a tattoo on one shoulder, a naturalistic design in dark jade. It looked like a rambling creeper, tendrils creeping toward her neck and down her arm. In the center was a small white flower with an inscription scrolling on either side along the fleshy vine. Charlotte couldn't make out the wording.

"Major was my rank in the military," Ash replied, buttoning her shirt before tucking it into her loose cargo pants.

Charlotte didn't respond. Her mind relentlessly gnawed on the revelation about Dani. There was so much she wanted to ask, but she couldn't bear to show how disturbed she felt. Shocked, she stared down at the wet, cracked concrete around her feet. Of all the emotions jangling in the chambers of her mind, the noisiest was one she had never expected to feel again as long as she lived. Naked, crushing jealousy.

CHAPTER NINE

As the Huey swooped over the rain-drenched emerald vegetation en route to Kwerba, Ash gazed out the side and told herself she had done the right thing. She didn't need a hassle and once Charlotte understood the kind of person she was, any naïve romantic delusions she might be harboring would evaporate.

Women like Charlotte were not cut out for casual relationships, and that was the only kind Ash could offer. If they were fool enough to fall into bed with one another out of sexual curiosity, it would only end in tears. They could kid themselves that they were just going to have a good time and move on, but they would both be fighting their instincts.

Ash already knew she had some kind of deluded fantasy going on about Charlotte, and the loss of Emma would only make her thinking even more screwed up. And Charlotte apparently thought if she admitted to the attraction and analyzed her inconvenient feelings to death, she could make them disappear. Ash had figured she could save both of them some grief by disillusioning her up front.

By now Charlotte probably detested her. She was a nice, well-brought-up middle-class woman with an obvious conservative streak. In matters of love and sex, things were black and white for her, Ash guessed. Gray was never okay. She would need to feel comfortable, even if it meant being bored. The Charlottes of this world chose safe partners who wouldn't challenge their beliefs or their understanding of themselves. They made rules and expected the people they loved to follow them.

Ash was not the type to get with the program and she'd made that very clear. Her admission about the threesome would cement Charlotte's poor opinion of her, and that was fine. Ash was happy to be written off as an uncouth, womanizing drunk if it meant Charlotte would keep her distance. She was not in the mood to resist temptation because it was the right thing to do. Right now she wanted to lose herself and not have to think about her life, her grief, and the decisions she needed to make. And in this frame of mind, she was going to be stuck in a tent for the next six nights with a woman who tempted her for reasons she could not fully fathom.

Ash was puzzled that she still felt this way. Normally Charlotte's weird control-freak behavior back in the hangar would have sent her running in the opposite direction and not looking back. Instead she found herself strangely thrilled that Charlotte had admitted an attraction to her, and the fact that she seemed quite undone by it only made Ash want to kiss her. Then again, she had always chased unattainable women. The difference now was that she was going to do her best to stay away from this one.

Ash allowed herself a grin, imagining how Charlotte was going to react to the news of their sleeping arrangements when she reached Kwerba. Obviously no one had bothered to tell her that, as the only two women on this venture, she and Ash would be sharing accommodations. The men would be sleeping four or six to a tent, and Miles Hogan had made it clear that Charlotte would have to be housed and guarded separately. It went without saying that a woman was preferred for that task. Tubby had been emphatic. Ash had to work the assignment for various reasons and that was one of them. She would just have to live with it until one of Nagle's few other female employees returned from her current gig on an expat wives' Coral Sea cruise. Some people had all the luck.

There was an alternative for tonight, Ash reflected. They would be in Kwerba and could sleep side by side on a mat inside a tribesman's hut, along with the rest of his family and any animals they kept, probably a pig or two. Germ-o-rama, no question about it. But she would offer.

"How's the forecast, boss?" Klaus asked as the Fojas started to occupy most of their window.

"Tomorrow morning is supposed to be clear," Ash said.

"So we're taking her into that lake bed?"

"It's the only way we can access the target zone."

Klaus glanced sideways. His bony, earnest face was anxious. "We're cleared to put her down?"

"Six permits, no less."

Dealing with the Indonesians was never easy. They didn't welcome outsiders flying into remote areas of West Papua, and permits had to be obtained from both government and the police. Ash wondered how much the expedition organizers had laid out in bribes to cut through the red tape. She knew Tubby had spent at least fifty thousand making sure the local military commanders wouldn't get in their faces, regardless of anything their government guaranteed. Those guys shot first and apologized later.

Ash looked back over her shoulder at the two NGD guards on this shuttle. She didn't know them. Both were leathernecks, according to Tubby, honorably discharged marines looking for a second income stream that didn't involve private contracting in Iraq. The other two members of the four-man detail were back at the hangar with the rest of the scientists. Ash knew one by sight and had worked with the other, a former CIA operative nicknamed Nitro, supposedly because he left nothing standing when a situation called for extreme measures.

She was surprised that Tubby was wasting one of his most credentialed snake-eaters on a local cakewalk like the Foja expedition. The last she'd heard, Nitro was pulling serious money in Azerbaijan on one of their BP contracts. The oil giant hired a private army of security contractors to ensure there would be no disruption to its Caspian Sea oil pumping, and Tubby had been making money hand over fist there since the democratic government was overthrown back in 1993. BP liked to distance itself from that privately funded coup, but there wasn't really any question who benefited. BP had promptly signed a "deal of the century" with the new regime.

Ash had thought about working that beat but she didn't like the political climate. Tubby's company was competing with the US contractor, Blackwater, so they couldn't be picky about assignments. Ash was aware of a couple wet teams in the region, hired to eliminate troublemakers. Nitro ran one of them.

Curious, Ash asked Klaus, "What's our friend Nitro doing down here?"

"There's some heat on him over that Armenian journalist. The one shot in the demonstration."

"Was that us?" Ash was disgusted. Taking out the occasional Chechen terrorist was one thing, but killing a woman whose only crime was criticizing a corrupt dictatorship? She had a bad taste in her mouth.

"No, Tubby says he turned it down." Klaus sounded like a believer.

"So why the heat?"

"There's a bid happening and all the PMCs are trying to lock each other out, so someone's blaming us."

"Another Ken Saro-Wiwa," Ash mused aloud.

Shell Oil was still trying to live that one down ten years later. As if they could pretend they had nothing to do with a bogus trial and execution of their most powerful critic in Nigeria. They bankrolled the puppet regime that had murdered him.

"Someone published Nitro's mug shot in the *Baku Sun*," Klaus said.

"You're kidding me." An unspoken accord existed between the various private military companies that they wouldn't knowingly endanger any contractor's life. "So he's blown? That's dirty."

"Yeah. He shaved his beard and got the hell out of there," Klaus said. "Brought the wife and kids, too."

"No shit." Ash supposed Tubby had tossed him this assignment as a consolation prize, a few weeks on easy street with a nice paycheck. "You still thinking about that Aegis offer?"

"Every time I say no, they increase the salary."

"What's the going rate for Baghdad now?"

"For me, fifteen a month for the Green Zone. More if I take on increased hazard. Tempted?"

"Maybe." Ash had been thinking about it since the funeral. She'd had a plan in the back of her mind for the past few years, but all bets were off now and that was probably a dangerous thing. She could see how it would be possible to let the years slip by as Tubby had, to build nothing else in her life worth a damn.

She stared out at the bank of cloud suspended over the ranges. "I need to get out before I have nothing to get out for."

"I hear you." Klaus took the chopper down under five hundred feet as they drew closer to their destination. "Three more years and I can pay cash for my farm. New Zealand, that's a good place for South Africans. And the land. You never saw anything like it." He gave a low whistle and behind his wire-rimmed specs, his hazel eyes were suddenly faraway. "Organic farming. That's the way of the future. The worse the pollution gets, the more people pay for natural food."

As he rambled on, Ash heard a homesick Afrikaaner whose family had been thrown off their land. Klaus was one of a generation of displaced young white South African men who had become soldiers of fortune, the elite of an emerging global phenomenon, battle hardened in the campaigns of Angola, Sierra Leone, and the Congo. No one called them mercenaries these days. They were security contractors who worked for global risk management organizations a.k.a. private military companies or PMCs. They worked and fought alongside regular military forces in conflicts that, since Iraq, were increasingly privatized.

There were 20,000 contractors in the Middle East. As well as carrying out regular security operations, they were active in the shadowy terrain of assassinations, intimidation, and dirty tactics, enabling honorable men to claim deniability. When they were killed by the enemy no one added their names to rosters of fallen heroes. Their families didn't get a flag. They did not die in the line of duty. But they didn't die for a lie, either.

Maybe a change of scenery would be good for her, Ash thought. She could keep her place in Madang and make sure she was home for the harvest each year. Her mind drifted, as it did all the time, insisting on sliding back to Emma as she died. Her chest rising and falling in diminishing increments, her pointed little face serene in the long good night. Around her, the machines fell still at last, unblinking mechanical angels witnessing her retreat from life. The frail hand in Ash's grew cold. The eyelashes fluttered their promise no more.

"You got a lot of farm girls there. They know how to work." Klaus was still visualizing his sunny antipodean future. "I'll get married. Have some kids. A farm is a good life for kids."

Ash said, "Sounds like a plan." She stared down into the relentless cascade of brilliant green beneath them, watching for their confined landing spot.

"How about you?" he asked. "What are you going to do?"

"Go somewhere clean and dry with no mosquitoes."

He laughed. "Hey, no mosquitoes in Iraq." He nosed down toward a small lake.

Ash checked their bearings. "You'll see a clearing beyond some thatched roofs."

Klaus swooped low. “That’s some rainforest.”

“Nothing like it on earth except for the Amazon,” Ash said. “You could lose a city in there and never see it again.”

“Heart of darkness,” Klaus muttered.

Ash pointed three o’clock where it seemed a hole was torn in the lush, unending tapestry. “Put her down there. Tight and sweet.”

Klaus grinned and called over his shoulder to their passengers. “Attention, everyone. Time to pray.”

❖

“I’m going to speak to Miles,” Charlotte said, surveying their modest tent some hours later as the long day was draining into night.

“This was his idea.” Ash thought it was worth mentioning.

“Then he can come up with a better one.”

As Charlotte made a beeline for the head of the expedition, Ash strolled to the mess area where one of the leathernecks, Billy Bob Woodcock, had dinner under control. She could smell coffee and rations already.

“The lady’s not happy?” The hulking, crew-cut Texan smirked as he handed Ash the coffeepot.

Ash found a mug and helped herself. “Can’t imagine why.”

“Just say the word and she can bunk in my tent.” Woodcock began doling beans into bowls. “Got ourselves a single woman’s paradise here. Two of you and twenty of us.”

“Keep it seemly.”

Grinning, the ex-marine yelled, “Chow time, bird watchers.”

Ash glanced toward the fringes of their campsite where Miles Hogan was being lectured on his antiquated chivalry. He had included a folding bed among their limited equipment so that “her ladyship” would not have to lie on a camp pad. Ash had been afraid to bring it into the tent.

“Poor bastard.” An Australian biologist rolled up. “Any danger we could just leave her behind by accident tomorrow?”

“She’s the sponsor’s golden-haired girl.” The baby-faced British butterfly expert shook hands with the few people he hadn’t greeted so far, announcing, “Simon Flight, shortly to discover a new species of *Ornithoptera paradisea* to be named after my humble self. If anyone wants their own winged tribute, I'm accepting bribes and sexual favors."

A few other team members arrived and stood out in the misty rain, gulping down beans. Ash traded her coffee for a meal. Charlotte and Miles were still talking. It sounded heated and the assembled dinner crowd diligently made conversation as if they weren't paying attention. Then, magically, silence fell at the perimeter of the camp. Like everyone around her, Ash stopped eating and looked up, half expecting to see Miles flat on his back with one of Charlotte's feet planted in the center of his chest. Instead Nitro was cutting a path toward the mess area with Charlotte walking ahead of him and Miles trailing behind. Both had their heads down.

Billy Bob Woodcock handed out beans and forks to the new arrivals. They ate in tense silence for a few minutes, then Nitro asked, "Anyone else not happy with their sleeping quarters?"

Amidst the mumbled denials, Ash exchanged a glance with Klaus. He'd been standing closest to the fray, so he'd probably overheard everything. He looked like he was busting to get it off his chest so Ash finished her beans, drank some more coffee, and casually excused herself, producing a cigar to justify her departure.

She could feel Charlotte's eyes boring into her back as she and Klaus moved away from the mess area.

"Okay, spill," she demanded as soon as they couldn't be overheard.

"Nitro said he'd have the chopper ready first thing in the morning to escort our lady friend back to Pom if she couldn't cope with the conditions."

Ash cut the cap off her cigar. "I'm guessing she didn't take that lying down."

"She threatened him and called him names."

Ash laughed quietly. Hadn't Charlotte noticed she was talking to a guy who looked like the poster boy for black ops? "I'd have paid to hear that."

"Nitro said she better work on her attitude and if it didn't improve he'd have no problem throwing her out of the chopper. That shut her up."

Nitro didn't come across like a man who made idle threats, and from the pinched look on Charlotte's face as they returned to the group, it seemed like she'd finally caught on. Ash chuckled and lit her cigar. She didn't offer one to Klaus. He was a health nut except when it came to his favorite recreational drugs.

They lounged against a huge tree trunk and watched several short, sinewy Kwerbans construct feathered headgear. So far the grass-skirted New Guineans had stayed well clear of the foreigners. They were shy, having seen very few outsiders, and technology made them anxious. Ash was liaising with them through the local guide NGD had hired, Pak Tony. He looked about sixty and was one of the few Kwerbans who had ventured far enough into the uplands to be of use to the expedition. NGD was paying him and the village in pigs. Ash would be flying the first six animals in with a supply run in a couple of weeks' time—assuming she was still in PNG.

Ash called to the guide in Bauzi, one of the fast-vanishing languages of the tribes around the Tor River, "Is there anything the elders wish us to gather for them from the uplands?"

Pak Tony consulted with a couple of wizened old people sitting just inside the doorway of a wood and flax hut, then said, "The powerful ruler Jared Diamond brought fine gifts when he came many years ago."

"Are they saying a white man was in the Fojas before the Conservation International expedition?"

Pak Tony pointed to a woman deeper in the hut. "Jared Diamond was in this village before she was born."

Intrigued, Ash strolled back to the rest of the group and asked if anyone knew their lost world had been found by another scientist thirty years earlier.

"Sure," Miles said. "Diamond was here in the seventies. Walked in. No chopper, nothing. He had a shit of a time, so no one was in any hurry to follow him." With a quick glance toward one of his colleagues, he queried, "Won the Pulitzer, didn't he?"

Pak Tony approached with something in his hand and displayed it reverently. "Here is one of his gifts."

Ash stared down at an ancient University of California ID card and felt sad all of a sudden. The tribes of this region had been living here for forty thousand years, undisturbed. Now they and the untouched world whose doorstep they guarded would be changed forever by the outsiders they were welcoming. In their innocence, they saw their visitors as marvelous beings from some far-off kingdom. They showed hospitality and expected little in exchange for the wisdom they offered. They had no idea of the Pandora's box they were opening.

West Papua's rainforests were second only in size to the Amazon and ripe for exploitation by the Malaysian timber barons who were steadily eliminating the rainforests of neighboring Indonesia. Right now, there were no roads into the dense interior and the Fojas were officially protected as part of the Mamberamo corridor, a territory closely monitored by Conservation International, one of Ash's few reputable customers. However, that didn't mean a whole lot. In this part of the world officials could be bribed to turn a blind eye to just about anything, and the Indonesian military worked hand in glove with illegal logging operations all over their own country and New Guinea.

Ash had no doubt that logging brokers would soon be beating a path to the Kwerba and their neighbors, trying to intimidate them into handing over timber concessions. China bought most of the sought-after hardwood smuggled out of the country. Ash had heard some 300,000 cubic meters was shipped to Zhangjiagang every month. The illegal timber was cleared through customs using Malaysian paperwork to hide its origins.

The timber barons were felling almost three million hectares of old-growth forest in Indonesia each year to supply demand. Local village committees who permitted timber felling received about nine dollars for each cubic yard of merbau felled on their land. In China, this fetched over $250.

Now, with the Olympics approaching, the Chinese were planning to build a giant timber processing factory in West Papua so they could speed up the deforestation. By the time they were done, most of Indonesia and West Papua's old timbers would be gone, along with the animals and tribes who had depended on the rainforests for millennia.

Ash supposed "progress" was inevitable, yet the methods these illegal operators used bothered her. Not so long ago she'd been hired by Hanurata, a timber company that kept a detachment of special forces troops barracked in its headquarters in Jayapura. These military personnel provided security for logging operations and intimidated locals who showed opposition. Ash had the job of transporting protesters to the nearest jail, where they were supposed to be locked up prior to resettlement. She'd subsequently learned that many had simply "disappeared," tortured and starved to death. The Indonesian military didn't like people who got in their way.

The more Ash saw of logging and mining operations in her adopted country, the less she believed any value came of "modernization." She wondered when hardwood buildings and furniture had become more important than entire cultures of people, and thousands of species of animals and insects? When did cutting down trees for money make more sense than maintaining the planet's climatic balance?

She almost laughed at herself. Lately she'd been thinking like a tree-hugger. She'd even visited a couple of hardware stores back home, wanting to see if American companies were participating in the disgraceful merbau trade. To her disgust she found that American customers were being duped into thinking they were buying hardwoods logged by sustainable methods. She wondered how her fellow countrymen would feel if they knew the companies claiming to guarantee this exercised no control at all over their suppliers.

There was simply no such thing as legal merbau. Every log supplied to an American company fell off the back of a timber baron's truck in PNG. Ash suspected Americans wouldn't be in such a hurry to install a merbau floor if they knew an entire village had probably been wiped off the map to provide it. And she should know—she'd been handling relocation transport for the displaced for years.

Maybe expeditions like this one were the only hope of preserving one of the world's last untouched areas. If what they found was rare enough and valuable enough, maybe the Indonesians could be convinced that it was worth more to protect the Fojas than to plunder them. Maybe, for once, they would enforce their own conservation laws. A laughable idea, but Ash kept hoping someone high up wouldn't be in government only to line his pockets.

"What exactly are you folks looking for?" she asked. "Are you just here to name butterflies after yourselves, or what?"

Miles Hogan gave an indignant snort. "You may not understand the scientific significance of the biodiversity in this region, but it's inestimable. There are almost no places on earth where the human footprint is nonexistent. Our surveys are merely scraping the surface, but what we aim to do is excite the global scientific community with the vast research potential of this rainforest."

Ash thought, *Sorry I breathed.*

Charlotte edged into the center of the group, slipping in front of a couple of the Australians. "I have a specific task some of you may be interested in, and I'd certainly welcome assistance."

She went on to describe in technical detail what she was doing on the expedition. It seemed to boil down to a pretty simple task. She was looking for a fig tree. Ash found this kind of ironic since they were in what was being referred to all over the media as a "garden of Eden." None of the scientists seemed to pick up on this.

They were all worked up over the prospect of seeing birds once thought extinct and some kind of tree kangaroo. The Australians had a frog fetish and enthralled the other science nerds with tales of poisonous skins and peculiar mating habits. Ash and the other NGD contractors took advantage of this bonding period to clean their handguns and sharpen their machetes. Between times they handed around the DEET and kept the mosquitoes at bay by helping the Kwerba pile damp mango wood and betelnut leaves on their dirt fires. Smoke was the only effective repellent used by the highlanders.

When the scientists began drifting to their tents, Nitro and one of the leathernecks offered to run the watch. Grateful for the chance to get some sleep, Ash checked once more that the Huey was secure, picked up the folding bed, and headed for her tent. She had managed to spend the entire evening avoiding Charlotte, an aim that seemed mutual. But all good things come to an end. She wondered what kind of first night they would have; certainly not the kind she'd imagined when they met.

CHAPTER TEN

Charlotte sealed the mosquito nets that shrouded the interior of the tent and hastily exchanged her clothes for a pair of thin cotton knit pajamas that were supposed to provide extra protection against biting insects. She hadn't thought about the malaria risk when she was preparing for the trip. Only when she and Tamsin were traveling in the Australian outback had it occurred to her that she would soon be exchanging arid desert for humid jungle in one of the mosquito capitals of the planet.

Normally, she would have found the constant application of DEET and the need to wear clothing that covered every limb intolerable in this humidity. But such inconveniences were a small price to pay for being in a biologist's nirvana.

Kwerba was a tiny village in the foothills of the Fojas, situated in a clearing surrounded by forest and jungle that seethed with life. Within minutes of arriving, the team had been stunned to see a bird of paradise come marching toward them, apparently interested in the equipment stacked near the helicopter. Miles had immediately waved for the film crew, and the ornithologists in the party had fallen over themselves to crawl close to the speckle-bibbed brown bird, which, Charlotte learned later, was a species thought to be extinct.

They didn't have to sneak up on it. The bird calmly walked over to one of them and climbed onto his hand. It was the first of many such encounters that afternoon as they explored the immediate environs of the village. Charlotte could hardly wait for tomorrow, when they would catch their first glimpse of the Foja uplands. If this location was any indication, they were going to find themselves in a world unlike any they could have imagined.

She lit the propane lantern and immediately turned it down low to conserve fuel. In the feeble light, she unrolled her sleeping bag and shook out the liner, dubiously eying the tent's groundsheet. This was going to be an uncomfortable night. She was hot already, the tent felt claustrophobically small, and very soon she would be sharing this inadequate space with another person.

Not for the first time, she entertained the possibility that she could blow this assignment because the conditions were so unbearable. At the very best of times, with state-of-the-art camping gear and five-star hotels in the vicinity in case she needed a couple of nights of comfort and a decent shower, she found sleeping in a tent deeply unappealing.

She had participated in wilderness adventures throughout her life because in her family there was no other option. Her parents and her older brothers liked nothing better than pitching camp in some godforsaken place, cooking bad food in unhygienic conditions, and drinking water treated with iodine. All in order to see a big starry sky and hear a world without traffic noise. Charlotte thought you could get the same effect watching the Discovery Channel in high definition while wearing Bose headphones, and save yourself a lot of sanitary wipes.

A voice called, "Knock, knock," and she grudgingly invited her tent-mate to come in. Charlotte knew she sounded snappish, but she couldn't help herself. She just hated that they were the only two women on the expedition and everyone took for granted that they would happily share accommodations.

Ash parted the nets Charlotte had just painstakingly secured and carried a folding bed into the tent. Placing it in front of Charlotte like a prize, she announced, "This is for you. The height of luxury."

"What are you going to sleep on?"

"My trusty three-inch pad. It's inflatable."

"Then I'll be fine with one of those, too."

"Oh, no." Ash shook her head emphatically. "I had to schlep this thing all the way up here, and I've already turned down an attractive financial offer from one of your colleagues to liberate it. So you are going to take full advantage."

"Look, it's not my problem if you people overdid the equipment. I told that boneheaded associate of yours earlier that I don't want any special favors, but he wasn't listening. Apparently he doesn't play well with others."

"Nitro is about getting results." Ash hovered at the tent flap. "What's it going to be— down among whatever crawls into the tent, or the smart choice?"

Charlotte hesitated, but being a few inches off the ground in a place teeming with insect life had its charm. Grudgingly, she said, "Okay. I'll take it." She moved her backpack aside as Ash unfolded the camp bed.

"Where we're headed, there's not a lot of even ground, so this might not even be an option after tomorrow," Ash pointed out.

Charlotte instantly pictured the two of them lying side by side in the narrow confines of this tent for the next week, and unease washed through her. Could this situation be any more awkward? Ash had been ignoring her all evening and while Charlotte wanted them to maintain a professional distance, they were now tiptoeing around each other like they had a crime to hide. In such a confined group, people were going to notice.

Also, irrationally, Charlotte found she resented Ash's impassive acceptance of the new rules. Her attitude seemed insulting somehow after the experiences they had shared. Yet what had Charlotte expected? Ash was a woman who had casual threesomes involving "dumb blondes." People who did that kind of thing were shallow. Just thinking about that episode cut loose a riot of emotions that crowded her mind, making her so agitated she was virtually hyperventilating.

She still couldn't credit that she'd stood in that bedroom, throwing Dani Bush out of Tamsin's house, and Ash had been a few feet away the whole time. It was one of those impossible coincidences no one would believe. Certain deluded individuals also attributed absurd significance to such strokes of fate, like they were messages from God. As far as Charlotte was concerned, the message was *Warning! Warning!*

She sat down on the camp bed and immediately felt foolish about her poor grace in accepting it. To her surprise the mattress was quite comfortable, certainly a step up from sleeping on a pad. Now that she thought about it, she realized she'd overreacted when Ash brought it into the tent. Having spent her entire life proving she could do anything her older brothers did, she was sensitive about being treated like a wuss just because she was a woman. The feeling was even more pronounced here, surrounded by males who all thought they were God's gift to the biological sciences.

Since her college days she'd been on numerous field trips, but never an expedition like this in such a challenging environment. If she were honest with herself, she had to admit she felt stressed. What if she failed to deliver the results Sealy-Weiss was counting on? What if she couldn't cope as well as the men, or made mistakes that people would attribute to her gender? Charlotte suspected she was probably being neurotic but opportunities like this one seldom went to women and having been given the chance, she wanted to prove herself worthy.

In her field women earned more PhD's than men, but there were still very few tenured female professors. Highly qualified women were routinely overlooked for the most coveted teaching posts. Originally, Charlotte had imagined herself teaching, but statistical reality discouraged her. In most of the best schools women only made up twenty percent of faculty, or less, a figure grossly disproportionate to their participation as students.

Things were somewhat better in the private sector. Talent was more likely to be rewarded and women who could embrace the commercial realities usually did pretty well, which was why Charlotte had ended up at Sealy-Weiss instead of taking the crappy option of tutoring mediocre males who would then be paid more than her. The last thing she wanted on this prestigious assignment was to have Miles and the rest of the expedition members reporting that she was a liability.

She thought through the evening's conversation, trying to figure out how she was perceived by the team. Most of her colleagues had been embarrassingly deferential to her. Charlotte pondered that fact. It certainly could be sexism, but she hadn't felt patronized and no one had made any stupid jokes about hair and beauty or scary insects. In fact, there were quite a few comments made about the quality of her research papers and her enviable new position at Sealy-Weiss. The men had talked about Belton Pharmaceuticals' financial commitment to the expedition, and how fortunate they were to have this giant commercial company dealing with the Indonesian bureaucracy and generally paving the way. They all seemed impressed that Charlotte's assignment was at Belton's behest, and everyone, Miles included, had been eager to offer her any assistance she needed.

In a flash of comprehension, Charlotte wondered if she was receiving special attention not because she was a woman, but because of her link to their major sponsor. She let that idea sink in. It made complete sense. Naturally she would be seen as a valuable commodity. Her presence contributed directly to the financial viability of the expedition. All the men she was working with were benefiting because Belton wanted their interests represented and she was the one chosen to bring home the bacon, so to speak.

She allowed herself a small smile of satisfaction. If she was as important as it seemed, perhaps she could apply some leverage. Why shouldn't she have her own private tent, whatever that "Nitro" individual said? He wasn't in charge. He was being paid to keep them safe. She almost laughed at herself for believing his deadpan threats to escort her back to Pom or throw her out of the helicopter. The guy had bullied her into submission and she had folded, believing this place was just lawless enough that a man like him could get away with anything. She should have been more assertive. From now on, she would be.

She glanced across at Ash, who seemed fully occupied with night-time preparations and had barely looked at her after setting up the camp bed.

"How many tents did we actually bring?" she asked and was irritated when her companion did not have the courtesy to look up.

"Enough for the whole party."

"No spares?"

"If we have a mishap, we can have replacements brought in with the supply drops."

Charlotte wondered if Ash had caught the dinner discussion about the aims for the expedition. If so, she had to know Charlotte wasn't just any member of the team, she was a key player. Ash had seemed detached while everyone was talking, making a show of cleaning her guns. But that didn't mean she wasn't paying attention. Charlotte had a feeling very little escaped her.

"I was thinking maybe a one-person tent could be brought in for me," she said, testing the waters. "I'm a private person and I'll have a lot of work to do, recording observations and writing up notes. I really need my own space."

"I'm sure all your pals on the team feel exactly the same way." Ash removed her holster and set it down next to her sleeping bag. "The bad news is we'll be in terrain that doesn't lend itself to a sprawl. Tent numbers have to stay at the minimum."

It made sense, but Charlotte couldn't shake the feeling that

Ash found her predicament amusing. Most people would have been mortified over what she now knew about the Dani Bush episode, but Ash seemed completely blasé about it. Maybe such conduct was just par for the course for her. Charlotte didn't think she'd ever seen anyone whose sensuality was such an out-in-the-open secret. In every way, from her animal physicality and self-awareness to her guarded but knowing stare, she oozed the kind of sexual confidence no one came by if they lived like a nun.

Charlotte allowed herself to watch covertly as she prepared for sleep. She had a lethal, unconscious grace that made it hard to look away. Every movement was automatic, as though she'd done the same thing hundreds of times. After checking the mosquito nets were secure, she sprayed some insecticide around the entrance to the tent, then removed various items from her pockets and arranged them neatly next to her sleeping pad. She then unfastened her ammunition belt, an action that made Charlotte's breath catch, and she stared, strangely riveted, as Ash rolled her sleeves down and buttoned the cuffs, then unbuttoned her shirt all the way, letting it hang loosely over a tank that advertised her lean muscularity.

Charlotte wanted to look anywhere but at the nipples that jabbed the thin cotton. They were hard. Was Ash turned on or just one of those women whose nipples never slept? She quickly lowered her gaze. Bad idea. She didn't want to look at the fly buttons of Ash's khakis and the fit of her pants around her crotch, but the thought that she could just reach out and unfasten the heavy cotton fly made her light-headed.

Ash seemed oblivious to her scrutiny, for which she was thankful but also strangely bothered. Part of her wanted to be seen, to hold Ash's attention the same way she had that evening at the Pongo Tavern, when they'd danced closer and closer until Charlotte had yearned for the mating embrace that never came.

How could this be happening to her? It was lust. Plain and simple. Normally, it never occurred and she was thankful for that. Lust was irrational and could complicate any situation. In one like this, it was a liability she could not afford. Charlotte hoped if she just ignored it, it would pass soon. Perhaps she was frustrated. It had been a while, after all.

She cast her mind back to the last time she'd had sex. Three months? No, six. The actual details of the encounter were now a little foggy. She'd been dating Dr. Hazel Robson and postponing the inevitable.

Finally their schedules coincided and they could take a weekend away. Charlotte wanted to go because it was healthy to have regular sexual activity and they'd already discussed whether they would be compatible in bed. It seemed they would and looking back now, she thought they'd had a nice time.

Hazel was attractive and fit, and a considerate lover with a competent oral sex technique. She was gentle and didn't seem worried that Charlotte took a long time to reach an orgasm, if she had one at all. They'd persevered and finally she had a very satisfying climax on their second night together. Hazel said she wasn't all about orgasm, anyway. She wasn't twenty anymore and found cuddling equally rewarding. That was something they had in common. In fact, after the weekend, they'd agreed that if they had to choose between a good massage and sex, the massage was more tempting.

They'd gone out a few more times after that, but the only nights they slept together, there was no lovemaking. They kept agreeing it would happen next time and there was no hurry, but in the end they hadn't got around to it again. Hazel met someone else, who shared her fondness for indoor bowling, and Charlotte was applying for the Sealy-Weiss job. So she wasn't even going to be in the same city anymore if she was offered the position. They'd parted as friends, without any acrimony, and since then Charlotte had been too busy to consider dating anyone else. It stood to reason that she was noticing her physical needs by now. She was a normal woman.

She watched Ash place the menacing-looking pistol close to her pillow, unzip her sleeping bag, and climb into it fully clothed.

Modesty? Or did Ash think she was so irresistible, stripped down, that any woman in her proximity would be putty? Butches like her appeared to have a diagnosable need to flaunt themselves. They were only interested in one thing and mistakenly assumed it was the same for everyone else. Well, Charlotte had news for her.

Acidly, she said, "I won't look if you want to get undressed."

Ash lifted her head and surveyed her for the first time in at least ten minutes. Her eyes shone like onyx in the poor light. "I sleep in my clothes. I'm paid to be prepared if the need arises."

"Whatever." Charlotte still thought the whole idea of a security detail was absurd, and now that they'd reached Kwerba the precautions truly seemed like overkill. They were in the middle of nowhere, deep in a jungle no one ever tried to penetrate, not even the tribes who lived here. From all accounts there were no large predatory animals and no militias. Who or what exactly were they being protected from?

Ash asked, "Need anything from your pack before I kill the lamp?"

"No. Thank you."

Charlotte knew her tone was ungracious, even sarcastic, and she was surprised at herself. Why was she letting this woman get under her skin? It wasn't like Ash was actually doing anything untoward. In fact, ever since their awkward conversation earlier that day, she'd treated Charlotte like a stranger. Given Charlotte's unwelcome physical response to her, wasn't that a good thing?

As Ash extinguished the lamp, Charlotte surrendered herself to the unfamiliar noises of the jungle. She could hear faint stirring sounds as Ash got settled in her sleeping bag just inches away, then the soft rush of a sigh and the din of her own heart pumping hot blood to places that distracted her. Outside, trees rustled and distant, eerie screeches cut through the night. The darkness was intense and heavy, the air in the tent stickily warm. Charlotte tried to get to sleep but after a few minutes she realized it was never going to happen.

She was agitated and tense, and it didn't help that she could not block out the sound of Ash's breathing, and the sense of her just feet away yet painfully distant. Squirming, she touched a fingertip to one of her bothersome nipples and found it stone hard and unbearably sensitive. So, too, her skin. Everywhere she touched, goose bumps danced a wild, clamoring response. She let her hand rest on her belly, trying to soothe herself by thinking of cool, clean water dripping from a fresh, crisp triple-washed salad.

Her mind retaliated with a lurid vision of Ash between her legs, giving her what she needed. Deep inside, her womb answered with a small implosion that made her stomach muscles clench. Horrified, Charlotte unzipped her sleeping bag and flapped it to relieve the heat of her frantic arousal.

Ash must have noticed this desperate measure because she said, "Don't worry. It'll be cooler in the uplands."

"I thought this was meant to be winter," Charlotte snapped. She could feel an orgasm stalking her, just waiting for a moment of weakness. This could *not* be her body.

"No, not exactly. We don't have four seasons in New Guinea.

There's the wet season and the dry season. You guys are here just before the start of the wet season."

"It feels hotter than Pom."

"That's the humidity. It's a hundred percent up here."

"Great." Charlotte could only imagine what it was going to be like fighting her way through the vegetation tomorrow, everything chafing. And more so because she was abnormally swollen. It had to be hormonal, perhaps a reaction to the climate. Delayed jet lag and homesickness. "I hope we're hauling plenty of water," she muttered.

"Yeah, we thought about that."

"I don't know how you live here all year round."

"I take breaks."

"Oh, that's right. You go back home and have threesomes."

Ash was silent. Charlotte thought she detected a slow sigh. She could kick herself for her comment. What did it matter to her what Ash did? Her annoyance wasn't about Tamsin. The damage to that relationship had happened long before Ash went home with Dani and her new girlfriend. No, Charlotte was peeved that Ash would sleep with a piece of work like Dani but walk away from her. Talk about lousy taste in women.

"Not that it's any of my business," she said, hoping she sounded nonchalant. "I just hope you get checked for herpes."

"What?" Ash sounded incredulous.

"Well, I have a right to be concerned," Charlotte said coldly. "It gets passed on by kissing, and if you're going to have sex with sluts like Dani Bush, who knows what STDs you might have."

A long, pregnant silence ensued, then Ash said, "Why do I get the feeling this is not just a health issue with you?"

"Because you can't imagine anyone taking responsibility for their sexual conduct?" Charlotte replied sweetly.

"Give me strength," Ash muttered. "Okay. For the record, I get tested and I make sure my partners do the same."

"Oh, right. You interview them before you jump into bed?"

"Actually, yes."

"How romantic."

"Romance is not a factor."

"Big surprise."

"Jesus." It sounded like Ash had thrown off her covers. Charlotte could hear metallic noises and she could make out a change in the deep shadows. Ash had sat up. "What the fuck is eating you?"

Her voice held a warning quality that made Charlotte's spine prickle. "Nothing. Other then the fact that I'm forced to share this sauna of a tent with a woman who was in my best friend's bedroom, having sex with her trashy ex *plus* the woman she's been cheating with. It doesn't speak well of you."

"God forbid I have consensual sex with whomever I like without asking her entire life history. Are you always so moralistic and judgmental?"

"We're not talking about *me*."

"Sure we are. You're the one who's pissed off. What exactly is the problem? Are you angry because I didn't sleep with you back in Pom?"

"Don't be ridiculous."

A hand snapped around her wrist. "Wrong answer. Try the truth."

Charlotte's stomach lurched and a hot shock of awareness seared every nerve ending where Ash's fingers dug in. She locked her knees together to counter the quiver that stiffened her clit. "Let go of me. I'll scream."

"And this entire camp will think you just found a giant millipede in your bra."

"Oh, God." Charlotte shuddered, distracted from her peaking arousal by that hideous image. She tugged her arm, trying to free herself. Breathing unevenly, she threatened, "I'll get you sacked."

"Be my guest." The hold relaxed just enough to catch Charlotte off guard, then Ash exerted a completely different kind of force, hauling her off her narrow cot and dragging her across the strip of canvas that separated them.

"How dare you," Charlotte gasped. "What do you think you're doing?"

She couldn't see six inches in front of her and her legs were tangled in the sleeping bag liner, but she swatted where she thought Ash's face might be and her free hand connected vaguely with bare skin before it, too, was ruthlessly captured. Squirming, she found herself drawn back to lean against Ash, both hands clamped together in front of her.

A voice in her ear, ordered, "Stop fighting me. I'm not going to hurt you."

Warm breath spread sensation over Charlotte's face and down

her neck. She tried to turn her head away but only ended up with her tingling cheek flattened against Ash's chest.

Forced to listen to the steady beat of Ash's heart, she said, "I don't know what you're playing at, but I'm not one of your dumb blondes."

Ash laughed softly. "Can't argue with that."

Then Charlotte found her hands released, but the arms that encircled her were so unyielding she couldn't get away. Ash had to notice how hard her nipples were, she thought miserably.

Her insolent captor said, "Now listen carefully. We're only going to have this conversation once."

Charlotte contemplated yelling for help, but somehow she couldn't summon the will. Instead she stopped struggling and wilted. There was something comforting about being held so tightly and maybe she was an idiot, but she believed Ash wouldn't hurt her. Stiffly, she said, "I'm listening."

Ash seemed lost in thought for a moment and Charlotte felt a tremor pass through the hard body pressed to her back. "I just lost the one person in my life I really loved." Ash's voice was leaden with grief. "The last thing I want to be doing right now is babysitting you and your nerdy pals. If there hadn't been a woman on your team, my boss could have replaced me. But no such luck."

As she spoke, her arms relaxed by degrees. If she moved fast, she could break away, Charlotte thought. But she did nothing. In fact, she sagged back into the body behind her own, listening despite herself.

"You've gone out of your way to be a bitch to me all day," Ash said. "And maybe I deserve it. But I really don't give a damn what you think of me personally. I have to be on my game for the next week and it's hard enough already without you on my case. So I'm asking you to show me some basic respect. Does that seem unreasonable?"

Ash was no longer restraining her, and Charlotte wasn't sure when that had changed, but she still had no desire to leave the sheltering embrace. She waited to feel anger in response to Ash's words. The trouble was, she just felt ashamed of herself. Ash was right. She had been a bitch. Petty, self-righteous, and controlling. She'd barely spared a thought for what Ash must be going through, having suffered the loss of her sister. She was too busy being angry.

Why? She wasn't normally like this. Something about Ash pushed her buttons. Yet again the memory of their kiss troubled her. She hadn't felt like herself since then. She'd been on edge. Prickly. Restive. And endlessly fixated on images of Ash in bed with her, of them having sex. It was like a sickness. All she wanted was to stop feeling this way. She'd been so exhausted by the end of the Kokoda trek, her fantasies had finally lost their immediacy and she could see an end to her strange fixation with the woman she'd thought was a man.

Then Ash had walked back into her life and ruined everything. That was why she'd been so angry back at the hanger. She had just been congratulating herself on getting a grip when her nemesis returned to destroy her peace of mind.

Charlotte sighed. "It's not unreasonable," she conceded in answer to Ash's question. "Please accept my apologies. I am truly sorry about your sister."

"We can make this easy or hard," Ash said. "I did exactly what you asked of me earlier, but it doesn't seem to be working for you. Is there something else I can do that would help?"

Kiss me again, right now. Charlotte shook her head emphatically. "No. Nothing."

"Okay. So are we good?"

"Yes." It didn't sound very convincing. Charlotte tried again. "We're fine."

She felt so stiff, Ash thought. And her voice was as brittle as glass. She let her arms drop, indicating that Charlotte was free to move back to her cot. Charlotte stayed where she was. Ash drew a deep breath. She could tell Charlotte was holding hers.

"I'm sorry I manhandled you," she said, and meant it.

She seldom lost her temper. It usually didn't pay off. Her approach was to watch and listen, and to roll with the punches unless there was no choice but to take action. In which case, she made her move swiftly and effectively.

She had planned to say a couple of things to Charlotte before lights out, such as: *What the hell is wrong with you?* Or that timeless reproach: *Grow up*. As it turned out, she was ready to throttle her over the camp bed, but the comments about sexually transmitted diseases and lack of responsibility had been the final straw. Ash could not believe she had finally made it to the tent, hanging out for some desperately needed sleep, and instead had some uptight prude telling her how to live her life.

Ms. Holier-Than-Thou was now hunkered against her chest like she was afraid to move, her tension palpable. Apparently she hadn't noticed that she was no longer being held against her wishes. Ash wondered what to say. *You can go to bed now.* Too parental?

She gave Charlotte's shoulder a friendly squeeze, hoping she would read this as an invitation to do them both a favor and quietly relinquish Ash's lap. Instead she flinched as if she'd been struck and her whole body stiffened. Shit. Ash wondered if she'd inadvertently probed an injury. The attitudinal biologist had hiked the Kokoda. It was possible she'd suffered some physical damage but was toughing it out because she didn't want to slow the expedition down. Ash wondered if she should speak to Miles, off the record. It wouldn't do any harm to rest up an extra day in Kwerba. She could do with the time out herself.

Maybe she could chopper the real zealots up to the dry lake bed, their landing zone on the western slopes of the Fojas, tomorrow. They could get settled and start catching beetles or whatever, and she would ferry the rest of them up the following day. Not a bad idea. Of course, Miles would never wear it. The guy was completely single-minded.

"I don't know about you, but I'm ready to catch some z's," Ash said.

Charlotte lifted her head and twisted slightly, leaning away to stare up at Ash. "Let's start fresh," she said with bedroom huskiness.

Ash wasn't sure what starting fresh meant in this context but she was too tired to ask for clarification. Some people made their interactions with others way too complicated. That wasn't her style. All she wanted right now was for her head to hit that micro-pillow.

"Works for me," she said, which seemed to go over okay.

Whispering an ardent thank-you, Charlotte moved away a little more, her hands glancing past Ash's thighs as she groped for the floor to orient herself. Ash resisted an urge to guide her.

"Everything okay?" she asked when she heard the creak of the cot frame.

"Yes, I'm fine. I'm sorry about…earlier."

Ash stretched out on her own pad. "It's done. No need to apologize any more. And don't lie awake thinking about it." That was the problem with brainy chicks. They took everything too seriously.

"I won't," Charlotte said. "Good night, Ash."

Ash said good night and stared into the pitch-black void of the low tent ceiling. Under normal circumstances, she might have been tempted to take Charlotte to bed regardless of the austere comforts of their lodgings. Charlotte's fast-crumbling resistance to being held, and her hesitance in moving away once she was freed, had been at odds with her protests. Ash could read an opportunity between those lines.

Yet that innocent shoulder squeeze had evoked an instinctive and emphatic *don't hurt me* response, and Ash never ignored those. Women often sent mixed signals and she was adept at second-guessing what they really wanted. But certain body language was crystal clear and she knew it well enough to recognize it instantly. She wondered who had stolen Charlotte's trust away through violence. A parent? A lover?

Ash got angry just thinking about it. There was never an excuse. Any time she heard that a colleague or one of her workers in Madang was hitting their wife or child, she did something to stop it. She knew a thing or two about bullies. She'd spent her first eighteen years living with one. Cartwright Evans had not beaten her or Emma severely, although he routinely terrified both of them with the possibility. But they knew what their mother's black eyes and stiff posture meant.

Ash could never understand why there was no divorce. As soon as she'd found out that parents sometimes separated and children lived with one or the other, she'd begged her mother to leave and take them with her. But Denise Evans was an old-fashioned woman who believed marriage was for good or bad. With the benefit of hindsight, Ash had concluded her mother was afraid Cartwright would hunt them down and kill her children. She was simply trying to protect them. Remaining in the marriage was the only way she thought she could.

Ash had been Cartwright's favorite, and that had created a wedge between her and Emma, despite Ash's efforts to support her younger sister. Emma lacked confidence and she'd never been able to stand up for herself against their father. When they were kids Ash used to push her to be more outgoing and to do the things that could win his approval. But Cartwright was capricious and cunning. He would reward one sibling and punish the other for the same thing, and Ash was always the one on the winning side of that equation.

Ironically, in the end, it was timid, obedient Emma who had tried to save their mother's life in the horrific attack that claimed it. Incredibly, after his arrest, Cartwright had seemed to expect Ash to take his side. It was as if he thought she regarded her mother and sister with the same contempt he did. He actually believed she was just like him.

Ash had never come to terms with that. She wanted to prove him wrong, yet she could not deny there were similarities. Cartwright was a charismatic bad boy with a dangerous charm women couldn't resist.

Ash knew she had inherited something of that from him, and, like him, she exploited it. She also shared his tall blond good looks and the recklessness that could add up to courage in a disciplined individual, but in him had manifested as callous self-indulgence. Cartwright Evans was a narcissist. He did as he pleased and didn't care how others were affected.

His wife had gotten in his way and he'd made her pay for it. Emma had tried to stop him, and she'd paid, too. Cartwright had attacked their mother with a baseball bat and when Emma tried to drag him off, he turned on her and chased her through the upstairs level of the house, finally clubbing her over the head at the landing. Emma had fallen down the stairs, unconscious. He left her for dead and returned to the master bedroom to finish off his wife, who had managed to call 911 by then. It had all come out at the trial, experts painting the full picture with photos of blood splatter and bodily injuries.

Cartwright's defense attorney had made a case that two African American men had broken into the house in a robbery that got violent and that he'd come home when the attack was in progress. Ash had testified against him, providing a history of his behavior that helped convict him. If she could, she would have killed him with her bare hands. Even that urge made her anxious sometimes. She was always aware of her genes, of a nascent Cartwright ticking like a time bomb inside her.

She'd gone to a shrink about it once, years ago, seeking some kind of reassurance that she would not turn into her father. The shrink had insisted on talking about irrelevant stuff like her lack of committed relationships, which was nothing more than a side effect of her working life. She wanted to read all kinds of significance into her love 'em and leave 'em pattern, instead of seeing it for what it was, a practical necessity. Ash had nothing to offer a woman who wanted a cozy domestic existence, and she didn't want to lead anyone to hope otherwise.

The shrink had said, *Conscience makes cowards of us all.* Her theory was that Ash felt responsible for what had happened to her family and she was afraid to start a new family of her own in case she fucked that up by behaving like her father. Ash could see where she was coming from, but she was wrong. Her biggest concern, if the apple hadn't fallen far from the tree, was that she would do something rash on an assignment, kill someone for no good reason and thereby cross that line in the sand she fought to preserve. She wanted to be able to live with herself, to retain some sense of honor.

That's what Emma had given her. A sense of honor, of being a good person. She let her mind drift to their last good day together at the Grove. Emma had laboriously baked banana bread and they watched a movie, then went out shopping for new clothes. In stores the clerks always made a fuss of her. She was petite and looked much younger than she was, with her pixie face and flaxen hair in bunches. When she was in a good mood, she was so sweet and lovable no one would believe she was also capable of stabbing a nurse and had to be supervised at all times.

Some days were better than others, and this was one of the best. Emma was sunny and affectionate and had asked Ash questions about Madang like she could actually imagine she might live there one day.

When it came time for her to leave, Emma had kissed her goodbye and said, as she always did, "Can I come with you?"

Ash said, "Soon." And for once she'd really believed it.

Medicine made constant advances. Ash had been sure that if she could keep Emma well long enough, a new treatment would emerge that would deliver real results. With Emma's gradual but marked improvement, it finally seemed possible that she could live outside of an institution.

"Don't forget me," Emma had called as she walked away.

Ash could still see her at that window, waving, holding the teddy bear she never let go of. Ash had the bear in her backpack, wrapped in a clean cloth. It still smelled of her sister. Tears stung her eyes and she rolled onto her side, facing away from Charlotte, her face muffled against her pillow.

Everything she did, the way she had built her life over the past ten years, the risks and everyday hazards she took for granted, had only made sense because of Emma. Now that she'd gone, Ash's life seemed pointless.

She had never felt more alone.

Chapter Eleven

Predictably, Miles didn't go for the idea of taking an extra day in Kwerba. He could see the promised land and was chomping at the bit. Ash tried to make an argument about cloud cover and the brief burn-off period when she could hope to put down safely on the lake bed. However, Miles wasn't hearing anything but mermaids singing. He looked twitchy just thinking about the possibility that they might not be able to start taping bird calls at five a.m. the next morning and asked what the big deal was. The flight was only a half hour.

So, as soon as the swirling mist seemed to be lifting, the Nagle team organized the field party, who had flipped coins to see who went in first. Crates of food and water would be dropped last because they could be pushed over the side without having to put the helicopter down on the soft sphagnum bog. Each landing was risky and they would need to get the Huey in the air again before its gear sank too far.

"Once we touch down, you'll have about three minutes to get out," Ash told her passengers. "So jump and run. Stay down. You don't want to get decapitated before you see your bow-wow bird."

"That's *bower* bird," Miles said like Ash had just disrespected the president or something.

Charlotte pointed to a stack of boxes, cages, and butterfly nets. "Can I get my things?"

"No. People first. We'll drop all the supplies and equipment in last."

"But what if you can't make it in again today? We'll be stuck up there with nothing."

Ash shrugged and gave Miles a pointed look.

With the confidence of a man who had never flown a helicopter in the New Guinea highlands, he said, "Don't worry. If it looks like conditions are deteriorating, we'll change our plan. You'll have everything you need. I personally guarantee it."

Ash almost laughed at Charlotte's expression. Even she wasn't kidding herself about the risks they were facing, but Miles was already climbing aboard the Huey, a man with a mission. He waved for the rest of the first group to follow.

Ash said, "Looks like we're moving out."

Charlotte mumbled something under her breath and picked up the bag Ash knew carried her microscope. "I'm not leaving this."

She was in fine form this morning, Ash reflected, all business but still sounding so seductive everyone fell into dorkish wonder whenever she opened her mouth. Over breakfast Ash had noticed Billy Bob Woodcock eyeballing her lasciviously. She wanted to smack him in the mouth but refrained. There would always be one guy who saw a sole civilian female as an invitation to help himself. She hoped his training had taught him enough to keep zipped up.

Just in case, she wandered over to him and said, "You're working, Woodcock. Remember that."

"Got it, Major. No handling the merchandise."

Ash disliked him already. She said, "Dr. Lascelles is the client's representative. I'm talking about our paycheck. Understood?"

That got his attention. "Yes, ma'am. Point taken."

Ash moved the conversation on immediately. She didn't want anyone thinking she had a personal interest. Money was the stakes everyone in the game understood. "You'll be going in with the second lift, Corporal. I'm counting on you to keep order in the meantime. Don't let any of these civilians run off by themselves chasing zoo specimens."

"I'm on it, ma'am."

He had seemed mindful of the mild reprimand ever since, keeping his eyes off Charlotte and his hands on the supplies. Ash cast a quick look his way as the last of the party climbed aboard. He was making wisecracks with one of the few macho scientists, an Australian not unlike Steve Irwin, the Crocodile Hunter.

Klaus moved to Ash's side. "Think he can keep it in his pants?"

Pleased she wasn't the only one who'd noticed the signs, Ash said, "If he doesn't I'll cut it off for him."

"You interested yourself?" Klaus had made her for a dyke about three seconds after they'd met.

Ash said dryly, "I'm interested in getting paid."

"You could do worse."

"That's a fact," Ash conceded.

Her colleague wasn't letting it go. "I think she likes you."

"She's a long way from home. Women like her end up with people who won't embarrass them at dinner parties."

Klaus lapsed into silence. They both knew what she was saying. Being honest about how they made a living was a guaranteed conversation stopper in polite circles. Once the novelty wore off, respectable women got fed up with hanging out with a social liability.

"I think they're waiting for us," Ash said.

She and Klaus shook hands, as they always did before a flight. The deal was if they ever had to ditch, this would serve as the respectful good-bye they wouldn't get time for. They'd known each other ever since Ash started running arms for Tubby Nagle, and she trusted Klaus. He was the nearest thing she had to a real friend in PNG.

There were folks in the Nagle organization who assumed they were an item. Ash neither confirmed nor denied unless she was asked, and no one ever got that personal, not even Tubby. It wasn't always diplomatic to mention family to a contractor. For various reasons, many didn't have one.

Ash climbed into the pilot's seat, next to Klaus, and sized up their takeoff area. There was enough room for a single bounce, and they would need it. They were loaded to the max.

As the Huey rose grudgingly away from the thatched huts and staring tribesmen, Klaus rotated a map to follow the compass heading and gave her some coordinates. Ash pulled into a hover and checked the gauges, then moved the bird slowly forward. With a slight shudder, the Huey sank and she let the skid toes bounce, then increased airspeed so the blades could bite into clean air. The strained rotor responded with the additional lift she was seeking and they gained altitude, a triumph greeted with audible relief by the passengers behind her.

Ash had done this so many times she no longer held her breath, but she knew everyone else in the Huey had just gulped a lungful of air and the overdue oxygen was making them giddy. They all started talking at once with exaggerated relief, as if no one had feared for a moment that they would end up dangling from a tree.

Heading due west on course toward the lake bed, Ash flipped on her audio switch so she could listen to her favorite flying music. She liked the oldies, maybe because she could remember her mother singing along to Joni Mitchell and Lynyrd Skynyrd. A cool wind floated through the Huey's open sides as the altimeter crested a thousand feet, and in her headphones Neil Young prophetically mourned Mother Nature in "After the Gold Rush." Ash stared out at one of the last true Edens on the planet and wondered what this view would be like in twenty years' time.

After they'd been cruising just on ninety knots for a while, Klaus lifted one of her earphones and protested, "You're making my nose bleed."

She dropped some altitude and patched the music through the intercom just in time for Pink Floyd. Why not display her age and outdated musical tastes to everyone on board? "Got a visual on the white treetops yet?" she asked Klaus.

Her copilot lifted his high-powered binoculars and visually prowled the dense canopy below for the markers Ash had noted on several occasions when she'd scoped this region out in a Cessna. One of them was a stand of trees covered in white flowers at this time of year. They would be hard to spot through the cloud cover, and she would need to find a safe spot to fly low if she hoped to see the other physical landmarks she'd recorded.

Keeping an eye on the shrouded slopes before them, she pulled the Huey into a climb to adjust to the rising topography. Flying in the mountains was always dangerous, but the dense cloud made the trip almost lunatic. Ash felt like calling back to Miles, *Having fun, smart guy? Still think flying into the uplands is no big deal?*

They were heading for the western summit of the ranges, an area deep in the unexplored heart of the island and often drowning in cloud for weeks on end. The field party had been warned that both supply drops and changes of staff could be compromised by weather, but Ash had the impression no one took this seriously. She wondered if their opinions were changing now.

"Nine thirty," Klaus said, pointing through a filmy break in the cloud. "That's your marker and I have visual on the lake bed."

Ash accelerated and dropped to a couple of hundred feet above the ground so she could verify. "Roger. We're going in."

The trees marked the beginning of the steep glide path into the landing zone. The approach angle was dangerous and she was coming in hot, the vegetation rushing up at her with alarming speed. Her heart pumping, she pulled more power and raised the nose a fraction to slow the rate of descent. They were already putting down on marshy ground. She didn't want them digging in any harder than they needed to.

She was vaguely aware of a deathly hush from behind, where her nervous passengers were no doubt whispering their Hail Marys. Laughing softly, Ash flared hard, demanding as much pitch as the blades were willing to deliver. She knew this low bird like no one else, knew every quiver and whine. The rotor rpm began to bleed off and the body shook in protest. The Huey succumbed to a small, sharp bounce, then remained in the air at a hover, about five feet above the ground.

There was nothing more awe-inspiring than executing a perfect in-ground-effect hover. Ash always savored the challenge, never taking for granted the magic of holding both altitude and airspeed as close as possible to zero, yet remaining airborne and ready to break free.

"That's a genuine bog down there," she told Klaus. "We'll need everyone out double time."

She pedal-turned until she faced across the slope of the ground, progressively lowered the collective, and kept the cyclic moving uphill until the gear touched down. Rolling off the throttle, she yelled over her shoulder, "Haul ass and keep your heads down."

Her passengers spilled out the side in an untidy scramble of khaki-clad bodies, and Ash caught a glimpse of Charlotte staggering across the spongy expanse with everyone else. She looked back toward the Huey and waved.

"I told you," Klaus said with earnest satisfaction. "She likes you."

Chapter Twelve

Charlotte opened her eyes in stages, letting them adjust to the beckoning light of dawn. They'd been camped a short distance from the lake bed for three nights and she still woke each morning with a sense of awe that remained with her all day. The morning birdcalls alone were like nothing she'd ever heard, a melodic cacophony that went on for at least an hour and was then repeated throughout breakfast as the ornithologists played back their tapes and argued over which vocalization belonged to this honey-eater or that fairy wren.

While all this was going on, Billy Bob Woodcock flipped pancakes over a propane stove and occasionally cast appreciative stares in her direction. The security guard made her uneasy. He was always scrupulously polite and never did anything untoward, but Charlotte hadn't seen him looking at anyone else the way he ogled her.

She had considered mentioning it to Ash but decided it was just a guy thing and she was being overly sensitive. She didn't want to get him in trouble. Ash was clearly the one handing down orders to the Nagle crew and Charlotte was sure if she complained the guy would be spoken to. She didn't want him feeling got at for no reason. Better to keep her powder dry until there was really something to complain about. Hopefully, it would never come to that.

She glanced across to the empty sleeping pad on the opposite side of the tent. Ash always rose before her and left the tent quickly out of good manners. Even though Charlotte was faintly disappointed to find herself alone, she appreciated the gesture. It was nice to be able to wipe herself clean with the large-sized antibacterial towelettes she'd packed for bathing, and get dressed in privacy.

Miles had organized volunteers to take turns looking for a safe pool along the stream that flowed near their campsite, so they would have a place to bathe and wash their clothes. But so far they'd only found sections they could wade in up to their knees. Today's searchers were planning to venture farther upsteam until they came to the source of their little tributory, hopefully a fork where a larger body of water divided. This could offer the kind of pristine pool that would enable swimming. Charlotte could hardly wait. Despite her best endeavors with the wipes, she felt like a walking microbe factory.

She finished dressing and left the tent to use one of the improvised bathrooms rigged up south of the camp. This was one Nagle-operated service she was thankful for. Their port-a-potty was housed in a small shack skirted with fleshy palm fronds. It would be replaced each time there was a supply drop. Not far from it, another mountain stream bounced over a small boulder, creating a natural faucet for washing hands and cleaning teeth. A spittoon nearby enabled them to do this without introducing toothpaste chemicals into the water.

Charlotte was bending over the stream rinsing her mouth when she became aware of large booted feet a few yards to her right. Forcing herself not to betray her nerves by jerking upright, she finished what she was doing, then slowly turned and said, "Good morning, Billy Bob."

"Ma'am." He flipped his black beret and flashed a wide set of teeth. He was well over six feet and had the beady-eyed satisfaction of a male who knew he was intimidating. "Must be hard on y'all, coping with this. Not a real positive situation for a lady like yourself."

Charlotte gave him a noncommittal smile. "Yes, but it's not for long and I'm thankful to be here."

"Some of us are mighty thankful, too." He delivered a heavy-handed compliment. "Looking at you beats the heck out of all them frogs and birds your pals wet themselves over."

Charlotte had heard enough. She tapped her wristwatch and said, "Speaking of which, the frog-hunting party must be back by now. I can't wait to see what they have in their specimen boxes this morning."

"Oh, yeah. Me either."

Charlotte's heart pounded a shade too quickly as he walked her back to the camp. But she kept her pace at a steady, casual stroll, determined to reveal nothing of her unease. As soon as she saw Ash, she made a beeline for her, thankful that her companion drifted off in another direction.

"Hello, stranger," she greeted Ash with a slight edge.

Despite the fact that they were sharing a tent, Charlotte had barely seen her since they'd arrived. Each night she tried to stay awake long enough to see her come in, but exhaustion claimed her almost as soon as her head touched the pillow and Ash was so quiet slipping in, whenever she finally got around to it, that Charlotte never woke up.

During the day, Ash was endlessly embroiled in getting the camp set up and helping build the platforms and walkways the mammal experts needed for their research in the upper canopy. She and the Nagle team had also created a perimeter for the expedition. No one was permitted to venture outside of this without an escort. Everyone was also equipped with 900MHz GSM cell phones and flares for emergencies.

The few occasions when she was free to talk were usually around meals, and other members of the team were present. For the first two days, Charlotte had been so overwhelmed with the surroundings and so excited by her work that she'd been able to be philosophical about the disconnect between them. But today, she didn't feel quite so contented, and the odd menace she'd sensed from Billy Bob had unsettled her even more.

Although they hadn't spoken beyond meaningless conversation for days, Charlotte had been constantly attuned to Ash's presence. She'd fought her awareness for about twenty-four hours, then she just gave in and decided to enjoy the sight of her whenever she could. Sweaty. Untidy. Stripped down to her tank to work on the various building projects. Head thrown back, laughing at something Nitro the nutcase said.

Charlotte had never encountered a woman who seemed so completely at ease with herself physically. When they sat together for a meal or when Ash stalked past her in the middle of some task, Charlotte never felt neutral. Instead she was so conscious of her she felt a sharp sense of loss every time their work took them in opposite directions. Even then, it seemed some invisible force connected them, and Charlotte could actually feel it grow stronger as Ash came closer again.

She wanted to believe the unconscious bond wasn't authentic; that with her senses on high alert and her mind constantly racing, what she was experiencing was a consequence of heightened survival instincts. Part of a larger picture. Charlotte could sell herself on that idea when she was being logical. The rest of the time, she was gloomily aware that her attraction to Ash was undiminished; in fact, it seemed to be growing exponentially. No matter how much or how little she saw of her, the feelings churned away inside. And lately, when she tried to convince herself this would pass, her reasoning lacked conviction. She just didn't believe it. Even more unnerving, she didn't want to believe it.

For the first time in years she felt alive, jolted out of her numb inertia by a current of anticipation so strong it delivered frissons of heightened awareness every time she saw Ash. The slow, easy rhythm of her voice filled Charlotte with contentment. And she knew the smell of her so well she could recall it when they were apart. It always made her think of that kiss, the one that had made it impossible for her to remain in her safe, comfortable, remote bubble.

Now, under Ash's questioning scrutiny, those knowing blue eyes narrowed, that hot, slow simmer of a smile tugging with the corners of her mouth, Charlotte felt a whimper rise in her throat. Her stomach churned and all she could think about was that mouth on hers. Those hands on her body. Ash's weight pinning her. The two of them in a sweaty tangle. Gasping. Coming.

Unnerved by the vivid images, she looked away and frantically tried to regroup. The power of these cravings threw her into turmoil. Since when did she allow sexual feelings to overtake her? Was she really as frustrated as she felt? Charlotte dismissed that idea with scorn. She had a perfectly normal sex life, admittedly a somewhat sparse one in recent times. But who was counting?

"I saw Billy Bob walking you back from the rest area," Ash said in a neutral tone, mercifully oblivious to Charlotte's lurid fantasies. "Everything okay?"

"Yes, fine." Charlotte's voice sounded thin and reedy, even to her.

She watched a pair of birds involved in an elaborate dance at the edge of the jungle. The male strutted around, flicking his wings and rippling the white plumes along his sides, whistling sweetly to attract the rather drab female watching this display. As she drew closer, he dropped low and hopped from foot to foot, his two-note song getting slower and hoarser. Their mating was inevitable, but still they danced as if nothing could be taken for granted.

"Can we talk somewhere?" Charlotte asked huskily. What exactly she planned to say was unclear, but she suddenly needed to get away from other people. She wanted Ash to herself for a few minutes, just to be with her. She didn't want to think about what that could mean.

Ash got to her feet. "Sure, let's walk."

Her expression was hard to read. Charlotte thought she saw a glint of anger, followed by a tension in her lower jaw. She followed Ash along a freshly cleared track toward a stand of mahogany trees far enough from the camp that they could not be seen or heard. As usual, she found herself mesmerized by the way Ash walked. Hers was a sensual prowl that spoke of harnessed energy and finely honed control. She would be a good lover, Charlotte thought, watching the firm muscles of her butt working beneath the khaki fabric.

Her heart sank when she glimpsed a subtle change in her body language, a rigidity in the set of her shoulders. She was suddenly tense, as if she'd just thought of something that annoyed her. Charlotte was almost ready to insist that they just go back to the camp when Ash stopped abruptly in her tracks and turned to face her.

"Tell me exactly what he did," she said.

Charlotte stopped walking, too. "What?"

"Billy Bob," Ash prompted sharply. "What did he do?"

"Nothing." Was that what Ash was upset about? Had she assumed something had happened? Hastily, Charlotte explained, "He creeped me out, that's all. He…stares."

"You want me to say something to him?"

"That's not why I wanted to talk." The compulsion that had seemed so urgent and irresistible just moments ago was fast seeping away, and Charlotte felt self-conscious all of a sudden. She didn't know what to say. Her mind told her one thing and her body another. "I'm sorry," she said, forcing herself to get a grip. "I know you're busy. Let's go back."

"Not so fast." Ash searched her face. "What is it, Charlotte? You didn't bring me out here for no reason."

Charlotte felt like a sleepwalker who had stumbled into a dream world unlike any she'd ever known. Everything seemed foreign, every step precarious. Delaying the inevitable, she allowed her eyes to roam the surroundings. The rainforest floor was heavily carpeted in moss, and where shafts of light pierced the gloom, Charlotte could see spores swirling and dancing. Even the air was alive.

Words would be her undoing, she thought. She would open her mouth and spill out some nonsense that would enable her to back out before she did something she would regret. With words as a barrier she could avoid the risk of touch. She would also deny something in herself. Ignoring the cautionary voices rattling their warnings in her head, she reached out and cupped her palm to Ash's cheek. Her hand shook.

For several deafening heartbeats they just stood there like that, then Ash placed her hand over Charlotte's and took a step toward her. In the forest shadows, her eyes glowed darker, the pupils huge and black within a gilding of blue. In a single heavy-lidded blink everything changed. Desire blazed from their depths, matching the fierce longing that flared in Charlotte's belly.

She lifted her other hand to Ash's hair, carving a path through thick white-gold strands that caressed her fingers. Ash's jaw was rigid. Charlotte could feel the twitch of a muscle in her cheek. She moved in to her until their bodies were fully engaged, their thighs and bellies claiming a home against one another, their breasts rising and falling in aching collision.

In the hush of the forest floor, far below the canopy, their breathing sounded loud. Ash's hand found the small of Charlotte's back, drawing her closer. Between them a question hovered, unspoken, swiftly overtaken by a low moan like a breath trapped in a plea. The sound came from Ash, and Charlotte answered it with her mouth, kissing tentatively at first, then giving in to Ash's hungry reply.

Ash walked her back a few steps onto higher ground, where their bodies were better aligned. Bracing them against a tree, she planted one hand next to Charlotte's head. The other yanked her shirt and tee from her pants. Then it was skin. The mercy of touch. Ash's naked hand on her naked flesh. And Charlotte didn't know if she was sinking or drowning. She couldn't resist and she couldn't withdraw. There was no place for her to run from her own desperate yearnings. Where had they been all this time? How had this part of herself, so ruthlessly banished, crept back to demand more?

She was wet, and sucking short gasps of air between kisses. Ash was barely touching her yet, just cupping a breast, eyes closed, face lost in concentration. Her thumb grazed Charlotte's nipple, her tongue intruded deeper. A knee nudged Charlotte's thighs apart. Reeling with desire, Charlotte caught at Ash's shirt, clumsily tugging the buttons open.

It occurred to her that someone brandishing a butterfly net would probably stumble across them at any moment, but she couldn't summon the willpower to stop. Urgently, she moved her hips down on the knee between her thighs, grinding her wetness against Ash, driven by some primal imperative that banished reason.

Both Ash's hands were on her now, caressing and exploring and making Charlotte quiver and gasp and want more.

"Please." She sought one and drove it firmly down.

Ash groaned and her teeth settled into the sensitive hollow at the base of Charlotte's throat. "You're so beautiful." The fleshy part of her hand slowly circled over Charlotte's center.

Charlotte added some pressure, clamping her own hand over Ash's, demanding more. Perspiration gathered on her top lip. With disbelief she realized she was close to coming. It would take nothing to push her over the edge. "Please. I want you inside of me."

She began fumbling with the top button of her pants, desperate to feel Ash's fingers sliding into her wet waiting flesh.

"Baby." Ash shakily halted her. "We can't do this here."

"Don't say that." Charlotte's voice seemed too thick to shape into words, her mouth too swollen to pronounce them.

"I don't want to stop, either."

"Then don't." Charlotte caught hold of the buckle of Ash's pants, only to have her hand gently seized.

Ash caught it to her cheek before planting a tender kiss in the palm. "I want our first time to be special. Not rushed. Not hiding in the dark like this."

"I don't care." In fact, being fucked hard against a tree sounded pretty good. Charlotte could not believe she could think such a thing, let alone lobby for it. Where was her self-control?

"Well, I care." Ash's expression was as naked and honest as Charlotte had ever seen it, the emotion heart-stopping. "I've been wanting to make love to you since the moment I first saw you. But this isn't what I had in mind."

"Does it really matter? We're here and we want each other. Isn't that enough?" Her cheeks burned. Having dragged Ash out here and tried to seduce her, she was now being refused. That was the icing on a very embarrassing cake.

"Charlotte, listen. Normally, it would be enough for me. Normally I'd be fine with having a quickie, then doing breakfast with the frog hunters ten minutes later." Ash cradled her face, a hand on each side. With laconic humor, she continued, "Ever since the airport hangar—

and before that—I've thought about fucking you more or less anywhere that's viable. The Jeep. The back of the Huey. Our tent…"

Charlotte's heart jumped. This was news.

"But this just isn't the right place or time." Ash glanced over her shoulder at the sound of something stirring on the forest floor. A small dark bird with yellow wattles emerged from a pile of moldy leaves with a huge beetle in its beak.

"You're right. It's not." Charlotte let herself slump against Ash's chest, and she was drawn into a warm embrace. Lulled by the hushed thunder of Ash's heartbeat, and fighting tears, she said, "I never let this kind of thing happen."

Ash stroked her hair. "I can see that."

"I think I'm afraid." The confession came out in a rush. "I'm afraid I might never feel like this again. Like I could just lose myself and be… here. In the moment. All of me. Not taking myself away somewhere." She broke off, feeling like she was talking nonsense and Ash would think there was something wrong with her.

Ash planted one small kiss after the next, on her cheeks, her hair, her lips. She felt so close, closer than anyone was allowed to be. It was as if she were drawing Charlotte to her, tenderly courting her inner self, inviting her to stay and trust. Charlotte fell into the bright ocean of her eyes and found nothing withheld. She sensed Ash was offering her a gift. That she found this closeness just as fragile and unexpected as Charlotte did. Yet she was not turning away, and somehow, by accepting this fledgling bond, they were both reaching into the unknown.

"I know exactly what you mean about going away," Ash said. Her voice was rough, fractured by a yearning that matched Charlotte's own. "And I promise you something. We won't do that when we make love."

Chapter Thirteen

"There's something I want to show you." Ash swung Charlotte's day pack over her shoulder. Her piercing eyes sought Charlotte's. The promise in their depths made her stomach plummet. "Come on."

Exchanging a few words with her associates as they went, she led Charlotte casually away from the breakfast crowd along a freshly cut trail that wound its way southeast of the campsite. After almost an hour, they broke through the darkness of the forest and charted a path down toward a natural opening in the canopy where several huge trees had fallen.

When they reached a vantage point on the slope just above the area, they paused to look out on an astonishing netherworld so lush it seemed thrown across the land like a sprawling quilt of emerald velvet dotted with flowers. At this time of morning, and probably for much of the day, it was a cloud forest, enveloped in thin swirling mists. The air was thick and damp, pungent with the bitter green secretions of plants and the drifting vanilla pear scent of crushed agar wood and rare orchids. The few remaining old-growth trees grew thick and gnarled, guarding the magical slope like ancient sentries.

"It's perfect," Charlotte breathed as they descended into a world bathed in mist.

After days in the dim underworld beneath the canopy, fruitlessly seeking a match for her leaf samples among the fallen array beneath the various strangler trees she encountered, Charlotte felt heady with delight to be out in the open. The shrills and clicks of countless birds and insects created a hum very different from the muffled calm of the rainforest floor, and the elaborate biome that had sprung up around the fallen trees was unlike anything she had ever seen.

The cycle of natural regeneration in this untouched place made it a virtual laboratory for reforestation research, from the toiling insects to the seedlings, epiphytes, and vines to the mosses and ferns. Fog drip converted rotting wood and leaves rapidly into layers of peat, infusing nutrients into the new growth, and Charlotte could tell the cloud mist was not completely persistent. Sunlight also tended this secret garden, fostering even more diversity and speed of regrowth.

Imagining the seed bank that must be buried beneath the rotting trunk they were skirting, she said, "This is incredible. I could spend a lifetime collecting data here and barely scratch the surface."

She caught a smile from Ash and her pulse responded by swapping its customary tempo for fits and starts that made her feel light-headed. In an instant she was transported back to the previous morning and could feel Ash's skin melting her own every place there was touch. She met Ash's eyes and saw in them an acknowledgement that she, too, was remembering.

Charlotte reached out to make their connection physical, but her hand met rubbery resistance from something that felt like damp fabric. She took a step back and found herself gazing at a huge spider's web dotted with crystalline dewdrops. It was at least five feet wide and eight feet high, a complex construction of pale gold silk angled and elaborately braced against the surrounding plants. Charlotte had encountered a part of it far from the center. She touched the web again experimentally, surprised that it didn't cling to her fingers and that she hadn't torn it.

"Simon would lose his mind," she said. Their butterfly expert also had an obsessive interest in spiders and had declared his determination to locate several of New Guinea's most famous specimens while he was here.

"See those?" Ash pointed to a row of insect husks arranged in a remarkably orderly line across the web. "That's to stop birds flying into it by accident. The way the spider sees it, they're homewreckers. No point catching something you don't want to eat and it tears your place up as well."

"So the spider makes its own safety strips." Charlotte was fascinated.

Ash pointed out the owner of the resplendent spider-palace, a narrow-bodied arachnid with a golden thorax and long black legs that appeared to be decorated with feather tufts. "Meet *Nephila*. The golden orb-weaving spider."

Charlotte laughed. "I was expecting a tarantula, at least."

"Tarantulas don't build webs. They burrow." Ash tapped her booted toe against the moss-covered tree limb they were crossing. "These dead trunks probably have a healthy population. Watch out for anything really huge and black with hairy legs and a bad attitude."

Charlotte shuddered. "Great. Is this what you wanted to show me—the valley of the spiders?"

Ash grinned. "No, it's better than that. But while we're here, just so you know, the golden orb's web is almost as strong as Kevlar. If you're ever in the field and you get injured, you can use one as a bandage or a tourniquet to stop bleeding."

"Are you serious?"

"Absolutely. Some of the tribes even turn them into fishing nets."

"You know," Charlotte gave her a long look, intrigued by her unexpected interest in natural history. Maybe they had something in common other than mutual lust. "You're a veritable encyclopedia about this place, and between you and me, I find that very sexy."

Ash seemed briefly startled by the flirtatious comment, then her eyes flickered and she replied warmly, "In that case, you're going to be all over me very soon. Come here, woman."

She lifted Charlotte over another dead limb and led her along a narrow thoroughfare between a fallen tree trunk of huge girth and a thicket of Cyathia tree ferns with extraordinary frond length. New Guinea was a large island, and something Charlotte found remarkable about evolution on such land masses was that plant species often grew larger, whereas animals became dwarfed.

Here in the canopy fissure, the additional light had given permission for the flora to run riot. Fleshy epiphytes sprang like a forest of green antlers from the moss-covered tree trunks; shrubs and small trees had found gaps in which to put down roots. Creepers festooned anything growing vertically, and birds and small animals wandered through the steamy lushness of it all, gorging themselves on grubs and seeds, then lolling back, sated.

None of these creatures fled as Ash and Charlotte passed by; they watched with vague interest, then returned to their snacking and snoozing. All the while, as they moved deeper into the cloud forest,

Charlotte sensed they were being observed by countless creatures concealed from the human eye, tarantulas among them no doubt. She paused as a flock of delicate little gray birds descended from a treetop and darted all over the path she and Ash had just trampled, apparently on an insect safari. Standing still, she stared back up at the Fojas, feeling dwarfed by the primeval grandeur of this unearthly place.

"It's so timeless," she said. "These forests formed in the Pliocene period. We're probably the first people to set foot here in five million years."

"And we live on borrowed ground," Ash reflected, surprising Charlotte again with the depth of her observation.

She thought about that. It said a lot about her attitude that she was startled every time Ash made a thought-provoking comment. Embarrassed by her own intellectual snobbery, Charlotte reconsidered its foundations. She knew a lot about some things, in fact, she could be called an expert. But she knew next to nothing about a great deal more, and she was just finding that out.

She had never known anyone like Ash and probably never would again. In Charlotte's narrow social circles, Ash would be a novelty, the real thing among people who only played at risk-taking. And Ash wasn't just a woman with some interesting stories to tell, she was an interesting woman.

Charlotte wondered what Ash thought of her. Was this pull of theirs only sexual? Did Ash like her as a person at all? They hardly knew each other, yet Charlotte could already imagine them being a part of one another's lives. Already, she could not conceive of leaving New Guinea in a few weeks' time and never seeing Ash again.

The thought shook her, and as she tried to come to grips with what it meant, she became aware of a sound she hadn't discerned before, a faint rattling swish.

"Do you hear that?" she asked.

Ash heaved a mock sigh. "I was going to blindfold you and make it a big surprise. I should have known you'd have hearing like a bat." Her gaze grew bold and her tone caressing. "Feel like taking a shower with me?"

Charlotte's breath died in her throat. Undone, but trying not to show it, she said, "Oh, let me see. Am I ready to wash five days of filth off my body or would I rather continue to be a human petri dish?"

Her attempt at flippancy drew a lazy smile. "I guess that's a yes."

❖

Ash kept thinking this was a mistake. She'd stumbled onto the secluded waterfall two days after arriving in the Fojas, and she'd known then that she would bring Charlotte here. At the time, she hadn't expected the place to hold any significance other than botanical. But here they were. Alone in paradise. And for the first time in living memory, Ash had performance anxiety.

She let her gaze slowly wander as she unlaced her boots, automatically verifying their solitude. The waterfall cascaded about forty feet into a tranquil pool overhung by a magnolia tree with enormous waxy white flowers. That alone was worth the trek, but it was chump change compared to the orchids that rambled over the entire area in a carpet of sensuous blooms like nothing Ash had ever seen.

As she'd expected, Charlotte flipped out the moment she saw them, gasping about new species and how there were more orchids in New Guinea than anywhere else on earth. She even delayed stripping for her shower so she could swoon over a silvery white flower she described as "like a ravishing gossamer star. The *Taeniophyllum* genus, I would say."

When she was finally done crawling around on her hands and knees, the face she lifted to Ash was adorably pink and framed by a mass of black waves corkscrewed into curls by the damp mist. A profusion of tiny white petals clung to her hair and if it hadn't been for the beige cotton vest and pants, the hiking boots, and the portable microscope, she could have passed for a bride.

That wasn't a thought Ash entertained every day. Neither was the one that followed. She wanted to kiss Charlotte and make love to her for the rest of the day, then take her home to Madang.

She told herself to get serious. There wasn't a chance in hell that this woman would walk away from a plants-are-us megastore in the middle of nowhere to shack up for a couple of months of passion with someone she'd never clapped eyes on until three weeks ago. They didn't know each other, and Charlotte held down a prestigious job, doing what she loved, on the other side of the world.

A romance between them was the kind of impossible scenario that only happened in novels, and even the women who swore by that stuff would probably find it a bit far-fetched. Sure, fact could be stranger than fiction—Ash's life was an unappetizing example of that principle. But she was a realist. A well-brought-up, overqualified girl from a normal family back East was never going to allow herself more than a brief brush with adventure. She would never consider settling in the tropics with a mercenary soldier-cum-pilot, and why should she?

Ash sensed that Charlotte might fool herself that they could have more. That was how women like her gave themselves permission to do things that would normally make them uncomfortable. But, in the end, she would go home and get on with her life. In due course, she would meet another impressively credentialed career woman and Ash would be nothing more than a fond memory. Hot sex in the wilds of West Papua.

Normally, Ash would have no problem with that. She always hoped her sexual partners would one day find love and happiness if that's what they were looking for. But in Charlotte's case…not so much.

She followed the swooping path of a fruit dove as it landed in the magnolia tree above them. An uneasy thought took shape as she watched the graceful bird explore a flower. What if her feelings for Charlotte weren't just a reaction to the loss of Emma? What if she was falling in love? Stranger things had happened, admittedly not often.

Ash rifled through her memory trying to find another time when she might have been in love so she could compare the two. At nineteen she'd had a relationship for a year with a girl she really loved. Things hadn't worked out. Posy's folks were religious and gave her a hard time about being a lesbian. They made a series of false complaints to the cops about her, just so that she would have the hassle of door knocks late at night and trips downtown to answer absurd questions about crimes she couldn't have committed.

At nineteen there's only so much you can cope with. She and Posy just gave up in the end and the last Ash heard, she had married a guy from the church and had a house full of kids. No doubt her parents were still congratulating themselves on their intervention.

After Posy, she'd had a succession of girlfriends, all short-lived. A career in the military made it hard to have real relationships, even for straight singles. Ash got used to limiting her emotional involvement, and by the time her world crumbled and she moved to PNG she seldom thought any more about finding "the one." Every now and then, when she lay next to another stranger whose body she'd just known intimately but whose heart and soul were entirely closed to her, a dark mood claimed her and she would have to leave immediately.

At those times she was aware of an aching void inside and a sense of isolation so profound all she wanted to do was bury it any way she could. Alcohol. More sex. Sex with fewer limits. Nothing ever made any difference and lately, she'd been finding herself even less satisfied than usual. Having sex, when all she ever shared was her body, simply brought home what was absent. Tenderness. A lover who knew who she was, not just what she could do. A mate.

Ash could swear that a part of her soul was shriveling. Neglected. Untouched. Starved of its needs and finding no safe harbor in another's arms.

"Hurry up." Charlotte's feet stopped not far from hers.

They were bare. So were her legs. Naked, she presented herself, hands shyly folded, one cupping the other, chest rising and falling at the mercy of her shallow breaths, eyes wide with apprehension.

Ash was so enchanted she forgot to be suave. "I am *so* not worthy."

"Does that mean I should shower alone?" This was spoken with a kittenish purr that made Ash feel like a country bumpkin mysteriously chosen by the May Queen.

"Absolutely not."

She got to her feet, feasting on the inviting grace of Charlotte's form, the girlish rise of her belly, the apple-perfect breasts and blush pink nipples, the delicate hollows where her shoulders flared. Arousal engulfed her senses and infused her limbs with familiar tension. But she was surprised by an unusual sense of tranquility where normally she was driven by a single-minded focus. The change was interesting. It meant she could slow things down. Sometimes that was difficult to do when desire overtook her.

Intrigued, she let her gaze fall to the shadow of dark hair between Charlotte's legs. Her desire was just as urgent and irresistible as it ever had been for anyone, yet another, deeper emotion was at work. Ash could feel it stirring in that starved inner self. Hope.

"Let me." Charlotte unbuckled Ash's belt with deft purpose. Her fingers played teasingly across Ash's torso, making the blood run hot beneath her skin.

"Temptress," Ash said, relishing her rare foray into flirtatiousness; it was so at odds with the woman the world saw.

She let Charlotte continue the ritual of undressing her, enjoying the changes in her expression from playful seduction to beguiling delight to moments of faltering inquiry. When she started to lift Ash's tank, she froze.

Seeking to reassure her, Ash said, "It's okay. Nothing hurts anymore."

"What happened?" A slight breeze swept the soft dark curtain of her hair away from the fine bones of her face. She lifted pained eyes to Ash.

"This big one was shrapnel." Ash took Charlotte's slender hand in hers and traced her forefinger over the knotted scars, wanting her to know it was okay to touch them. "The three holes are from bullets. And these stripes are machete wounds."

"Machete?"

"It's a long story," She gave a deflective smile. "I'll tell you sometime over a civilized meal."

"You lived," Charlotte said softly.

Ash could not take her eyes off that full, pursed bow of a mouth. She was made for kissing. It needed to happen soon or that fortuitous sense of calm would evaporate and Ash would probably blow everything by grabbing her.

Holding herself in check, she asked the question that kept repeating in the back of her mind. "Charlotte, why me?"

Charlotte took a while to think about it, then answered, "Honestly? I don't know."

Ash shrugged. She didn't want to give the impression that the answer had mattered. She let it go, and because Charlotte seemed hesitant, she pulled her tank off for her and said, "You know this is killing me, don't you?"

Charlotte withdrew her hand and regarded her gravely. "You don't like it?" She sounded genuinely anxious.

"Quite the opposite. You're making me so horny I'll probably drown in that waterfall, thanks to the distraction level."

To her relief, Charlotte's uncertainty vanished and, after a long look at Ash's breasts, she shifted her attention to the briefs that stood between them and a real skinny-dip.

"I should tell you something," she confided as she edged a finger around the waistband. Pink flooded her cheeks.

Wondering what this babe in the woods could possibly need to confess to, Ash murmured, "Yes?"

"I'm not as experienced as you."

Ash smiled. Tracing a solitary finger from Charlotte's throat to the bony recess of her heart, she said truthfully, "I like that about you."

The two small dark eyebrows angled together like butterfly wings, joined in the center by a narrow crease. "I'm mentioning this because I don't want to disappoint you."

Her quaint formality made Ash think before answering. Normally she would have treated this conversation as play, but she sensed Charlotte wasn't teasing. She watched the shifting expressions on her face, the tiny giveaway signs of emotion. No, she wasn't pretending. Her anxiety stemmed from a lack of confidence. She was trying to be honest and open about something that must have been an issue before, with other lovers. And maybe she had some far-fetched ideas about what butches expected from their sexual partners. Over the years Ash had run into all the usual stereotypes in that department.

Hoping to cover as many bases as she could, she adopted a casual tone and said, "How about if I just tell you what I want. I think I'd find that quite a turn-on."

The chest beneath her fingertip rose and fell with a slow, deep breath and Charlotte's beautiful mouth relaxed. The pressure was off. "I'd like that."

Ash stepped toward her and curled a hand behind her neck, cupping the base of her skull. "See how easy it is." She brushed her lips back and forth over Charlotte's. "Any time you're not comfortable, just tell me."

She tilted Charlotte's head back a little more and pressed closer, taking in her creamy oriental scent. Delicious. Even in this humid zone. Even with some perspiration. She placed the tip of her tongue a fraction beneath Charlotte's upper lip and slowly sucked until she was invited inside.

Caressing gently with her tongue, she moved against Charlotte, letting her know she was wanted. Charlotte responded with a soft whimper of anticipation, her nipples peaking marble hard against Ash's chest. The response kicked Ash's heart into an up-tempo beat that pounded through her body. Blood rushed south and she let both her hands slide to Charlotte's butt, cupping the firm cheeks and lifting her just enough so they connected completely.

Charlotte ended their kiss by catching her breath. Dazed gray eyes stared into hers.

Ash said, "Let's wash. I need you."

Charlotte shuddered and the arms wrapped around Ash fell. Somehow they stumbled into the chill cascade, where they washed and licked and caressed each other, imprinting taste and smell. Ash could feel every pore contract as Charlotte's hands brushed over her. The delicacy of her touch was maddening. Her small hesitations and careful avoidance of breasts and groin made Ash ache for her relentlessly.

A stream of sunlight seeped through the leafy vault above, bleeding reflected color onto the water's surface, and Ash stared around at a paradise so vivid and sensuous it could have flowed from the palette of a master. The ceaseless drone of the jungle pounded in her ears, surging with the ebb and flow of blood in her veins. She caught Charlotte beneath the arms and lifted her onto one of the natural stepping stones leading down into the pool.

They returned to the spot beneath the magnolia tree where their clothes were piled. Ash unrolled the sleeping pad she'd strapped to her backpack that morning and positioned it on the spongiest patch of interlaced vines she could find. Then she spread her spare cotton sleeping bag liner over the top. It was clean. That, she'd made sure of.

Orchids clamored on all sides and Ash was drunk with their scent. She couldn't help but be struck by the blatant sexual allure of the plants. Petals splayed wide. Moist, softly parted pink lips hungering toward rigid little shafts.

"It's a bower," Charlotte breathed. She clasped her hands behind Ash's neck and allowed herself to be lowered onto the improvised bed.

They stared at one another.

Ash asked, "Are you sure?"

"Yes, very sure."

Charlotte's mouth was orchidlike. Ash wanted to feed her tongue over the fleshy folds. She closed her eyes and breathed in Charlotte's scent, an animal tang in a heady floral sea. Kneeling, bending down, she sealed their lips together, at first in tender pledge then in silky, searing demand. Charlotte tilted her head in yielding compliance, inviting Ash to linger in the dusky almond wetness of her mouth. Still, she thirsted for more, her blood pulsing furiously through her body.

Charlotte felt new and good, all hers. There was something remarkably innocent about her for a woman of thirty-some years. Ash touched her. Smooth strokes, down the long pure line of her throat and the supple curves beyond. Her breasts. Her sides. Her hips.

"You're beautiful," she murmured, dragging a nipple beneath the tip of one finger, back and forth, watching it extend and pull at the pale skin around it.

The soft sounds in Charlotte's throat urged more. Ash wanted to take her time, she wanted to tease and caress her along a well-plotted course toward perfect satisfaction. But her self-control was slipping. Holding back was torture. Her body was tight and swollen, bent on a course of its own. At this galloping rate, she would come first. Not what she was planning.

She slid a hand between Charlotte's thighs, grinding gently into her flesh. Charlotte opened eyes dark and heavy with languid promise. Wordlessly, she parted her legs. Ash pressed harder. Something in Charlotte's expression altered and she reached up and slid her hands over Ash's shoulders, insistently drawing her down until they were rocking and sighing together in the ancient cadence of lovers.

Ash was completely undone by the thrilling shock of Charlotte's body, opening to her, the slippery blush of flesh sealing around her fingers, the squeeze and pulse that matched her own. And she was startled when Charlotte's hand slipped down between their bodies to embark on her own exploration.

She didn't arrest the first tentative strokes as she would normally. Instead, catching a flash of apprehension in Charlotte's gaze, she guided her hand along the narrow ridge where her tension centered.

"Oh, baby. That's good," she groaned. "You'll make me come if you don't stop right now."

Charlotte's eyes glowed and she became intent about the firm gliding strokes. Resigning herself to the inevitable, Ash let go of her control and watched her lover's face flush with delight when she discovered how easy it was drive her straight off the edge. She was still convulsing when Charlotte whispered in awe, "Was that…?"

"Yes." Ash lifted her small hand away from the exquisitely sensitive postorgasmic parts, explaining hoarsely, "Afterward…I find it too much."

"Oops. I'm sorry. Normally no one lets me do that, so I'm…kind of inept."

Ash couldn't remember ever having a discussion like this during sex. But nothing else had gone exactly to script, either, so she expressed her opinion frankly. "Well, you've been sleeping with the wrong people."

She kissed Charlotte deeply and slowly, giving her own breathing time to settle. All the while she kept her fingers poised inside, awaiting a return of focus. When Charlotte arched her back in reminder, she said, "I should punish you for distracting me."

Charlotte draped one of her legs over Ash's hip and bucked a little against her hand. "Punish me some other time," she responded throatily.

"Be careful what you wish for." Ash eased her fingers slowly free of their slippery sheath until the tips barely teased inside.

Charlotte whimpered her name.

"Want something?" As she said it, she was back on track, that familiar hunger grinding inside. Heart pounding, she slid her left arm beneath Charlotte, gathering her close. Gazing down at her, she thrust inside.

"Yes!" Charlotte bore down on her. Avid concentration stilled her face.

Ash could feel the pressure building inside her, the rippling and gathering of muscles, and the stiffening of her body. She was almost there, losing herself. Panting. Moaning. Eyes closed. Head thrown back.

One of her outflung hands gripped an orchid. Slowly, inexorably, she crushed it as she began to spasm. And while she rocked and shuddered in release, a stain of amethyst juice trickled between her fingers. Eyes the same color frantically sought Ash's.

"Hold me," Charlotte begged, and burst into tears.

❖

Many hours later, lying in Ash's arms in their tent, Charlotte said, "I was thinking about that night."

Ash shifted a little to get more comfortable. They'd joined their inflatable pads and zipped their sleeping bags together. "What night?"

"Back home. At Tamsin's house. When you were in the bathroom listening."

"What about it?"

"You slept with *both* those women?"

Ash sighed. "Charlotte, I haven't lived like a nun. I'm sorry you ever had to know about it. Okay?"

Charlotte hesitated. "I just hate the thought."

"You have nothing to be jealous about, trust me. It was just sex. And when that's all it is, who cares whether it's with one person or ten?"

Charlotte felt queasy. Britt's excuses echoed in the corridors of her memory. *It's just sex. It didn't mean anything.*

"Is that what today was?" she asked. "Just sex?"

Ash rolled them both onto their sides so they faced each other. "How can you think that?" She placed a hand on Charlotte's belly. "What does your gut tell you?"

It was more, so much more. At least that was true for her. If Charlotte were honest with herself, she had to accept that there was no way she could measure what she'd experienced. It was completely new.

By any standard, Ash was an exceptional lover. Charlotte knew that much from having close friends who talked about sex. Most of them had much more interesting encounters than she ever did. But until now she'd thought some of their accounts exaggerated. Obviously sex was a highly subjective experience. Those recalling it through rose-tinted spectacles could be expected to claim transcendent physical and emotional pleasure. But even with Britt, Charlotte hadn't come close to such delusions.

Ash was another story, a tale her body insistently told even now, in the damp tenderness between her thighs and the honeyed heaviness of her limbs. The impression of Ash's kiss, her tantalizing scent, the pledge of their joined flesh, was written where there had only been blankness before. It could not be erased. Charlotte could not return to the way she was before Ash—numb, a stranger to the passionate self within. Everything had changed.

She only wished she could trust that the change was rooted in reality. She'd felt alive with Britt, too. She'd fallen in love and handed her common sense in at the door. Britt had been a player, too, but insisted their relationship had changed all that because they were in love. Charlotte had believed every lie she was told. She had happily fallen sucker to every self-serving promise. Incredibly, whenever her doubts began to harden, Britt would sense her withdrawal and yank an emotional rabbit out of a hat. She knew exactly what Charlotte needed to hear at those times and, like the successful trial lawyer she was, she delivered.

It had taken Charlotte far too long to realize the promises and declarations were nothing more than the currency it took to keep her in the relationship. They were words. Closing arguments. Britt never had any intention of following her promises up with actions. Charlotte would not be made a fool of a second time, with another woman who thought the way Britt did.

In the end, she'd understood that Britt felt entitled to have it all—the wife who meant something and the extracurricular sex that meant nothing. Thank goodness they'd been unlucky with the turkey baster. She'd been bitterly disappointed back then and she still wished she had a child, but she was thankful it hadn't happened with Britt. The Fates had done her a favor.

Inhaling the scent of Ash's skin, she nestled closer, comforted by the fading traces of her clean spicy fragrance. A strange melancholy had corroded her joy. Puzzled, she allowed herself to be cradled, parting her legs to scissor with Ash's.

"You haven't answered me." Ash paused. "Or maybe you have."

Charlotte said. "I don't know if I can."

She wanted to believe there was more to this than two lonely people unanchored in a world without consequences, each enjoying the other while she could. But she'd kept herself safe for the last five years by remembering the lessons of history, not repeating them.

Yes, she thought their lovemaking was far from mere physical union. And yes, she had feelings for Ash. That alone meant her judgment could not be trusted.

CHAPTER FOURTEEN

When she finally came face-to-face with the fig, Charlotte understood exactly what Eve must have gone through, seeing the apple and wondering if she could trust the snake enough to sample the forbidden fruit.

She had almost walked straight into it, busy cleaning her binoculars as she slowly moved along the route she'd been mapping out. The strangler fig, once an epiphyte but now a sprawling monster, blocked her path, corded thickly around a low-hanging branch of its host tree. And there, dangling right before her eyes, was one of its succulent wares, hanging far below the upper canopy where all the fruit and seeds usually grew.

Mesmerized, Charlotte could only stare. Her heart went wild in her chest and her legs wobbled. She was tempted beyond belief to seize the plump ruby-black fruit and cram it into her mouth, knowing she would be the very first woman on earth to taste it. She fought off the urge to run back to the camp immediately and share her triumph with Ash. The last thing she needed right now was another lapse into daydreams about the woman she could not shake loose from her mind.

Forcing herself to focus, she reached for the fruit, instinctively checking behind her. Yet again, she had the odd feeling she was being watched. She'd spoken with Ash about her constant sense that she was not alone. She suspected her imagination was running away with her because she felt like a burglar in a hallowed citadel, a spy in the secret bower where Mother Nature seduced Father Time. Not that she'd phrased it that way to Ash, who could not be expected to empathize with such flights of fancy.

Ash had pointed out the obvious—that the Nagle team was discreetly patrolling the area, making sure everyone was safe. It was likely someone had been nearby periodically, checking on her but trying not to disturb her. If she wanted, Ash would tell her team to make themselves known to her. Charlotte had declined, dismissively insisting that it was nothing and that she knew if she needed help all she had to do was use her cell phone, yell, or fire one of the flares everyone carried.

She turned slowly on the spot, surveying the musty, dripping forest floor around her. "Hello?" she called in a casual voice. "Who's there?"

When no one answered, she took a long look behind her, then swiftly plucked the fruit and sniffed it, the first test of toxicity. Any wild plant that smelled of peaches or bitter almonds was probably poisonous. The fig had a very different scent, somewhere between crushed grape skins and maple syrup.

Fascinated by her discovery, she traced the strangler branch ten feet down a steep slope to its source, a vast web of aerial roots that had encased its victim like a living coffin. This specimen was huge, perhaps a thousand years old. Overwhelmed, Charlotte sank down onto the ghostly root structure and leaned back against the damp, solid trunk. She had started to wonder if she would ever find the *Ficus* species she was looking for or if the reports of its presence in the area around Kwerba were mere speculation.

She stared up at the vast columns of wood rising some hundred feet above her. *Ficus lascellesae*. A tree named after her. She might have wished for a less macabre species; however, strangler figs had always fascinated her. She examined the small reddish black fruit, looking for signs of a fig wasp. That, too, would be a discovery, because each *Ficus* had its own dedicated species that only pollinated those particular trees.

Another amazing thing about tropical *Ficus* was that they bore fruit all year round. This made the trees important players in the battle to regenerate rainforests that had been destroyed, as they were incredibly hardy and could provide food for birds and animals when there was a seasonal shortfall.

In addition to the wasps, most *Ficus* had vertebrate dispersers, usually small mammals like fruit bats. That was something she could look forward to, Charlotte thought with wry amusement, picking up countless samples of droppings to identify which animals were involved. Perhaps she would recruit one of the naturalists to help her with that grubby task. Someone was bound to want a break from the physical slog of rigging up platforms at a hundred feet to study the mammals and birds that lived in the rainforest's upper canopy.

Or there was Simon, the entomologist. He could only hunt his giant birdwing butterflies for about an hour each day because there was not enough sunlight the rest of the time. He was always hovering, looking for someone he could latch on to.

She let her hand glide over a cool smooth ridge of wood. In rainforests the biggest trees tended to grow straight up, not branching until they'd reached the canopy and long hours of sunlight. Below canopy level, trees didn't need protection against water loss or plummeting temperatures and the bark was so similar in many species that they could not be told apart, except by their flowers. The near-naked trunks and roots were satiny to the touch and ghostly silver white, making the forest seem somehow enchanted with its deep shadows and monochrome vegetation.

The crisp snap of a twig made Charlotte freeze and lift her head. All she could see was the massive buttressed roots of the towering trees and the dense latticework of lianas and epiphytes entangling the lower canopy. She suspected the sound had been made by one of the remarkable golden-mantled tree kangaroos that followed expedition members around like dogs. It was truly astonishing to encounter animals that had no fear of humans. They had never been hunted or harmed, and innocently approached the visitors to their world, curious and willing to be touched. Even the birds were gregarious and inquisitive. The knowledge that humans were dangerous had never been acquired. Every creature they'd encountered here trusted that no one was going to harm them.

Yesterday, in front of her tent, a tree kangaroo had sat in her lap and offered her some of the berries it was eating. Until that moment it had never occurred to Charlotte that a caring accord between humans and animals in the wild was not only possible but could be a natural state of affairs. The birds and animals in these enchanted mountains knew nothing of the reign of terror humans had inflicted on every living creature sharing the planet. Their behavior was as close as possible to nature's intent, and fear was not genetically encoded. The Fojas were a living illustration of the global paradise humans had lost.

Ever since that moment of realization Charlotte had swung

between awe and desperate sadness, knowing what might have been and hating that, no matter how good their intentions, the expedition was a threat to the serenity this region had known since the beginning of time. She knew she was not the only one who had this on her mind. After their first day of frenzied field work and startling discoveries, conversation around the mess area had been surprisingly sparse, the atmosphere one of quiet reflection.

The initial jittery elation they'd felt from the moment they tumbled out of Ash's helicopter had given way to a sober realization people slowly began to articulate. By the end of the evening they'd all agreed that the last thing they wanted was for their work here to open the floodgates to numerous research teams, tourists, business, and the whole unstoppable cycle.

A couple of the moodier team members had even suggested they return to Kwerba and devote their lives to circulating stories of a giant man-eating spider and a species of anaconda so huge they disguised themselves as tree trunks. They'd even come up with a name for the fearsome predator, *Eunectes rex homicides.* The group discussed the idea quite seriously for several minutes before concluding that such speculation would only be an invitation to poachers and Hollywood movie producers.

Charlotte looked around again; then, satisfied that she was completely alone, she opened the fig and probed the pulpy contents with the tip of her tongue. If it was poison, there would be a reaction. She waited for the telltale numbness, burning sensation, or bitter taste. The tiny sample was a little sour, but no worse than the subtropical tamarillo fruit. Remarkably, it bore a hint of the muskiness found in the best fig cultivars.

Thinking, *This is a historic moment* and *Perhaps this is what the very first figs tasted like to Neolithic woman*, Charlotte sank her teeth in. She hadn't even chewed the first momentous mouthful when another fruit landed in her lap. She started in fright and choked on her sample as a bizarre creature, neither man nor beast, stepped out from behind a mahogany tree.

Charlotte had taken courses in evolutionary biology and sedimentary petrology at college, contemplating a career in paleoanthropology if her first love didn't pan out. Nothing could have prepared her for what she saw. The individual appeared to be a hirsute male hominid who possessed primitive skills—he had woven a grass covering for his genitalia. His entire body was smeared with dark clay as though in an attempt to mimic the appearance of a West Papua tribesman; however, the skin tone was Caucasian. Charlotte's first thought was *Bigfoot!* but there was one serious problem.

The creature had a head that could only be described as a nightmare mutation. Covered in a mop of reddish hair that suggested Neanderthal origins, it was peculiarly elongated, the facial characteristics reminiscent of a marsupial. This tragedy of genetics had adorned itself with a large collar of leaves and feathers, perhaps another sad bid to be seen as belonging to a local tribe.

Despite her apprehension, Charlotte felt sorry for him. She and the kangaroo man regarded each other for several seconds, then Charlotte had a brainwave and took out a small flashlight she could offer in exchange for the fruit gift he'd thrown. She wondered if the individual had any language. And what if he had a family? Imagine how famous the expedition would be. The Flores Island "hobbit" would be chopped liver compared to a find like this.

Charlotte tried some sign language, cupping her hands to her heart and lowering her gaze in case the creature saw eye contact as a challenge. Very slowly, she looked up again and pointed toward herself, saying gently, "Charlotte."

The creature did the same thing and said in a thick Aussie accent, "Bruce the Roo at your service."

Charlotte knew her mouth had fallen open, but she was so shocked she could only stare.

Eventually the kangaroo man said, "Dr. Lascelles, right?"

"That's right."

"A pleasure and a privilege. I read your paper on the healing properties of the Peruvian *Eustephia*. Bloody fascinating, although I take issue with your argument about the ethics of hiring local *curanderos*. It's still biopiracy, doesn't matter how you want to dress it up."

Charlotte was lost for words. What did one say to a man in a fake marsupial head, wearing a grass loin-pouch and trying to debate ethnobotany in the middle of a lost world that was supposed to be inaccessible by foot? And he looked like he lived here. How was that possible?

"Why the fake kangaroo head?" she asked, for lack of a more erudite response.

"The kangaroo has a symbolic meaning in shamanism," he said. "Because of its jumping ability it helps us overcome fears and inhibitions that stop us doing what we really want."

"Similar to alcohol?" she observed dryly.

"Sarcasm does not become you. There's also a New Guinean myth," he continued intrepidly. "A female roo saw the very first human couple here in the Garden of Eden after they'd just finished doing the wild thing and it ate the leaves they'd been lying on. It got pregnant from eating sperm and gave birth to a human boy called Sisinjori."

"So this is in honor of the myth?" Charlotte concluded.

"Yes, and I don't want anyone to see my face."

"Why not?" Charlotte imagined a disfiguring accident.

"Because there's a price on my head."

Wonderful. She was out here with a felon. Charlotte contemplated screaming but her companion shook his snout at her.

"Don't scream, Doctor, or I'll have to shoot." He raised a weapon.

"That's a tranquilizer gun," Charlotte said disdainfully, not sure whether to run or try to talk her way out of whatever mess she was in. Was this a kidnapping? Had there been a reason for all the security after all? And where were the Nagle guards now that she really needed one?

"Imagine what could happen while you're out cold as a mackerel. Maybe your friend Billy Bob will wake up and find you before the cavalry shows up."

"Billy Bob?"

He gestured toward a shape lying inert in the darkness behind him. "Your minder."

"Oh, my God. Is he dead?"

"He can be." Calmly, he offered her the weapon.

"Are you insane?" She didn't mean for the question to be taken literally but he appeared to consider a reply necessary.

"Sanity is relative. Your president invaded a country so that his friends could make money from a war. Is that sane?"

"Immorality and insanity are not the same thing."

"What do you call a sane man who chooses villainy instead of honor?"

"A criminal," Charlotte replied.

"My point exactly." He walked over to Billy Bob and nudged

him with a toe, coaxing, "Wakey, wakey." When there was no sign of movement, he cajoled, "He wouldn't feel a thing."

"No!" Charlotte spluttered. "What on earth would make you think I could do such a thing?"

"You're afraid of him, aren't you?" When she hesitated he said, "My animal instincts are seldom wrong."

Charlotte was not entirely surprised by that assertion. "I don't go around killing people, even ones I don't like. What about you, Mr. Roo? You said there's a price on your head. Are you a criminal?"

"It depends who you talk to." He took Billy Bob by the ankles and dragged him to an intensely shadowed spot, then kicked a layer of leaf mold over him. "I am a thorn in the side of corrupt authority, an archenemy of the Indonesian death merchants, defender of the forests…"

"You're an environmental activist?" she interpreted.

"I prefer Knight of the Order of Gaia."

He *was* crazy, she thought. "What do you want with me?"

"Just a small favor."

Charlotte had a bad feeling about this. "Let's get to the specifics. I have a *Ficus* to document."

"You're connected with Belton Pharmaceuticals, aren't you?"

"Yes, my employer is conducting one of their key research projects."

"What would you say if I told you I know where there is a compound every pharmaceutical company in the world would kill for?"

"I'd say what's in it for you?"

He waved an arm around. "This. I want a guarantee that this will never be touched. No loggers. No mining companies. Soldiers stationed at every point of access to keep the murdering, lying, thieving bastards out of here."

"I have no control over what happens here politically."

"True," he conceded. "But you work for the people who could make it happen. And that's why I'm talking to you."

"Well, I don't think I can be of any help. I'm not a lobbyist. Once I've completed my study, I will be making various recommendations, but it's not as if I can start demanding the kinds of things you are suggesting. I'm a researcher, not—"

"Let me show you something," he interrupted. "I think you're in for a shock."

He offered his muddied arm and Charlotte took it reluctantly and allowed herself to be escorted away from the approved research perimeter, in the wrong direction from the camp, where she would never be located. She could hear Ash already.

"I'm not so sure about this," she said, staring up into a pair of glassy, unblinking brown eyes. She wished he'd take off the mask.

"Ever done any rappelling?" he asked.

"Yes. My family went hiking and caving a lot when I was a kid."

"No worries, then," he said cheerfully. "It's only eighty feet down."

❖

Ash called Charlotte's cell phone yet again, ignoring her own directives to the team about not wasting battery power and confining calls to real emergencies. When Charlotte still didn't pick up, she sent a text message.

"Hey, beautiful. Where are you?"

She continued to search the pegged-out area Charlotte was supposed to be working within. It was too soon to sound the alarm or involve anyone else. At the best of times most of the scientists were vague about boundaries and prone to plunging headlong into the forest if they thought they heard one of their endangered species. No one went looking for them and reported them missing after two hours. Ash would be inviting speculation if she treated Charlotte any differently.

After what had passed between them, she found it very disturbing that Charlotte hadn't returned to the camp at any point during the day. Ash had said she would be around. She had to make up some supply lists for the helicopter drop tomorrow so she could call in the order to Klaus. They would be changing places, too, with Ash flying the Huey back to Kwerba. Klaus was bringing in the female contractor who was Ash's ticket out of here.

Only, she now felt uneasy about leaving. She didn't understand what was going on with Charlotte. Ever since they'd made love she'd been acting strangely, keeping her distance. Ash thought maybe she was overwhelmed and needed some time to come to terms with the change in their dynamic. Things had happened pretty fast and Ash sensed Charlotte was somewhat disoriented.

Perhaps she felt the need to scuttle back inside her scientist shell for a while. Ash was trying to respect that, so she gave her space and hadn't spent all day following her around, waiting for some affection. She trusted Charlotte would return to her, happy and together, when she was ready.

Stifling her disappointment, Ash peered into the sullen gloom where she'd expected to see her new lover doing something with a leaf. Twilight was fast fading and the forest seemed more sinister than ever. The trees rose with ghostly menace, their upper limbs knitted together in a murky wickerwork ceiling high above.

Maybe Charlotte had been suckered into helping one of the other scientists who needed an extra pair of hands. It wouldn't be the first time. She was always generous about that compared with some of her colleagues. Lately Ash had noticed her and Simon Flight working together on and off. Maybe he'd taken her to the upper canopy for a change of scene. Charlotte had mentioned she wanted some time up there in the sunlight and he'd offered his company.

Ash decided she was being overly possessive. She didn't have a whole lot of practice at ongoing situations with a woman. The most she'd managed in many years was an occasional repeat encounter with a one-nighter she genuinely liked. There were no regular girlfriends, and now that she thought about it, she realized how much easier that had made her life. Who needed the complication? Her first lovemaking with Charlotte was not twenty-four hours old, yet here she was, torturing herself like a teenager waiting by the phone.

There was no reason on earth why Charlotte should suddenly start reporting in to her because they'd had sex. Normally, Ash never got an ownership complex about any woman. But part of her reveled in this new possessiveness because it proved the existence of emotions she thought had been extinguished in her. At the same time she was aware of being far outside of her comfort zone, in unfamiliar territory, trying to find her bearings in a new landscape.

She was certain Charlotte was equally unstuck, and she could see a certain irony in their situation. Charlotte, she suspected, had never had really great sex, physically speaking. And Ash had never had great sex, emotionally. Their lovemaking had been a revelation for her because she felt whole and complete through every moment of it. For once, she'd had sex with her feelings involved and it felt wonderful. She and Charlotte had made love for hours after their first union, and it only got better. She could hardly wait for the next time and she had thought, when they left the orchid garden, that Charlotte felt exactly the same way.

But now she wasn't so sure. One thing was pretty clear: Charlotte was discovering for the very first time the passionate, sexual woman she could be with the right lover. Maybe that had unsettled her. It had to be a shock to find out that your sexual self had barely functioned in previous relationships.

Ash was amazed every time a woman confessed how little pleasure she'd had with other lovers. How she faked it. How she had sex as a way of getting affection. What kind of deadbeats did those women sleep with? It wasn't rocket science to find out what your partner wanted and give it to her. Her own motto was if in doubt, ask. Then do.

With Charlotte, she had quickly realized there was no point asking. When a woman's only yardstick was dull sex with well-meaning partners, she wasn't in a position to state categorically what worked for her. How could she know? Ash had sensed something else, too.

Someone had destroyed Charlotte's sexual confidence.

It didn't happen in a vacuum. An intelligent, sensitive woman with normal appetites did not just decide she was a failure as a sexual being. Someone made her feel that way. Probably the same person whose physical violence was encoded in Charlotte's reflexes. There were places she could not be touched without warning. Ash had carefully charted them for herself and when she read the completed map she knew exactly what she was looking at. Her own mother's had been almost identical.

Whoever had used Charlotte for a punching bag had also beaten her up emotionally, and Ash knew all too well that in many ways, that was worse. A physical beating left scars but everything could return to working order. Emotional trauma was different. It continued to exact a toll because the damage could not be undone. Those who suffered it lived with wounds that kept opening. The ones who broke out of the cycle usually avoided making themselves vulnerable to more injury. As she had herself.

Ash wasn't sure if Charlotte knew how much her past was a factor in her present. But it was obvious in the ways she protected herself. The layers of learning. The "rules" about this and that. The harsh judgments passed on weaknesses, especially her own.

Charlotte had wondered out loud what they had in common. Ash thought, *We're both survivors.* She had the distinct feeling that she understood some aspects of Charlotte better than Charlotte understood them herself.

But perhaps that was arrogant. Charlotte didn't see herself as a victim. People who grew up in bad homes, with violence and alcohol, were victims. But those who chose a bad partner were accomplices in their own misfortune. Charlotte blamed herself, and while she did she would always live in relation to her past.

Ash wondered if she wanted to sign up for that in a partner. She had problems of her own, not least her constantly pressing grief.

Maybe taking the break away from the camp was a good idea. She needed to think things through without the distraction of Charlotte's presence.

With a final despondent glance around the area, she shouldered her backpack and set off for the camp. Charlotte was probably waiting there. Ash walked faster. She wouldn't be able to rest until she held her again.

CHAPTER FIFTEEN

Charlotte's eyes had already made all the adjustments they were capable of and her night vision was still virtually zero. Skeletal forms shadow danced before her, forest wraiths in claim of their domain. She clung tightly to Bruce's rough, sinewy arm.

"Maybe we should stay where we are and find the camp in the morning," she suggested when they fell over a twisted root.

"It's not far," he said.

Charlotte stared dubiously into the pitch dark. She wasn't sure which idea was more insane—trusting her new best friend to lead her back toward the lake bed through a rainforest with no visibility, or spending the night camped out in the open with him, knowing he would probably leave her alone in the bewildering forest to find her way back the next morning.

"I have a GSM phone and a flare," she reminded him.

"If we get lost or fall into the wrong hands, I'll use the flare for self-immolation," Bruce replied with the confidence of a man who had departed far from societal norms.

Charlotte was about to make a snippy reply when he caught hold of her shoulders and made a shushing sound. Slowly he turned her ninety degrees to her left. Charlotte squinted and could just make out a zone where the darkness seemed less intense.

"Is that moonlight?" she whispered hopefully.

"Walk straight ahead for a hundred paces and you will be near your tent." He released her.

"Oh, my God. How did you do that?" She could see pale blobs, tents illuminated with low-lit lanterns.

Bruce said, "Humans have a homing instinct. We just don't use it."

"Like the sixth sense," Charlotte noted.

"I have that, too," he said.

"You're a spooky guy, Bruce."

He gave a low chuckle. "I can live with that. So…do we have a deal?"

"I wish you'd let me tell Ash."

"Like I said, she works for scum. I don't trust that mongrel."

"What if I just come right out and ask her. I mean, she'd know if this Tubby individual has a contract out on you, wouldn't she?"

"Probably."

"Then I'll be discreet. I'll just ask her in passing. We're… friends."

"Is that what they're calling it these days?"

Charlotte rolled her eyes. "I hope you weren't spying on us."

"I stopped looking when you stripped off and started groping each other under that waterfall."

"Oh, God," Charlotte muttered, hoping he was telling the truth about ceasing his voyeurism before they made love.

"It's the truth," he said, adding mind-reading to his list of paranormal accomplishments. "I'm not a perv."

No, you just wear a kangaroo head, call a rainforest home, and have made the discovery of the millennium. "How will I find you again?" she asked.

When she didn't get an answer, she groped around in her immediate radius and found her companion gone.

"Bruce?" she called into the night.

"No worries." His voice drifted back. "I'll find *you*."

Fixing her gaze on the tents, Charlotte hurried through the forest, breathing hard, flooded with relief and guilt. Some time earlier, she'd heard her name being called and had seen the frog hunters wasting precious flashlight beams on her. But Bruce had insisted on taking her all the way back to the campsite himself instead of making contact with them. He seemed to think people were out to get him. Against her better judgment and only because of what he'd shown her, she'd indulged his paranoia and hoped for the best.

She also thought it would be better if she located Ash before Ash found her wandering around like a lost soul. It was only two hours after the usual evening mealtime. She could argue that she'd fallen asleep when she only meant to take a short nap.

She felt uncomfortable not telling the truth, but Bruce had sworn her to secrecy and for the moment Charlotte had decided to respect his wishes. She needed some time to consider what she'd just seen. She was still reeling from it, her mind refusing to accept the evidence of her eyes. If she knew Ash better, she would tell her, if for no other reason than to be reassured of her own sanity. Having another person see what she'd just seen would confirm that it hadn't been a dream and that she wasn't crazy.

The cave Bruce had dropped her into was only accessible via the chimney they'd used or through a tiny entrance on a jungle-clad slope with a clear drop below. Its inhabitants climbed a web of lianas to access their front door. Charlotte and Bruce had no hope of doing the same. They were far too big.

No one will ever believe you.

Charlotte tried to picture herself addressing a Sealy-Weiss meeting. "The Foja cave dwellers are of small stature, rather similar in size to the so-called hobbit of Flores. It would appear that they represent a living family of *Homo floresiensis* and not a group of aberrant or pathological individuals. Their facial features are primitive, and it may be possible that they are descended from *Homo erectus*, the species known to have populated the region some 800,000 years ago.

"These hominids have language, tool-making skills, and fire. But of most interest to the Institute is their apparent longevity coupled with unusual youthfulness. Further research is necessary, but one of the individuals in the group claims to be the same age as a mature mahogany tree situated close to the cave. I estimate this tree to be two hundred years old. The Foja hobbits attribute their long lives to the extract of an orchid they cultivate, a species previously unknown."

She would need an arsenal of hard evidence to support these claims, preferably one of the individuals and, of course, specimens of the orchid. How she was going to accomplish this in secrecy was a mystery to Charlotte. But she could see why Bruce insisted she tell no one. Living prehistoric humans was one thing. But an orchid that could turn out to be the elixir of life—the ramifications were staggering. If Charlotte could take back proof, she would be the most famous botanist alive. She could write her own job description. Belton Pharmaceuticals would put a statue of her in their lobby.

Meantime, she had to keep her mouth shut.

As she headed for the tent, she repeated what she was going to say to Ash. She would be casual. Give her a moment to be annoyed, then apologize.

A hand clamped her shoulder and Charlotte jumped with fright.

"Where the hell have you been?" Ash demanded. "I've been out of my mind."

"I fell asleep," Charlotte said. "Then I got kind of lost."

"Lost?" The fingers in her shoulders dug in. "And you didn't phone me?"

Before Charlotte could summon an answer, Ash made an entirely different demand, crushing her in a fierce embrace and claiming her mouth without ceremony. For several long seconds she kissed Charlotte hard and deeply, then she all but dragged her off her feet, propelling her into their tent.

"Don't ever do that to me again," she warned as the tent flap dropped behind them.

Charlotte tried to move away from her, but there was nowhere to go in the cramped confines. Ash caught hold of her once more, pinning her hands together behind her back so Charlotte couldn't jerk away. Her mouth found Charlotte's throat and, as she bit down, she tore her shirt and bra away with one hand while the other maintained its grip on her sandwiched wrists.

"Ash, don't," Charlotte cried as she felt her belt being undone and her zipper tugged down.

The reply was swift and shocking. Ash pushed her onto their makeshift bed and dragged her pants off. Her weight pinned Charlotte as she quickly shed her own clothes. Then, when they were both naked, she jammed a knee between Charlotte's legs.

"It's not that easy," she bit out. "Do you think I'm one of those tame house pets you can let into your bed once in a while? And when you're bored I'll wait in a corner?"

Her fury made Charlotte shiver. Fear tangled with excitement, knotting in her belly until she was helplessly aroused, crazily aware of the welling at her core. Already her body was molding itself to Ash's, hungrily reclaiming what it knew. Ash's mouth returned to hers, hard and relentless, forcing her lips apart, making her accept the onslaught of tongue and teeth. At the same time, her hands were seizing possession.

She opened Charlotte, compelling her way inside with short sharp thrusts.

When Charlotte pushed at her chest, the kisses ceased and damp, hot breath rushed across her cheek. Ash spoke into her ear.

"Don't fight me."

She gave no quarter. Every small flutter of resistance was met with unbending authority until Charlotte stopped struggling and lay still, panting and shaking, her body no longer in concert with her mind.

She dragged a shaky hand past one of Ash's rigid shoulders to stroke the fine hair clinging damply to the base of her neck. With her other hand, she traced several fingertips delicately over her lover's face, trying to read what the darkness concealed. The piercing eyes and defined cheekbones. The straight deliberate nose and sensual mouth. Her fingertips remembered every crease and shadow. Her heart remembered the glinting challenge and tender intensity.

When she found moisture where tears would linger, remorse formed a lump in her throat. Had Ash been crying?

"I'm sorry—"

"No, I am," Ash rasped. "Forgive me."

Charlotte could feel the beginnings of her withdrawal and begged, "Don't." She lifted her hips and drew Ash insistently down. "I can't bear if you leave me now."

She slid a hand down the taut straining muscles of Ash's back and moved with her as their bodies fused in passionate accord. Ash's strokes slowed to a languorous rhythm that made her shudder with yearning. A flood of liquid bathed the fingers inside her, bidding them deeper.

"Kiss me," she whispered, almost sobbing with the sudden force of her emotions. She couldn't think. All she could do was crave. And be.

Trembling, she offered her lips, then her breasts, cupping them for Ash's possession. The torture of wet heat and gentle teeth compressing her nipples one at a time only increased the pounding pressure at her core. Moaning, Charlotte arched her back, needing more. Harder and faster. She was sweating, wracked with desire, her nerve endings telegraphing every miniscule sensation to the crushing tension at her core.

"Oh, baby." Ash was shivering, and Charlotte could feel a change in her body.

Through the haze of her own cresting response, she realized Ash was on the brink, too, and she slid a questing hand down between their bodies.

"No," Ash choked out. "Wait."

She moved back a little and nudged Charlotte's legs further apart. Leaning over her, she said, "You smell so good, I just have to have it all."

Charlotte could scarcely stifle the cry torn from her as Ash's mouth added unbearable sensation where she needed it most. She could feel herself falling. Her stomach plummeting. She grabbed for something to anchor herself, curling her fingers into Ash's hair.

"Ash," she gasped, and a strength-sapping flume of pleasure spiraled from her womb to her clit, where it broke free in shattering convulsions.

For a long while, they clung to one another. Charlotte felt Ash come hard against her at some point and realized she'd tended to herself. She made an attempt at apology for this, but Ash silenced her with kisses so exquisitely sweet, Charlotte understood she'd done nothing wrong.

"I would never hurt you." The broken whisper pierced her heart.

She sensed Ash had more to say, and wanted to tell her there was no need. Explanations didn't matter. But she was drifting. A deep contentment stilled her mind and soothed her body. For the first time in her life, she felt known by her lover.

❖

The cloud forest called to Charlotte, awakening her from a deep slumber. She rose with painstaking care, listening for any change in Ash's breathing that could herald her surfacing. Watching her face, naked in sleep, she almost stayed. But she knew if she did, she would never be able to clear her mind enough to unearth the truth of her emotions. In the light of day, she doubted all she'd felt the night before and she was afraid of the choices she might make, the bridges she might burn, if she pushed Ash away again.

Anxious not to cause pain, she scribbled a quick note telling Ash she was taking a long walk and wanted them to talk when she returned. Tucking it in the top of Ash's backpack, she stole one last long look at the woman who changed the way her heart beat, then picked up the clothing she needed and crept from the tent.

She fled quickly into the forest and as soon as she knew she'd escaped detection, she paused to change quickly into her work clothes and boots. Her time was limited. She had to get there and back well before the clouds burned off in the middle of the day and the Nagle helicopter arrived.

The route to the waterfall was etched into memory, and she had also mapped it out with subtle markers as she and Ash made their way back to the camp two days earlier. It took a little under two hours for her to find the ridge again, and she stood there for a while, calming her breathing and allowing time to slow down. She hadn't understood until right now why she needed to be here at this moment in her life, poised on the edge of pure beauty in a place unchanged for millions of years.

The lost world found here, secreted in the heart of Mother Nature, was a painting of her own interior. Its truth was her truth, and resonated inescapably. Here at this timeless ontic threshold, one reality became another. Earth touched sky. Primal displaced urban. The lowlands were press-ganged into mountains. Heat rose and descended as mist. Life ended and began in an unstoppable, eternal cycle of which she was a part. She, too, trod a line between one universe and another. Innocence and knowledge. Past and future. Solitude and union.

Sandwiched between heaven and earth, the cloud forest seemed trapped, a surreal layer at the intersection of the planet and its atmosphere. Light drained through the mist, painting the verdant undergrowth every shade of wet luminous green. The yearning trees stretched toward the sun. Each tiny organism seized its moment, finding its equilibrium and embracing its part in the whole.

Like a witness to her own dreaming, Charlotte descended into the mist, drinking in the smell of a world destined to be lost almost before it was found, the pungent ooze of fallen layers rotting down to peat, the perfumes of species doomed to extinction. Was that to be her lot, too? Would she uproot love before it had time to bloom?

She sank down onto the mossy floor beneath the magnolia tree and felt the spray of the waterfall on her face. She could almost hear the forest breathing, feel the movement of the earth—the restless shift of continents, the rise and fall of the oceans. Curling against the roots of the tree, she let herself cry.

They were old tears, for the woman she had been and the one she had become, tears she wanted to leave in a place where they could find rebirth in beauty. There was no going back. She could not change the past. But she could change the future. And suddenly, intoxicatingly, she understood how.

For a long time, she lay there thinking about the woman who had made her want that changed future more than anything. Superficially they had little in common, but there was a deeper understanding at work between them, a mysterious tie neither could escape. Charlotte had felt it all along, and fought it. Last night, fighting Ash physically, then surrendering, had been a revelation.

The symbolism stole Charlotte's breath away. That struggle of her will against Ash's echoed so closely the struggle within, between heart and mind. She needed to let Ash come close, yet at the same time she denied that need and pushed her away. In doing so, she was punishing the self that made her vulnerable. She was denying her own nature.

She stared through her tears at the orchids spilling around her and thought about the larger battle for control of nature, the one waged by machines and men. And she knew something else. She would do what Bruce had asked of her. It would be a crime not to.

Charlotte sighed, recognizing how easy it would have been for her to contact Ash that afternoon. Instead she'd decided to treat her like any other member of their party and rush off with Bruce, leaving Ash to wonder where she was. Her behavior was a denial of everything that connected them and of the truth discovered right here in this spot—that she was in love with Ash.

She had, Charlotte reflected, been in denial about one thing or another the whole time they'd known each other. In acknowledging that, she finally understood why she had believed Ash was a man. The self-deceit was necessary. Her unconscious mind had tricked her conscious. Her soul had put her in blinders so she would not be afraid.

A sweet contentment enfolded her as she revisited the question Ash asked her when they first made love. *Why me?* Here, in the very place it was asked, resting in the bosom of Mother Nature, lulled by the heartbeat of life, she could finally answer.

My soul chose you.

Chapter Sixteen

"The weather's closing in," Klaus remarked from the pilot's seat as they climbed away from the lake bed. "Good thing we made the swap today."

Ash nodded. The lump in her throat was so big she couldn't speak.

"By tomorrow, it's going to be a mess down there," he continued. "Could be zero visibility for weeks. Lucky you got out now, my friend."

Ash stared at the monsoon clouds rolling in from the northwest. Klaus was right. Once the weather set in, supply drops would be a crapshoot. Visual flight rules applied all over New Guinea. If you couldn't see through cloud, you didn't fly into it. The expedition would just have to cope without extras for as long as it took to get a clear day.

Fuck it. What did she care? She was never going back anyway. After this, she intended to spend a few days hunting around Kwerba for Bruce the Roo, just so she could tell Tubby she'd tried, then she was going back to Pom to sell her apartment and make arrangements to put a manager on her coffee plantation. She would spend some time in Madang, securing her belongings, then catch a plane, and flip a coin to choose her destination. Maybe she would just take the latest offer from Aegis and head for Iraq. The whole place was going up in smoke. Civil war was a profitable time to be a soldier of fortune.

Her thoughts drifted to Charlotte and she found herself ground down by sheer misery. To awaken and find her gone had made her crazy. She'd scoured the immediate vicinity of the camp, frantic to find her before the Huey arrived. There was no way Klaus could put down on the lake bed for any longer than it took to offload his cargo, namely Renee Gunderson, the woman who would be taking Ash's place in Charlotte's tent from now on.

She had called Charlotte's cell phone repeatedly only to endure the sound of her lover's smoky lilt inviting her to leave voice mail. She didn't. Charlotte had made it pretty plain that she didn't want to hear from her. No explanation. No kiss good-bye. She'd slipped from their tent like a thief, depriving Ash of the chance to explain herself. And she'd desperately wanted that much.

There was no way she could make up for what had happened the night before, she knew that. Her loss of control was a shock to her, too. She'd never forced herself on a woman and she wanted Charlotte to know she would never let it happen again. Her whole life, she had dreaded this day, the day her father's genetic legacy would steal something precious from her.

Who could blame Charlotte for running away? Ash had known full well she was pushing her buttons as they wrestled for physical control, but her emotions had been running white-hot in those fraught moments. She should have walked. She should have seen where it was going and had the good sense to remove herself from the tent. But Charlotte's blithe unconcern for her feelings had messed with her head. Something beautiful had happened between them only the day before and it seemed as if Charlotte had done her best to ruin it ever since. Bad enough the strange conversation about the Dani Bush incident that very night, but then the unexplained vanishing act. What was up with that?

Now she'd gone off somewhere to examine ferns under her microscope, knowing full well that Ash would have to leave without seeing her. It was the last thing Ash had expected. She'd been so sure that despite her poor handling of the situation, she'd somehow broken through to Charlotte on a deeper level. In those moments, she'd felt as close to her as she'd ever felt to another human being. Had she completely misread the perfect intimacy between them?

Charlotte's latest ploy had certainly dispelled any illusions. Ash could take a hint. If Charlotte wanted nothing to do with her, that's exactly what she would get.

❖

"I don't understand." Charlotte stared down at the depression in the earth where her tent used to be. "Why do we have to move the camp?"

As if it weren't bad enough that she'd arrived back to find Ash gone and no reply left for her, not even a verbal farewell to be passed on by one of the others, now there was this—the entire camp taken apart?

"Are you sure there wasn't a note in the tent for me?" She surveyed her rolled-up sleeping gear with dismay. Maybe there was something but it had been discarded by mistake.

The woman methodically stacking the equipment said, "I spoke with Major Evans at some length during the handover. She didn't give me any message to pass on."

Charlotte picked up her tightly rolled sleeping gear and started undoing the Velcro fastenings. "I think I'll check for myself. I'll try not to hold you up."

Her companion, a Minnesotan who looked like a prison warden and acted like she'd been separated from Nitro at birth, got impatient. "I'm sure if there was a message she would have asked me to deliver it. She was surprised you weren't around when she left." Placing the lamp on top of the folded mosquito nets, she added, "I'm setting off for the new site in four minutes. Anything not in order will be left here and you will need to transport it yourself."

Where did they find these people? Charlotte unfurled the pad and sleeping bag and carefully searched them. Then she had a better idea. Hastily she rolled the bedding up again and stacked it with everything else. They had phones. Charlotte located hers and hit Ash's number on speed dial.

No one picked up. Meanwhile, the prison warden, whose name Charlotte was too distracted to remember, was loading their tent and its modest contents onto a crude sled. When she was done she gave Charlotte a curt nod and set off up the mountain, apparently expecting her to follow. Charlotte stayed where she was. She'd spotted Miles standing with Nitro on the track down to the lake bed. Just the unappealing pair she wanted to see.

"I'll catch up with you later," she told her new minder, then marched off to find out if Ash had given Miles a message for her.

The conversation she overheard as she approached was all about the change in campsite, apparently Miles's brainwave. Nitro thought it was a dumb idea. Both men were high on testosterone. Miles was shouting as she reached them.

"I take full responsibility. This is my expedition and you guys are the hired help. Get used to it."

"In matters of personal security, you agreed to abide by the recommendations of Nagle Global Diligence personnel," Nitro replied. "Do I understand that you are declining to do so?"

Charlotte had heard the same speech shortly before he threatened to throw her out of the helicopter.

Miles blurted, "You bet I am. We're the customer, and that means we call the shots."

"You're placing your party at risk." Nitro was keeping his cool. "The present campsite can be evacuated more easily in an emergency, and it doesn't show flash flood damage. We've got rain coming."

"Which is precisely why I'm moving us to higher ground!" Miles's tone was contemptuous. "I suggest from now on you leave the thinking to the smart people."

Charlotte couldn't help but feel that talking down to Nitro was a mistake. The guy was well over six feet, a hunk, armed, and had all his hair, qualities that probably didn't endear him to Miles. But putting him down was no way to deal with jock envy. Miles was spoiling for a broken jaw.

"You're making a mistake," Nitro said with icy composure. Charlotte thought, *Here we go*.

"What are you going to do?" Miles kept right on pushing his luck. "Shoot me?"

Nitro looked tempted.

Charlotte decided it was time to defuse the situation. Politely, she interrupted. "Excuse me. I was wondering if Ash left a message for me with either of you."

Both men stared at her blankly.

Miles said, "What kind of message?"

Charlotte shrugged. "It's not important. We were supposed to have a quick chat before she left, but I got kind of lost coming back from my new sampling site."

"Where's Gunderson?" Nitro asked.

"Who?"

"Your bodyguard."

"I don't have a bodyguard."

Nitro looked past her and made some kind of hand signal. Both Charlotte and Miles turned around, and there was the warden, standing with her loaded-up sled, looking like she was itching to put Charlotte in solitary for a month.

Miles seemed just as taken aback as Charlotte was. He directed his wrath at Nitro. "Would you mind explaining what the fuck is going on?"

"In the light of the security lapse and Dr. Lascelles's risk profile as the immediate representative of Belton Pharmaceuticals, Major Evans revised Gunderson's job description."

"What does that mean?" Charlotte demanded.

"From now on Gunderson will be escorting you at all times."

"Oh, no she won't." Charlotte wasn't wearing *that* for a minute. What was Ash thinking? "That will not be necessary. I can explain what happened. I fell asleep, that's all. It was dark when I woke up, and I had trouble finding my way back to the camp."

"You're lying," Nitro asserted.

"Hey, pal." Miles leapt gallantly to her defense. Sticking his unspectacular chest out, he rose to his full height, which was about five feet eight in hiking boots. "If Dr. Lascelles said she fell asleep, *she fell asleep*!"

Nitro's sphinx-like calm was unshaken. His response fired bullets through her story. "When the Major and I searched the area, we found one of our staff wandering in a disoriented manner. Billy Bob Woodcock. We did not, however, find you."

Charlotte blinked. How much had Billy Bob told them? Had he seen anything? Ash must have known she was lying that night when she claimed she'd been lost. What must she think? Why had she really assigned a bodyguard? Was she spying on her because she knew something about Bruce? Charlotte made an effort to compose herself. She didn't want the all-too-observant Nitro guessing there was something she needed to hide. If Bruce was right, all the Nagle security guards wanted to put a bullet in his head. Did that include Ash?

Bruce said she worked for a mongrel with the ethics of a death adder. Even if that were true, Charlotte could not believe Ash would kill anyone. She wished she'd trusted her with the truth about the cave. Surely Ash deserved that much from her. She needed to convince Nitro that there was nothing to be paranoid about, and she needed not to have a Nagle person trailing her everywhere she went. She also had to get ahold of Ash and explain what was in the cave. She could leave Bruce's name out of it and just act like she found it herself. Ash obviously cared deeply about this land and its people. Charlotte could not believe she'd do anything to jeopardize the cave dwellers or their environment.

A plan took shape in her mind. She knew exactly how to create the smokescreen she needed and maybe even shake herself free of her new watchdog at the same time.

Producing a flustered sigh, she said, like the truth was being dragged out of her, "Okay. I was not *asleep*, exactly. For crying out loud, can't a person have any privacy? I'm sick of sneaking about. Simon and I didn't want to create a situation, but obviously it was only a matter of time…"

Let them make of that outburst what they would. Her two companions seemed genuinely lost for words. Nitro showed rare signs of an emotion, humorous derision perhaps, and Miles was downright flabbergasted. His flush extended right over the balding dome of his head.

"You're talking about Simon Flight?" he marveled.

"At least have the decency to keep it to yourselves," Charlotte said huffily. "We were hoping not to have the entire camp gossiping about us. Now, if you'll both excuse me, I have a tent to put up."

Trying not to snort at her own performance, she stuck her head in the air and flounced off toward her grim-faced "bodyguard." Within half an hour, the gossip would be all over the camp because Miles was incapable of keeping his mouth shut. And Charlotte had no doubt Nitro would keep his colleagues apprised of the situation. She wished she could see the shock on Billy Bob Woodcock's face. He was always calling Simon a faggot behind his back and imitating his mannerisms. Maybe now he'd keep his eyes off Charlotte and zip his mouth about her butterfly-obsessed colleague.

She hoped she would get to Simon before Miles did. If she was going to be able to blow off her minder long enough to connect with Bruce again, she needed for Simon to play along with her story.

Marching up the steep gradient toward the new campsite, she tried Ash's number again. She was just going to keep calling until she got ahold of her. And when she did, there was a lot she wanted to say.

❖

At first, the faint patter of rain on the tent was comforting. Charlotte was having trouble sleeping. She could smell Ash on her sleeping bag, and the scent was making her restless for several reasons. Uppermost, she was despondent. She hadn't been able to reach Ash on the cell phone and in the end she'd given up when several team members said the heavy cloud cover was interfering with the signal. Their phones weren't working either.

Compounding her despondency, she felt strangely unanchored without Ash. Being single had never bothered Charlotte. She enjoyed her own company and she didn't need a partner's approval to feel good about herself. But this was different. Without Ash she felt strangely diminished. It made no sense and her logical mind harped on that all the time. She had only known Ash for a few weeks, including the gap in between, so it was impossible to be in love with her. And if Ash cared about her, surely she would have stayed. And even if they did get together, what could possibly come of it, long term? They were two very different people with very different lives.

Charlotte let the constant clatter wash over her. Since her time in the cloud forest, she had a whole new perspective on her emotions, one she wanted to share with Ash. Being apart from her had only magnified that desire—and every other one. Her body was in a state of readiness she could not ignore. Her nipples were tight with neglect. Her limbs were twitchy. And every time she thought about last night's wild coupling, her stomach nose-dived. Inhaling Ash's scent for the past hour had made it impossible to think about anything else.

As the straining tension between her legs tugged tighter, Charlotte crossed one leg over the other, which only succeeded in making her thighs slippery and adding more pressure exactly where she needed the relief of Ash's mouth. Miserably aroused and unrequited, she peered across her tent and cursed the lousy timing of Ash's flight to Kwerba. They should have been together tonight, talking, making love, clearing the air so they could move forward with a new understanding. But no, she had to be lying next to a stranger sleeping flat on her back, fully clothed, and snoring in raspy little hitches.

Charlotte wondered what it would take to wake Renee Gunderson. The dour Minnesotan didn't sound like a light sleeper. Would she notice if the woman she was guarding quietly had an orgasm? Charlotte had never been much good at reaching a climax single-handed, and it usually took ages. But she knew that would be different now, with her body still in a state of tender thrall from Ash's touch.

She caught her breath. She wanted Ash so badly she felt like crying. The swelling volume of the rain had intensified, and she opened her sleeping bag to enjoy the unusual cooling of the air. Beneath her, the ground reverberated with the rolling drumbeat of thunder. Rain hammered down, making the tent panels flap. Condensation began to fall in splats.

Charlotte wiped at some of the water landing on her thighs, and the motion made the seam of her pajamas brush her clit. She reacted with a stifled gasp. The elemental din of the storm drowned out her next response, a small whine of relief as she slid a hand down inside her pants and let her middle finger drift over the drenched parting of her flesh. She imagined Ash, moving between her legs, sliding in and out of her. Those deep groans in her ear. Ash's lips exploring her face and throat.

She stroked herself harder, arching her back, allowing herself the soft noises she couldn't contain. Her muscles stiffened and her breathing changed. She closed her eyes and lifted her hips. Any moment now.

"Christ!" A voice exploded right next to her.

Charlotte stopped dead and guiltily jerked her hand away. Disoriented and trembling, she stared around.

Fingers caught her arm. "We have to get out of here."

The lamp abruptly bloomed pale gold, hurting Charlotte's eyes. Renee shoved a pair of boots at her and said, "Get your feet in these. Just do it."

"What's happening?" Charlotte's heightened preorgasmic focus was rapidly giving way to panicked awareness, but she was still a beat behind. She could hear thunder, louder and closer. The storm must be directly overhead.

Renee wasn't waiting around. She pushed one of the boots onto Charlotte's right foot and yelled at her, "Move!"

Charlotte shoved her left foot in the other boot and tied the laces as fast as she could with her hands shaking uncontrollably. Renee efficiently tied her own boots, then grabbed one of her guns, her backpack, and Charlotte. She ripped the tent flap apart and they charged out into the heaviest rain Charlotte had ever seen, a wall of water slashing at all in its path.

Renee paused and swung her gun in the air, firing three shots. "Get out!" she yelled as a lamp came on in one of the other tents. "Run!"

Dragging Charlotte along with her, she tore open the fronts of the main tents and shouted at the occupants. Then they were running east and uphill, tripping over roots and slithering helplessly as the ground beneath their feet became a water-jammed slick. Charlotte fell behind when Renee let her loose so they could both keep their balance. Losing traction, she caught hold of a tree trunk and hauled herself upright, trying to see around her.

"I'm here." Renee dropped back and took her hand. "Hang on tight."

They continued steadily upward at an angle, getting distance from the campsite. Charlotte's heart crashed against the walls of her chest. She was breathing so hard her head spun.

She cried, "I have to stop."

"It's okay." Renee was gasping for air, too. She steered Charlotte toward a tree and yelled through the thick tropical darkness. "We can rest here. I think we're safe."

They both sank down. Charlotte could hear nothing but a deafening, almost explosive crashing sound. "Is it always like this in the monsoon?" she shouted.

"It's not the monsoon," Renee yelled in her ear. "It's the stream."

They stayed where they were as the storm raged on. The ear-shattering boom subsided after a while, and Charlotte heard grunting sounds. A shape broke through the night just a few feet in front of them.

Renee called, "Hello?"

The figure fell to the ground and crawled up. A male voice inquired, "Gunderson?"

"Yeah, and I have Lascelles. What's happening?"

It was Nitro. He said, "I have eight of them from the big tent."

"What about the others?"

"No idea."

"Fuck." Renee repeated the expletive several more times, then said, "I left a Coral Sea cruise for this."

A big hand found one of Charlotte's and pressed something into it. She felt a crinkly wrapper. Nitro said, "Eat."

Charlotte didn't argue. She was weak and shaky and the high-energy chocolate hit her bloodstream in a rush. A narrow beam of light played across the tree trunks around them. Renee had her flashlight on and was pulling stuff from her backpack. A moment later she passed her a small pile of dry clothes.

"There doesn't seem much point in getting changed while it's still raining," Charlotte said, flicking water from her face.

"I have a raincoat you can wear once you're dry," Renee said.

She and Nitro held the coat over her while she dressed, then helped her pull it on. Thankful to feel clean again, Charlotte sat back down and drew the hood over her head.

"Sunrise in three hours," Nitro remarked.

All Charlotte could think about was Ash. She had to know if she was okay. "I left my phone behind," she wailed, unable to stop several big sobs. "I need to call Ash."

"We can use mine." Renee foraged in her pack once more and produced their link to the outside world. "What do you know," she said after dialing. "We have a signal."

Charlotte took the phone from her and jammed it to her ear.

CHAPTER SEVENTEEN

"Charlotte?" Ash elbowed herself up. Blood throbbed a martial tattoo in her temples. She checked the caller ID again, alarmed. "Where's Renee?"

"She's over by another tree with Nitro." Disappointment infused Charlotte's voice. "Do you want to talk to her?"

"Not right away. What's up? Is everything okay?" There had to be a very good reason why Charlotte was calling someone she obviously didn't want to talk to, at two in the morning.

"The storm is really bad up here," Charlotte answered tearfully. "We had to leave the new campsite."

"What new campsite?"

"Miles found a big pool upstream for washing and he wanted us to move closer to it."

How did some people ever get a PhD? You didn't park your tent in the fork of a stream on a slope in monsoon country. What did Miles think would happen when it rained? Disbelieving and horrified, Ash said, "So where are you now?"

"I have no idea. We just ran away as fast as we could."

She sounded stunned and frightened. Ash stopped with the twenty questions and asked, "Are you hurt?" Bile rose in her throat. "Charlotte?"

A snuffling sound came down the phone. "Yes, I'm hurt! Why didn't you leave a note for me?"

That was rich. "I could ask you the same thing."

"I left a note in your pack!"

The hot indignation would have made Ash smile any other time. Now it jarred her conscience, cutting through the self-torturing assumptions she'd made. She pictured herself getting ready to leave that morning, throwing her gear heedlessly into her pack. She'd spent so much time hunting for Charlotte she had to rush. If there was a note, it had either fallen out or been stuffed to the bottom of her belongings.

"I didn't see it," she said, groping for her flashlight.

"Oh." A winded sigh.

"Hang on a second." Ash's hand connected with rough, bristly hair and mud-caked skin. The pig sleeping a few feet from her didn't stir. Oriented now that she could feel its proximity, she located her boots and pulled the flashlight out from inside one of them. The other contained her Sig. She was off duty, with Klaus guarding the Huey, and here in Kwerba, away from the expedition, the risk factors were low. So, for a change, she hadn't slept fully dressed and ready to roll.

Directing the beam carefully so she didn't stir the two elderly people whose hut she was sharing, she pulled her pack over and shoved her hand deep inside. Her fingers trawled through the familiar contents until she felt the Nagle insignia on a shirt toward the bottom, one of the first things she'd shoved in during her hasty departure. Underneath lay a folded piece of paper.

"Damn," she muttered beneath her breath.

"Did you find it?"

Ash responded to the hopeful inquiry with a subdued "Yes" and held the note to the light.

Ash, I need to clear my head so I'm going for a long walk. I wish you weren't leaving today. I hope we can talk this afternoon before you go. Please don't worry. Everything is fine. I'm not angry about last night. I just feel a bit overwhelmed and I need some space. Everything seems to be moving so fast between us. See you soon. Charlotte.

It certainly didn't sound like a kiss-off.

Ash croaked dryly, "I wish I'd seen this before I left."

"Me, too." Charlotte's voice broke. "I wish we could have talked. I stayed too long in the cloud forest."

"You went back there?" Ash's mind jumped to the two of them standing naked and awestruck in the chill purity of the waterfall, like they'd just beamed down into paradise.

"I had to," Charlotte said. "It's hard to explain. But I feel like I know who I am, there."

"Yes." Ash understood exactly. From the moment she'd set foot in that enchanted place, she'd been able to see her deepest self with astonishing clarity. Long-buried dreams came alive. Hope chipped away at her doubts. It was a scary, exhilarating state of mind.

"There were some things I needed to figure out," Charlotte said.

"And did you?" Ash was almost afraid to hear the answer. It was all wrong that they were having this conversation at opposite ends of a cell phone in the middle of a tropical storm. She wanted to see Charlotte's face. She wanted to hold her and let nothing harm her.

"Ash." Charlotte's voice dropped lower. It was charged with emotion. "I think I'm falling in love with you."

She had to hear this heart-stopping declaration sitting in a thatched wood hut with a pig snoring next to her. Could her life be any less storybook? Elbows resting on her knees, Ash cradled her head in her hands, the phone cupped close. Charlotte's words floated like oxygen. She gulped them down into lungs deprived. She could hear Charlotte breathing raggedly from the risk she'd just taken. It was time to respond.

She put it out there in all its corniness, unable to come up with a better way to explain the slingshot to her soul that day in the bar. "I fell in love with you at first sight."

"Oh."

Ash could see her mouth parting in kissable awe. She wanted to touch it, to carve the full pout of that bottom lip into her fingertips so she could feel it forever. "I don't even believe in love at first sight," she said huskily.

"I don't either," Charlotte murmured. "I think it was love at second sight for me."

They laughed softly.

Ash said, "What was I thinking leaving you in that hotel room?"

"I seriously considered chasing you down the hall," Charlotte informed her. "But I was too drunk to get to the door."

"I'm glad we waited." Ash meant it. Sex in a hotel room with a woman under the influence usually only ended one way. They both deserved better, and maybe on some level they'd known it, even then.

"I tried to find you," Charlotte said. "Before I left for the Kokoda Trail. You're not listed."

"No. Mostly I don't want to be found." Ash was amazed. The uptight woman so horrified to see her at the Sarmi airstrip had actually sought her out after their night on the town? Clearly, they had more catching up to do, sometime when they didn't have to worry about killing a cell phone battery. Gently, she said, "Baby, I want to continue this conversation, but right now I'm guessing Renee is worried her cell phone is going to die at any moment."

"I don't care."

Ash laughed. "That's my girl." Adopting a sterner tone, she said, "Come on. Say good night and put her on."

"What do I get in return?"

"What do you want?"

Charlotte's shaky breath teased Ash's ear. "Take a wild guess. And since I'm not alone that's all I'm going to say."

"I think they've heard enough." Ash knew her colleagues must have been straining their ears this whole time.

They'd both been intrigued by her instructions to Renee to keep Charlotte under constant surveillance. Being professionals accustomed to following orders, they hadn't questioned the decision, but Nitro had given her a sharp look. He'd examined Billy Bob Woodcock the night they'd searched for Charlotte and had a few theories of his own.

He wasn't the only one. Ash still had some questions for Charlotte to answer. Every time she thought through those events, she felt like she was missing something. She'd raised the alarm as soon as everyone rolled in for the evening meal with Charlotte not among them. Notably, Billy Bob had been absent, too, a fact that had made her sick to her stomach at the time. However, the burly Texan hadn't been hard to find. She and Nitro had barely arrived in the area where Charlotte was last seen when he lurched out of the undergrowth talking gibberish.

At first his dazed condition seemed to be explained by a lump near his temple where he'd suffered a blow. He said he must have tripped and hit his head on a tree. That was all he could remember. He'd woken up in a pile of leaves.

None of which explained the puncture mark Nitro subsequently found in his neck. "Tranquilizer dart," he said.

Ash took his word for it. The guy knew more than she ever would about how to immobilize human beings, temporarily or for keeps.

"Do you think it's a kidnapping?" Ash's blood ran straight to her feet.

"Could be. But they left him and took her, so there must be a reason. He's got to be carrying a ransom note, only I'm not seeing it."

They searched Woodcock's clothing carefully and combed his body in case the kidnappers had decided to write their demand in felt tip on his chest or something. Billy Bob then decided to have hysterics because he thought headhunters might have been coveting his meaty skull.

Leaving him to his lurid imaginings, they kept up the search until the intense darkness made it futile. Ash had been pacing around outside the tents when Charlotte finally showed up, unscathed and telling some bullshit story about falling asleep in the very area they'd been patrolling for hours.

No wonder Nitro was suspicious. Ash wasn't comfortable either. She hoped her evasive lover planned to come clean and tell her what had really happened that night. Ash wondered what on earth she could be hiding. Had she discovered the ultimate fern and wanted to keep it to herself? One thing Ash had noticed about the scientists—they were incredibly competitive with each other in their own nerdy way.

She switched the phone to her other ear as the signal faded out a little. Renee was on the other end, relaying their circumstances. By the time she'd finished telling her tale, it was clear that she'd probably saved Charlotte's life.

Ash said, "You did good. Thank you."

"It could be worse," the intrepid hero remarked with irony. "I was sick of playing deck quoits, anyway. And their calypso band sucked."

Ash grinned at this rare display of humor. Renee Gunderson, according to the Nagle rumor mill, had iced her husband over an affair with the babysitter. She'd been acquitted on a technicality but was dishonorably discharged from the army. Now she was working cream-puff assignments that called for a female contractor.

"Phone me tomorrow with a report on the damage. Okay?"

"You bet." Renee was all business again. "My guess, it's going to be ugly."

❖

The day after the storm, Charlotte stared down at the two bodies laid out on the only clean sleeping bag liners they'd managed to salvage from the far-flung detritus of their camp. The bloodless pallor of their faces, and the gaping cuts and abrasions, would haunt her all her life. Simon had gone back for a butterfly. Jeb Tanner, the other Texan on the Nagle team, had gone after him. They were washed away when the stream became a lethal torrent and breached its banks. The two men were thrown hundreds of yards downhill, smashing into trees and rocks. They had no chance, Nitro said.

The team had decided to bury them here, near the lake bed, where they could easily be brought out in a recovery operation if that's what their families wanted. Everyone had gathered in a fine drizzle of rain to pay their final respects. Charlotte felt eyes on her as the bodies were lowered into their graves. She didn't know what to say. With the exception of Nitro and Renee, who seemed to have added two and two, the entire field party now thought Simon had been her boyfriend.

All morning people had been coming up to her, giving her embarrassed hugs and shoulder squeezes. It seemed to help them all cope to have someone they could offer condolences to, so she kept her mouth shut. It was ironic. She'd learned more about Simon in the few hours since his death than in the past week. Everyone who consoled her had a story to tell about him. It sounded like he was a genuinely good person. Charlotte wished she'd laughed at more of his jokes.

After the men were in their graves, the Australian mammal experts led the group in a simple rendition of "Amazing Grace," then anyone who knew the British national anthem sang it in honor of Simon. The Americans followed this with their anthem in salute to Jeb Tanner, who had tried to save a life and lost his own.

Billy Bob produced a tinny CD player and cranked up the volume to play Jeb's favorite song, "Take Me Home, Country Roads." Everyone knew at least some of the lyrics and sang along out of tune. Miles stood a short distance away, staring at nothing, wiping tears off his face. He'd been throwing up all morning.

As Nitro and several other men shoveled earth into the graves, Charlotte sensed a restless expectation in the ranks. They all wanted to give their dead colleagues as much dignity as they could, and without a priest something crucial seemed to be missing from their simple ritual. So, to the soft thud of falling earth, she did her best to recall the words everyone expected to hear at a funeral.

"We hereby commit the bodies of our two dearly departed brothers Simon and Jeb into the ground. Earth to earth. Ashes to ashes. Dust to dust."

It was all she could call to mind, but a solemn sigh ensued and the tension dissipated. Life was short. Charlotte hoped each dead man had found his measure of happiness.

CHAPTER EIGHTEEN

Time slithered by. The field party subsisted in a veil of rain and cloud. Grim. Oppressive. Unrelenting. Day after day.

The flash-flood waters had run off into small tributaries all over the affected area of the mountain. These fingered a sea of mud in which most of the supplies and equipment were buried. Each day, in shifts, the team dug with any implement they could find, trying to unearth food and phones. Most people had lost theirs and the camp's small generator had been destroyed, so there was no way to recharge the batteries of the few that still functioned.

Charlotte felt miserably guilty that she had consumed most of Renee's charge while she was confessing her love to Ash. But Renee never complained. All she said was that they could only phone Ash once a day to check in, and they had to save power for their most important call, when the clouds finally parted and a helicopter could land.

Each morning over breakfast, the entire camp gathered at the edge of the lake bed to stare up at the sky like the faithful awaiting the rapture. They had a carefully mapped-out plan for the day the weather looked like changing. There were flares set aside. Nitro thought at least some of them would work. An array of brightly colored items was piled up ready to be laid out in the middle of the boggy landing area. Nitro said Ash would need some markers if she had to come down in thin mist. And they'd drawn straws to see who would leave on the first shuttle.

Planning their departure and discussing what they were all going to do when they got back to civilization kept their spirits up. Several of the team had also evolved a scheme for walking out of the Fojas if they had to. Kwerba was a twenty-day hike, they'd calculated, perhaps thirty, and Jared Diamond had done it all those years ago. Maybe they could, too. Whenever they got carried away with that conversation, Miles reminded them that Diamond had guides with him, whereas theirs had flown back to Kwerba once they'd established the camp and mapped out their research area.

The post-flood camp had been rebuilt on the original site Ash had chosen. One of the large tents had been recovered and the men had rigged up bivouacs for everyone who could not be accommodated. Charlotte and Renee slept side by side in the tent. They didn't talk much. Everyone was in mourning, Charlotte thought. For the men lost and for the expedition itself. They had plans to regroup and start again, but this journey of discovery was over. When people died, it was time to go home.

Charlotte got despondent every time she thought about returning empty-handed to Sealy-Weiss. Of course, she had some basic data and there was a good deal she could bring together from memory. She could confirm the existence of the *Ficus* they were seeking and she intended to collect a new set of specimens today. But there was so much more she wanted to do. She couldn't help but imagine how she would be received if she took back the prize she really wanted. The orchid of life.

The more she thought about it, the more desperate she became to make contact with Bruce again and get back to that cave. The rain had finally stopped and a heady optimism had seized the breakfast crowd. The sky seemed brighter, the clouds thinner. Maybe they would have liftoff tomorrow.

Charlotte was both thrilled and alarmed by the prospect. She would see Ash. At last. But she would be leaving the Fojas before she could gather the evidence she needed to announce the discovery of a lifetime. What if Bruce was murdered by one of the various parties he claimed to be hiding from? The Indonesian military. The big mining companies. The timber barons. His ex-wife.

She paced the perimeter of the camp, conscious of Renee's watchful regard. She usually kept a discreet distance but she was always there. Today's digging parties were setting off, all in high spirits for a change. The few people remaining were on latrine and maintenance duty. Among them was Miles, whose heart seemed to have gone out of him since the catastrophe. His face had thinned and he had let his goatee run amok. His wispy brown hair was weighed down with mud.

Charlotte watched him drag his feet as he transported buckets of fresh leaf mulch and twigs around the camp to spread over the pathways, their attempt to prevent their thoroughfares becoming slippery mud trails. An idea took root as he worked, and with a nonchalant smile at Renee, she strolled toward him.

"Miles, hey. How are you doing?"

He straightened up and regarded her uncertainly. Charlotte could understand his apprehension. He blamed himself for Simon's death, and she was the supposed girlfriend.

"I have a favor to ask," she said.

He seemed cheered by this, perhaps seeing an olive branch. "Anything to help."

Charlotte decided her plan was a win/win. Miles would get to feel good about helping her and she would get the chance to see Bruce, if he was still around. She had a feeling he was.

"As you know, I lost all my data and specimens in the flood. And my camera. And microscope." She kept her tone soft, not wanting to sound accusatory. "But I believe I can still gather some extremely useful specimens of one key species I'm here to research. It would probably be in both our interests to provide Belton Pharmaceuticals with a reason to fund another expedition."

"Do you see that happening?" He sounded dubious.

"Absolutely. But we don't have much time if the weather is going to clear, so I thought if I had some help…" Charlotte cast a pointed look toward Renee and lowered her voice. "The problem is, she slows me down in the field and right now, time is of the essence. I was hoping you might be able to work with me."

Miles, as Charlotte had expected, relished the chance to score a few points against the Nagle crew. "I'm your man," he said. "Let's lose the guard dog."

Charlotte gave him a big smile. "Okay, here's the plan. You're going to tell her you're walking me up to the dig. We'll say we're really bored down here and we want to see if they've found our laptops. Then I'm going to suggest she takes the morning off since I'll be up there with Nitro and everyone else."

"You think she'll go for that?"

"She has period cramps and there's no Motrin. She'll go for it."

Miles beamed. "That's very resourceful."

Charlotte offered her hand and he got emotional shaking it.

"I just wanted to say," he stammered as they approached Renee, "I'm terribly sorry about Simon."

"It was a tragic accident. Try to stop beating yourself up about it. Okay?"

He nodded effusively.

Renee greeted them with a suspicious stare, but she didn't put up much resistance. The cramps, Charlotte surmised, must be really bad.

❖

Miles got with the program immediately. His backpack had survived the storm and he offered up its contents the moment they arrived at the *Ficus* tree. Specimen bags. Energy bars. Pocket knife. And best of all, sanitary wipes.

These he handed her, saying, "Take the whole box. It's not like I ever use them."

Charlotte shuddered to think she'd shaken his hand. She stared down at the unopened box. Two hundred lightly perfumed antibacterial towelettes. All to herself. She'd died and gone to heaven.

"If you're fine starting with the bark samples, I think I'll take a walk and go clean myself up," she said, beyond thrilled. Clean, good-smelling skin. She'd almost forgotten what it felt like.

"Knock yourself out." He was already labeling a stack of bags, looking as happy as a clam. "I'll be right here."

Charlotte couldn't believe her luck. She'd been wondering how she was going to find an excuse to vanish for a reasonable period. Having her own private sponge bath would buy her as much time as she needed. Miles wasn't going to do anything to undermine their new rapport. He would not have the temerity to come looking for her while she was having the next best thing to a shower. She could probably take hours if she wanted to.

Humming to herself, she waltzed along the route east of the *Ficus* until she came to a pleasant little clearing about five minutes away. On one side, large buttress roots provided a natural screen. On the other, liana creepers formed a tangled curtain between two broken branches.

Charlotte discarded the T-shirt she'd been wearing since the storm and flinched at the smell of her armpits. Disgusting. She opened a wipe and inhaled the sharp citrus promise of germ-free skin. Languorously, she ran the wet fabric all the way down one arm. Oh, God. When had anything felt so good?

She lathered it up and down a few times before setting it aside. Two hundred wipes. She could use fifty now and have another hundred and fifty to last her until they were picked up. At least, when she finally got to be in Ash's arms, she would smell clean, DEET notwithstanding.

Charlotte tore open several packets and whipped out the towelettes, flipping them open and bunching them into a luxuriously large wipe. She finished cleaning her arm, then continued with the back of her neck, and her other arm. If Bruce came now, she would tell him to go wait behind one of the trees until she'd finished. She opened more wipes and got started on her chest, sighing with pleasure as her skin prickled at the slight astringent. This, she decided, was the best bathing experience she'd ever had.

She knotted a couple of wipes together so she could clean her back using a seesaw motion. Her filthy skin thrilled to the cool liquid and Charlotte heaved a huge sigh. She would never take plumbing for granted again. Stretching, she gave the center of her back some extra attention, then undid her pants. She was about to lower them when the snap of a twig made her freeze.

"Don't stop on my account." The voice came from the other side of the broken branches, the accent unmistakable.

Billy Bob Woodcock stepped out from behind the creepers, smiling with beady-eyed threat. He had a gun in his hand. Stroking the barrel suggestively, he said, "Well look at you, all naked, and no one around to appreciate the pretty picture."

Charlotte snatched up her T-shirt and held it to her breasts.

He chuckled. "Aw, don't go getting shy on me now."

Charlotte tried to slow her breathing. With polite authority, she said, "I'm not sure what you're doing out here, Billy Bob, but I think it's time you went back to the camp. I'm willing to forget all about this."

"Oh, no. You're never gonna forget, and that's a promise. When I show a lady a good time, she remembers."

Charlotte considered her options. Miles was just a few minutes away. If she ran she might make it. Or she could attempt to reason with this hormone-driven creep. It was important not to show fear, she decided. Men like him got off on it. They counted on their power to intimidate.

"Billy Bob, we'll probably be leaving here tomorrow," she said reasonably. "Let's not do something we might regret. It's been a stressful time. I understand that. But an episode like this can follow you around."

He shrugged. "The way I see it, I got nothing to lose. I'm out of here anyway, real soon. Going to Iraq." Incredibly, he wheedled, "Don't you want to give me something hot to remember?"

"No. I'm not attracted to you."

Billy Bob seemed to find that funny. As he chortled, Charlotte started walking, glancing over her shoulder.

"Hard to get. How did I guess?" He caught up to her in a couple of quick strides and grabbed her arm.

Charlotte yelled, "Miles!"

Billy Bob laughed harder. "Last I seen, your buddy Miles wasn't moving."

Charlotte felt winded. "What did you do to him?"

"He's okay. He'll just have a sore head tomorrow. Now, are you gonna be nice to me or do I have to make you?" This time he aimed the gun.

Shaking, Charlotte begged, "Let me go. Please."

Her mind seemed to be breaking into fragments, each one playing through different scenarios like movies on fast-forward. Incredible how fast the one dark question transcended all—could she stay alive? She was going to be raped. That was inevitable. Did he plan to get rid of the evidence, too? Would she be better off making nice, or would he see through her? Was killing her part of his fantasy?

In the traffic jam of her thoughts she was jerked back in time to the floor of her kitchen. Crawling away from Britt, asking the same dark questions about how she would survive and whether, this time, Britt would go too far and kill her.

Making nice, being obedient, had never done a thing for her then. Cold rage infused her. This nobody thought he could invade her world without her permission and violate her. He thought he was entitled to take what he wanted. Maybe she wouldn't be able to stop him. Maybe she would be seriously injured. But she was damned if she was going to acquiesce. She would mark him. He wasn't going to be able to walk back to into the camp like nothing had happened.

Billy Bob pushed her down onto the ground and ripped her T-shirt from her hands. She needed for him to put the gun down, just for a minute.

"Please," she disguised her intent with a soft beg. "Don't hurt me. I'll do what you want."

His eyes glittered. He was pumped up now, feeling strong. He said, "You're gonna love it." He transferred the gun to his left hand, so he could get busy unfastening his pants. His eyes shifted from her to the task and he announced, "Look what I've got for you."

She kept the gun in focus, watching it droop as her assailant distracted himself, admiring his own organ. It took her only a split second to move. Grabbing his left arm with both hands, she swung it across a tree root. The gun flew from his hand. Howling, off balance, he crashed down and she scrambled up, screaming ear-splitting screams. Claiming the gun before he could get to it, she ran.

But he was bigger and faster, and tackled her around the neck. She kicked back. He had her by the wrist, squeezing, preventing her from turning the gun. In her ear, he yelled filth. She swung an elbow back, jabbing him in the gut. A hand covered her mouth to silence her. Stinky, sweaty skin compressed her nostril and lips, filling her with revulsion. Charlotte bit hard. He yelped and cursed and Charlotte knew she couldn't hold on to the gun much longer.

She squeezed the trigger, announcing their human presence with a gunshot that splintered the ancient silence of the forest. He mashed the gun from her hand and threw her to the ground, pinning her with his weight. As he grappled to keep her still, she swung her elbow into his mouth. Blood drooled down his chin. She wanted to write his crime all over him, damage him so he would be branded with what he was doing. With fierce determination she jerked her knee up and landed an inept shove to his groin, not enough to disable him.

Grunting and moaning, he choked out, "You wanna play rough, you fucking bitch? I'll show you rough."

His weight constricted her breathing. He tore at her pants. The gun was limiting him, leaving only one hand free. He didn't bother trying to silence her anymore, so she screamed again, eyes closed, face rigid, diverting all the oxygen in her lungs into the loudest noise she could make. And while her own alarm still reverberated in her chest and her head, something exploded and she knew the gun had gone off.

His body seemed to fly off hers and she reacted instinctively, elbowing herself up, stunned and blinking, her whole body trembling. Her attacker was lying in a heap next to her, his brains blown out, Nitro standing over him. He checked the dead man's pulse, then picked up Charlotte's T-shirt and handed it to her.

Returning his gun to its shoulder holster, he said, "The bodyguard was for a reason, Dr. Lascelles."

CHAPTER NINETEEN

Klaus wasn't happy with the plan and explained his objections during the flight back to the Sarmi hangar.

"The group is descending into anarchy," he said as they cruised along at six hundred feet, below the scudding clouds. "The disaster caused a breakdown in order. In a vacuum people make up new rules. You've read *Lord of the Flies*."

Ash thought his gloomy assessment gave the expedition too much credit. They'd never had much order in the first place, and a group of civilians losing the plot in a crisis was only to be expected. Some sound leadership would contain the situation, and that's exactly what Nitro had imposed. Billy Bob Woodcock's behavior was not part of a big picture, it was all about one man's lack of character. Now he would never bother a woman again. She owed Nitro.

Ash kept her emotions firmly in check. She'd given in to an initial outburst and a spell of impotent rage when Renee called her just after daybreak. But even then, she'd kept a lid on herself. Renee knew she'd let her down. She'd allowed Charlotte to give her the slip, and Ash didn't need to spell out how much worse the consequences might have been. Fortunately for Charlotte, Miles had staggered back to the camp after being pistol-whipped, and raised the alarm. Nitro was already there, looking for Billy Bob, who had not returned to the digging team from a bathroom break.

The rest was history and Ash could not allow herself to dwell on it. She had not been there to protect Charlotte from a sexual predator, and there wasn't a damn thing she could do about it. All she could offer was comfort after the fact, and if it was humanly possible she would get to her lover today. Meantime, indulging herself in recrimination and self-blame was a luxury she could not afford. If she was going to put this bird down in the conditions Renee had described, she would have to be flying at the top of her game.

This was the easy part of her plan. She'd called Tubby to arrange a rescue operation, and a team would be arriving in Sarmi the next day. Klaus was going to wait at the hangar so he could guide them to the site. Ash hoped to extract at least some of the party this afternoon if possible. She would only get one shot at it, given the weather, and she knew she might not able to land the Huey at all.

"They can wait another day," Klaus urged.

"Yes, but I can't."

He looked sideways at her. "You are serious about this woman?"

"I never thought I would say it, but yes."

He gave this a moment's thought. "What will you do? Is there work for her over here?"

"I doubt it. We haven't discussed the future, but her job is in Chicago. The weather sucks there."

"You're leaving PNG?"

"I will if she wants me to."

He was silent for a while, then pronounced, "Billy Bob was lucky."

"How's that?"

"It was quick, yes?"

"One to the head is what I heard." Nitro was not a man who wasted time or bullets.

Her copilot nodded. "You would not have been so considerate."

"Not even close." She started her descent.

"Is she okay?" he asked cautiously.

"Just cuts and bruises."

She'd put up one helluva fight, Renee had told her, and that bought them critical minutes. Ash hoped Charlotte felt good about her own role in defending herself. She planned to make sure of it.

The airstrip loomed and Ash dropped the Huey effortlessly onto the landing gear. Before Klaus bailed out, they shook hands and, because it was pointless to let self-consciousness prevent her, she said, "If anything happens, tell her she's the love of my life."

"You have my word," Klaus gravely assented. "And if there is a cremation, I will make sure she receives the urn."

On that cheerful note, they parted company and Ash headed for the Fojas with her heart in her throat.

❖

They heard the helicopter before they saw it. Ash was circling, Charlotte thought, trying to see down through the jigsaw of gaps in the cloud. A fine mist shrouded the lake bed. She would never be able to land in this.

Nitro was on the cell phone, trying to talk her down. He handed out flares to several members of the team and had them stand in the landing area. On his signal they fired them, and a cluster of small orange explosions broke overhead. A few seconds later, the noise of the chopper blades whooped and thudded like huge bird wings smacking into plastic.

Charlotte felt nauseous. She was desperately afraid for Ash, but something else was going on, too. She had awakened that morning aching all over, and her body temperature had been swinging from freezing to feverish ever since. Teeth chattering, she squinted up into the fog and held her breath as a dark shape came into view northwest of their position. Ash was approaching the lake bed from the opposite direction of the one she'd chosen almost two weeks earlier.

Nitro was talking fast and Charlotte tugged at his arm, reading the tension in his face. "What's wrong?"

"It's a steep angle. She's trying to come in for a low hover."

Charlotte wanted to run out into the middle of the marshy clearing and wave her arms. Everyone had turned around, facing away from landing area to watch the dark khaki helicopter dropping into view. Ash steered it toward the lake bed. Amidst the cheering and premature elation, Nitro barked off an urgent "No," and Charlotte could see why.

Something very strange was happening. Ash had started to hover above the lake bed when the helicopter began to swing around as if something had caught it by the tail. It seemed to wobble in the air.

Nitro muttered, "Fuck."

"What's happening?" Charlotte wailed as a hand landed squarely between her shoulder blades and she was flattened to the earth.

Nitro yelled, "Everyone, get down!" and shielded her with his body.

The helicopter veered sideways, nose dropping. The air vibrated as if the sky itself were shuddering. The Huey was heading straight for the forest south of the team. Charlotte couldn't move. She wanted to close her eyes, but they were locked wide open. She couldn't draw breath. Ash was going down right in front of her.

"Do something," she cried.

Nitro placed his hand over her eyes and held her tight as a dull boom shook the earth and the sky fell quiet.

They lay frozen for no more than a couple of seconds, then he was on his feet again. Ordering her to stay where she was, he charged off across the lake bed followed by most of the team.

Flames licked up over the trees and a plume of black smoke blended with the mist. A hand touched her shoulder and Renee drew her into a sitting position and gingerly hugged her.

"I'm sorry, Charlotte." She was crying.

They stayed in a shaky crouch for a few seconds, then lurched to their feet by unspoken consent and started walking.

"Are you sure you want to see this?" Renee asked as their feet sank into the bog.

Charlotte had no answer. All she knew was that she could not believe she'd lost the woman she loved. She had to see Ash, no matter what.

❖

The acrid smell of petroleum and damp, burning wood assaulted Ash's nostrils and lungs, but she could feel every part of her body. The undergrowth at the rim of the lake bed danced before her eyes in a blur of greens and browns. She angled her head. Above her, the forest canopy swung back and forth with the gait of the man carrying her, slung over his shoulder.

She craned awkwardly to see the back of his head and instantly recognized what looked like auburn dreadlocks. Her rescuer was half naked, his skin covered in earth. When they'd made it into the concealing gloom of the forest, well away from the wreckage of her bird, he deposited her on the earth, propped against a tree trunk.

Ash gazed up, her head swimming. "Bruce. G'day."

"Yeah, g'day." Glassy brown eyes regarded her with fixed marsupial tranquility. "It's always the bloody tail rotor."

"I tipped a tree on the descent angle," she said, hardly able to believe she'd lost her bird. "Something must have been caught up and tangled. Thanks for getting me out."

"No worries." He leaned his back against the tree and slid down next to her. "Could you give Charlotte a message for me?"

Ash stared at him. "You know Charlotte?"

"I have the honor of her acquaintanceship." He paused. "I wouldn't have let it happen. I want you to know that."

"You were there?"

"About the same time as the Terminator. I would have offered to help, but he didn't need my services."

As her mind foggily processed this information, Ash ran an exploring hand over her pounding head. A lump the size of a golf ball protruded above her right eyebrow. Very attractive.

"What do you want me to tell her?" she asked.

"I'll meet her at our special place tomorrow morning."

"Your special place?" Ash could not be hearing this. Charlotte had been hanging out with the most wanted man in New Guinea?

"I have the specimen she'll need," the Roo said.

"Wait a minute. You're selling plants to her?"

"It's a gift." He sounded affronted. "I should get going."

"Bruce." Ash put a hand on his shoulder. "Some advice. Get out while you still can. Time's up."

"I feel the heat," he conceded. "I know that cretin you work for wants to serve my head on a plate to the corporate villains. What am I worth?"

"He offered me fifty to bring you in, and I don't think the Terminator was sent out here to light the campfires."

"I figured."

"You can do just as much somewhere else," she said. "Maybe more. The people here need voices on the outside."

"I'll think about it."

Ash took a card from her pocket and handed it to him. "If you need a ride, that's my number. I have a spare bird in Madang."

He tucked the card into his woven loin pouch and got to his feet. "Don't forget to tell her."

Ash stared after him. Charlotte had some explaining to do.

❖

"I still can't believe it." Kneeling next to Ash, Charlotte ran a sanitary wipe over the gash on her head. "I mean that you're here and everything is all right."

They were finally alone, in the fading light of day, in the privacy of a smaller tent Nitro had found among the items dug up the day before. Charlotte was more placid now, having spent the first few hours after the crash attached to Ash like a limpet, revisiting her fears and relief over and over.

"It is all right, isn't it?" Ash checked in again. They'd talked about the attack, and she didn't want to keep bringing it up, but she need to be absolutely certain that Charlotte wasn't hiding anything from her.

"I'm fine. Truly. I told you, he was dead before he could do what he wanted and it's weird, I don't really feel a thing about it. Maybe I will one day, but right now, all I'm interested in is you. And us." She delivered another stinging dab.

"Okay, you've tortured me enough." Ash slid an arm around her waist and drew her down onto the sleeping pad. "Stop fussing and lie down. You're sicker than I am."

Charlotte didn't resist. She placed her prized box of wipes carefully in the corner of the tent, wrapped in a torn piece of cloth, and they both slid onto their sides, facing each other. Ash stroked back the dark strands that clung to Charlotte's forehead. She was flushed and her eyes seemed too bright.

"I don't know what's wrong with me," she said, meeting Ash's eyes. "Do you think its malaria? I don't see how it could be. I haven't been bitten and I think the DEET's soaked through every layer of my skin by now. All that mefloquine I've been taking is probably in my liver. Maybe that's why I'm sick."

Ash gave her a reassuring smile. "I'm sure you don't have anything serious. As soon as we're out of here, you'll be seeing a doctor."

Ash didn't want to scare her with speculation about the nastiest suspects. Malaria. Dengue fever. Ross River fever. She knew Charlotte must have had every shot in the book, so she couldn't have any of the other serious conditions. Chances were, she had picked up the flu that was epidemic in Pom. Her symptoms matched those Ash knew all too well from her own infrequent bouts. Locals seemed to build up a resistance, but visitors usually took the virus home with them as a parting gift.

Charlotte nuzzled into her shoulder. "Don't leave me again."

"I won't." Ash kissed her cheek. Her skin felt hot and damp. She would fall asleep soon, and Ash still hadn't asked the question she'd been putting off while others were around. Keeping her tone casual, she said, "There's something we need to talk about. Tell me how you met Bruce."

Charlotte stiffened in her arms. "How do you know—"

"I spoke with him. I think it's time you told me what's going on."

"I was going to as soon as you got here." Charlotte sounded upset. "I would have told you on the phone but with the batteries—"

"I know. It's okay." Ash rocked her gently. "I'm not angry. Just talk to me."

"When did you see him?" Charlotte demanded.

"It doesn't matter." Ash wasn't going to give her the opportunity to make anything up as she went along. She wanted to hear the unvarnished truth.

Charlotte sighed. "I was trying to find him yesterday when…it happened. It's a long story, but you know that night when I didn't come back and you were angry?"

How could she forget? "Yes."

"I was with him. He took me to see something."

She sounded so uneasy Ash assumed Bruce had mentioned the price on his head. "You can trust me," she said, wishing she didn't need to assert that to the woman she loved. But she had to be real. Charlotte knew enough now to wonder about anyone who worked for Tubby Nagle. "If I wanted to kill Bruce, I've had the opportunity. Last time I saw him, he was fine."

"Well, I know you probably won't believe me, but he's made maybe the most important discovery of this century."

"Bigger than your fig plant?"

"Huge," Charlotte said. "If I hadn't seen it with my own eyes I would just think he was crazy, and that's what the scientific community would think, too, if he tried to tell them. That's why he told me."

Her teeth were chattering and Ash could tell from her rapid, shallow breaths that talking was hard for her. "Slow down, baby," she said. "Just tell me what he's found."

Charlotte scrunched her face like she could hardly bear to give up the information. "He found little people who keep themselves young with an elixir of life from an orchid species unknown to science."

It was a movie. Ash hardly knew what to say. "Dwarfs?"

"No. A primitive species of human."

"Like the hobbit?" Concussion, she thought. It had to be.

"Yes, in fact, they are probably the same species, only living. Can you imagine?"

Strangely, Ash could, despite her immediate disbelief. She had heard stories about "little people" but had assumed they were simply the stuff of legends, like leprechauns in Ireland. But West Papua was perhaps the last place on earth where a tribe of people could exist, unknown to the outside world.

"So Bruce has contact with these people?"

"He took me to see them."

"Oh, God."

"I know." Charlotte placed her hand to Ash's face. "I was frightened to say anything. I'm so afraid of what could happen to them."

Ash could understand that. She wasn't sure what she would do with such knowledge either. "Thank you for telling me."

"I should have trusted you," Charlotte said. "I'm sorry."

"You did what you thought you had to. We all have to make decisions like that. I promise you something. Once we get out of here, I'll do anything I can to help. Okay?"

Charlotte made a small sound of relief. "I wish I knew exactly what to do about it. I mean, I have no proof, but Bruce expects me to get a huge company to do all kinds of things to protect the Fojas. They're not going to unless they think it's worth their while."

Ash smiled, finally clear about the Roo's gift. "Good news. Bruce has a plant for you."

"The orchid of life," Charlotte whispered in awe.

"He seems to think you'll know where to meet him so he can hand it over."

Charlotte nodded. "At my fig tree. I can take you there."

"Good. We're meeting him tomorrow morning."

When Charlotte was silent for a long time, Ash got worried and shifted a little so she could see her face more clearly. "Are you okay, baby?"

Charlotte clasped her hands behind Ash's neck. "I know I'm sick and it means you'll get my germs, but please kiss me."

"How can I say no to an offer like that?"

Laughing, Ash rested her lips against Charlotte's, then kissed her softly, content to feel the slow burn of desire and not act on it. There would be better times. Right now, she was thankful beyond measure. That she was here. Alive. And, most astoundingly, loved. After they made it off the mountain, she didn't plan on letting Charlotte out of her sight for a while.

"I want you," Charlotte murmured. "But I think I'd probably pass out."

"I want you, too." Ash kissed her again, this time making sure she would know how much she was desired.

When they drew back breathlessly, Charlotte said, "When I thought I'd lost you, I couldn't imagine living my life without you. I want us to be together, Ash." She worked her way more tightly into Ash's arms, until their bodies were fully entwined. "Will you take me home with you? After this."

There was nothing Ash yearned for more. She longed for Charlotte to be with her, in her home. To wake in the morning and find Charlotte in her bed. To share herself as she'd never shared herself with anyone. She knew it could not be permanent. Charlotte had a life far away and she would have to go back to it, but until then, Ash could have her all to herself.

Happier than she had ever been in her life, she said, "I'd love to take you home."

Charlotte gazed into her eyes, blinking away tears. "I love you."

"You've no idea what it means to me to hear you say that." Ash wished she had words for the feelings that washed over her. "One day soon, when we are not in a bug-infested tent and when you don't have a fever, I'll show you."

A tiny flicker of mischief entered her lover's expression. "Give me a clue."

Ash rolled her onto her back and let her weight descend just enough to make her squirm. "It's paradise," she said, planting small, urgent kisses over Charlotte's face and throat. "And loving you the way I do, feeling what I feel…that's more than paradise. It's a whole new way to live."

"Oh."

Ash couldn't resist that perfect mouth. Claiming it once more, she let herself imagine everything. Love. Marriage. A whole life together. She could see it all and, for once, she trusted.

CHAPTER TWENTY

Ash's aging houseboy, Ramon, padded across the wood boards toward Charlotte, carrying a tray. He set this down on the coffee table next to her and inquired in Tok Pisin, "*Kaikai long nait*, Charlotte?"

She smiled as she always did over the local pidgin for the late-night supper snack served without fail in this part of the world. It didn't seem to matter what crazy hours she kept, if she rose from her bed and went out onto the balcony, Ramon was always at her side within minutes, serving hot chocolate and some kind of dessert. This evening, he'd prepared the treat that had become a favorite of hers during the week she had been at the plantation, a warm black rice pudding made with coconut milk.

After she thanked him, he said in the careful English he used most of the time with her, "Ash will come this night."

"You think so?" She glanced back into her room to the mantel clock. It was eleven. The sun had set a long while ago and the Bismarck Sea was now inky black. Ash would not be driving her Land Rover along the unlit dirt roads to reach her home at this hour.

"We are waiting," Ramon said, as if this were reason enough for her to make the hazardous twelve-hour journey from deep in the highlands.

For the past few days she'd been in Goroka, meeting with a group of coffee growers. Her plan was to join a small consortium and obtain some additional supervision for her plantation during her long absences. She'd hired a manager who worked for several of the local owners, but she wanted to make sure the place didn't fall apart every time she left the country.

Charlotte sipped her hot chocolate and stared along the balcony to the French doors that led into Ash's bedroom, as yet unshared by her. It hadn't been their intention, but Charlotte's fever had kept them apart and she was still weak from her flu when Ash left for the meeting. But tonight, for the first time since they'd left the Fojas, she felt her strength returning, and with it, a need so powerful she had no idea how she was going to get through another night alone. She was therefore putting off bedtime, waiting for her head to droop and her body to sleep no matter what.

On an impulse, she moved inside once more and cracked open the door that joined her bedroom to Ash's. The rooms were halves of a master suite built by the German aristocrat who had once owned the plantation. Like many gentlemen of his era, he had not expected to share his wife's bed more than a few times a year. It was obvious from the design of the home that they'd lived separate lives. The front parlor was a room intended for needlework and pianoforte, and the library smelled faintly of cigars and whiskey. Its walls were crammed with books and tribal art.

Charlotte's bedroom was a pale, airy space trimmed with light-colored woods. The furnishings were too busy and flowery for her taste, the art on the walls insipid and the bed, a brass four-poster draped with heavy mosquito nets, rather a cliché. By contrast the room next door was darker and simpler in its décor. Ash had assembled a collection of unique handcrafted furniture, mostly in Australian timbers, and the paintings on her walls were innately sensuous. Nudes. Voluptuous orchids. Undulating modern landscapes. One innocent exception stood out, the portrait of a sweet-faced girl with flaxen braids and Ash's piercing cobalt eyes.

Charlotte stepped farther into the room and stared at the painting for a few minutes. She'd seen the same face in the library, in photographs on the desk and mantel. Emma, Ash's sister. They'd never spoken about her, except for brief allusions to her death. Like most aspects of Ash's life, family seemed to be off-limits. Charlotte hoped that would change sometime soon. She wanted to know who her enigmatic lover was, not just who she appeared to be.

With a weary yawn, she wandered over to the bed and parted the nets so she could sit on the edge. The cover was linen, in a pale coffee tone, the bedding ivory. She liked the clean simplicity of it. Everything in this room was unpretentious and practical. The choices said a lot about the owner. Charlotte ran her hand across the fine, cool cotton sheeting, then looked up with a start as the door swung open.

Ramon walked in carrying her robe and her house slippers. With a note of approval, he said, "You sleep here now."

"No." Charlotte shook her head. "I was just looking around."

He draped her robe over a small triangular chair in one corner of the room and indicated a tall, narrow dresser. "Tomorrow I will bring your clothes."

Charlotte had no idea what to say. She was still getting used to the idea of domestic staff. In the seedy decadence of this postcolonial nation, she knew it was taken for granted that those who could provide such employment did so. But she certainly didn't want a grown man running around after her like she needed to be waited on.

Ramon must have detected her unease because he said, "If you like, tomorrow I will bring *meri* for you. Wash clothes. Make hair very nice."

"That's a kind offer," Charlotte said. "But no, thank you. I don't need a lady's maid. I prefer to do those things for myself."

"*Oke.*" He placed the slippers next to the bed, but on the other side. "*Gut nait*, Charlotte."

She bade him good night in pidgin and slid resignedly beneath the covers, shifting across the bed to sleep on the side Ramon had designated. Ash's presence was tangible in the room and it comforted her. She smiled drowsily as Ramon moved around the bed, fixing the nets, then extinguished the lamps. The darkness here was intense, no city lights haloing the sky, no pinprick flickers in the distance. There was no road from Pom to Madang. You had to fly in, and the drive north along the coast to the plantation was on an unsealed road.

Charlotte could see why Ash had made her home here. It was beautiful, tranquil, and very hard to find.

❖

In the salmon tint of dawn, Ash stumbled in the front door and dropped her car keys on the hall table. She was dead on her feet. Ramon immediately rushed out of his room and tried to press hot tea on her, but she patted his shoulder and told him to go back to bed.

She showered quickly in the bathroom downstairs so the creaking harmonics of the upstairs plumbing would not disturb Charlotte. The hot water didn't do much for her tension, but she felt human again with the grime and sweat and layers of DEET scrubbed off. As she dried herself, she was foggily aware of her muscles twitching and her stomach churning. She'd grappled with this jumpy anticipation all the way home, trying not to be distracted as she drove along hair-raising roads through jungles full of dark, watchful eyes. There were places between here and Goroka where she wouldn't want to get a flat.

Although they made it a challenge to concentrate, she reveled in her feelings. She loved the thought of coming home to Charlotte. She loved knowing that she was only hours away from possessing her physically. Most of all she loved the sense of belonging, the unshakable certainty that her world would never be the same again, because Charlotte would now be a part of it.

Ash had no idea how they were going to manage the practicalities, and the truth was she didn't care. She planned on making it easy. No guilt. No pressure. She would let Charlotte make the rules. If Charlotte needed space and time, Ash would give it to her.

As for the here and now, Charlotte was upstairs, just a breath away. Ash's heart assaulted the walls of her chest. She dragged on a toweling robe and took the stairs two by two, intoxicated with a mix of exhaustion and helpless passion. As silently as she could, she opened Charlotte's door and peered into her room, seeking out the shadow of a dark head on the white pillows. The bed was empty.

Ash swung the door wide and stalked across the floor, trembling with the force of her emotions. In sheer panic, she wrenched the mosquito nets aside. The bed hadn't been slept in.

"Charlotte?" The cry escaped from her.

She strode to the antique wardrobe in the opposite corner and almost took the door off its hinges. As she plunged a hand into the void, she heard the bedroom tone she'd played over and over in her mind since the first time Charlotte spoke her name.

"Ash." She was standing at the connecting door. Her smile had a fuzzy half-awake quality. "I was in your bed."

As she came stumbling across the room in her white tank and panties, her guard down, her hair messed, Ash could hardly think straight. She caught her in a fierce embrace and for a long while they just stood there, clinging to one another. Then she remembered to be a responsible adult and asked, "How are you feeling? Has the fever gone?"

"I'm not sure." Charlotte drew back only enough to stare up at Ash with sleepy-eyed mischief. "I just got all hot."

"That sounds serious." Ash couldn't quite stop her voice from shaking. "Maybe you need to lie down."

She did, then, what any self-respecting Romeo would do. She swept Charlotte off her feet, one arm under her knees, and strode into the next room. There, she lowered her tenderly onto the bed. At least that was the general idea.

Only she didn't feel tender. The demure temptress sprawled against the fine pale sheets had summoned a predatory passion Ash could not fully control. And she didn't try. She wanted a home in Charlotte's arms without having to kill off parts of herself. She wanted Charlotte to know her. Yes…she'd just spent the entire trip home planning a slow, gentle return to intimacy. Maybe just kissing and cuddling to begin with. But now, she had a whole other agenda.

Uncertain how she should handle this homecoming all of a sudden, she moved onto the bed and propped herself on an elbow, leaning over Charlotte. "You know, we could give it a day or two. I mean, we're not going anywhere."

"Why wait?" Charlotte shifted so their bodies were aligned. Her eyes met Ash's. She said, "Do something for me. Please."

"Anything you want," Ash whispered.

"Be who you are." Charlotte ran a fingertip over Ash's lips. "I want to know."

Ash's throat closed. She caught Charlotte's hand, placed a kiss in the palm, then gently placed it on the pillow above her head. "I love you," she said, stripping away the fabric barriers between them. Her robe. Charlotte's tank and panties.

"I love you, too." Charlotte dropped her other hand up on the pillow. Both nestled above her head, the posture lifting her breasts. She opened her legs, offering herself.

Ash's breathing changed as she laid claim to the body she could not stop craving. Charlotte's nipples bumped against her palms. She was wet, the dark hair between her thighs clumped in a single mat. Ash had to be inside of her. She dipped her fingertips. A brief pang tore across her concentration as she thought about what had almost happened, how she wasn't there to protect the woman she cherished.

Charlotte's hands smoothed over her head, caressing their way down to her shoulders. "I'm yours," she said. "No one else's."

Their lips met and as Charlotte took her deep inside, Ash lost herself in the kiss she had always known was waiting for her somewhere. Their bodies rocked in wordless accord, gradually inevitably building the bridge to bliss they would soon cross together. Then all thought was consumed and they were groaning and shuddering, pushing and straining, harder and faster, until time seemed to stop entirely. Flushed and shivering, they stared at one another, eyes wide with knowing.

Ash thought, *This is how it's meant to be.* And in that second they collapsed in shuddering release, their hearts racing together, their bodies pulsing as one. Unable to move, unable to speak, they huddled together in the conspiracy of lovers, inscribing a language of their own in the secret hallways of their twinning souls.

When Charlotte could eventually summon words, she said in wonder, "It was always you. I always thought someone was out there, just waiting for me."

Ash nodded. "I thought that, too. And I kissed a *lot* of frogs trying to run you to ground."

Charlotte laughed and gave her a small prod. "Those days are over."

"Really?" Ash wanted to hear it. A promise—maybe not the ultimate promise. It was too soon for guarantees. Yet nothing about their love had happened logically so far. She ran caressing fingers over the soft planes of Charlotte's face and prompted, "Tell me what you want for this…for us."

Her lover angled her head pensively. "I want to say yes." She covered Ash's hand with her own. "Whatever this chance is, I want to take it."

Ash brushed her lips over Charlotte's in silent affirmation and once more they devoted themselves to pleasure. Hours later, when they woke from another sated sleep, Charlotte followed the tattooed jade tendrils along Ash's left shoulder to the white lotus flower above her collarbone. Now that she was close enough to kiss the skin it adorned, she could finally read the inscription.

No one can flee death or love.

About the Author

New Zealand born, Jennifer Fulton resides in the Midwest with her partner, Fel, and a menagerie of animals. Her vice of choice is writing; however, she is also devoted to her wonderful daughter, Sophie, and her hobbies—fly fishing, cinema, and fine cooking.

Jennifer started writing stories almost as soon as she could read them, and never stopped. Under pen names Jennifer Fulton, Rose Beecham, and Grace Lennox she has published fifteen novels and a handful of short stories. She received a 2006 Alice B. award for her body of work and is a multiple GCLS "Goldie" Award recipient.

When she is not writing or reading, she loves to explore the mountains and prairies near her home, a landscape eternally and wonderfully foreign to her.

Jennifer can be contacted at jennifer@jenniferfulton.com.

Books Available From Bold Strokes Books

More Than Paradise by Jennifer Fulton. Two women battle danger, risk all, and find in each other an unexpected ally and an unforgettable love. (978-1-933110-69-1)

Flight Risk by Kim Baldwin. For Blayne Keller, being in the wrong place at the wrong time just might turn out to be the best thing that ever happened to her. (978-1-933110-68-4)

Rebel's Quest, Supreme Constellations: Book Two by Gun Brooke. On a world torn by war, two women discover a love that defies all boundaries. (978-1-933110-67-7)

Punk and Zen by JD Glass. Angst, sex, love, rock. Trace, Candace, Francesca...Samantha. Losing control—and finding the truth within. BSB Victory Editions. (1-933110-66-X)

Stellium in Scorpio by Andrews & Austin. The passionate reuniting of two powerful women on the glitzy Las Vegas Strip, where everything is an illusion and love is a gamble. (1-933110-65-1)

When Dreams Tremble by Radclyffe. Two women whose lives turned out far differently than they'd once imagined discover that sometimes the shape of the future can only be found in the past. (1-933110-64-3)

The Devil Unleashed by Ali Vali. As the heat of violence rises, so does the passion. A Casey Clan crime saga. (1-933110-61-9)

Fresh Tracks by Georgia Beers. Seven women, seven days. A lot can happen when old friends, lovers, and a new girl in town get together in the mountains. (1-933110-63-5)

The Empress and the Acolyte by Jane Fletcher. Jemeryl and Tevi fight to protect the very fabric of their world…time. Lyremouth Chronicles Book Three. (1-933110-60-0)

Erotic Interludes 4: Extreme Passions. Thirty of today's hottest erotica writers set the pages aflame with love, lust, and steamy liaisons. (1-933110-58-9)

Storms of Change by Radclyffe. In the continuing saga of the Provincetown Tales, duty and love are at odds as Reese and Tory face their greatest challenge. (1-933110-57-0)

Sleep of Reason by Rose Beecham. Nothing is as it seems when Detective Jude Devine finds herself caught up in a small-town soap opera. And her rocky relationship with forensic pathologist Dr. Mercy Westmoreland just got a lot harder. (1-933110-53-8)

Grave Silence by Rose Beecham. Detective Jude Devine's investigation of a series of ritual murders is complicated by her torrid affair with the golden girl of Southwestern forensic pathology, Dr. Mercy Westmoreland. (1-933110-25-2)

Erotic Interludes 3: Lessons in Love ed. by Radclyffe and Stacia Seaman. Sign on for a class in love…the best lesbian erotica writers take us to "school." (1-9331100-39-2)

Justice Served by Radclyffe. Lieutenant Rebecca Frye and her lover, Dr. Catherine Rawlings, embark on a deadly game of hide-and-seek with an underworld kingpin who traffics in human souls. (1-933110-15-5)

Justice in the Shadows by Radclyffe. In a shadow world of secrets and lies, Detective Sergeant Rebecca Frye and her lover, Dr. Catherine Rawlings, join forces in the elusive search for justice. (1-933110-03-1)

A Matter of Trust by Radclyffe. JT Sloan is a cybersleuth who doesn't like attachments. Michael Lassiter is leaving her husband, and she needs Sloan's expertise to safeguard her company. It should just be business—but it turns into much more. (1-933110-33-3)

Chance by Grace Lennox. At twenty-six, Chance Delaney decides her life isn't working so she swaps it for a different one. What follows is the sexy, funny, touching story of two women who, in finding themselves, also find one another. (1-933110-31-7)

Stolen Moments: Erotic Interludes 2 by Stacia Seaman and Radclyffe, eds. Love on the run, in the office, in the shadows…Fast, furious, and almost too hot to handle. (1-933110-16-3)

Distant Shores, Silent Thunder by Radclyffe. Dr. Tory King—along with the women who love her—is forced to examine the boundaries of love, friendship, and the ties that transcend time. (1-933110-08-2)

Beyond the Breakwater by Radclyffe. One Provincetown summer, three women learn the true meaning of love, friendship, and family. (1-933110-06-6)

Safe Harbor by Radclyffe. A mysterious newcomer, a reclusive doctor, and a troubled gay teenager learn about love, friendship, and trust during one tumultuous summer in Provincetown. (1-933110-13-9)

Honor Reclaimed by Radclyffe. In the aftermath of 9/11, Secret Service Agent Cameron Roberts and Blair Powell close ranks with a trusted few to find the would-be assassins who nearly claimed Blair's life. (1-933110-18-X)

Honor Guards by Radclyffe. In a wild flight for their lives, the president's daughter and those who are sworn to protect her wage a desperate struggle for survival. (1-933110-01-5)

Love & Honor by Radclyffe. The president's daughter and her lover are faced with difficult choices as they battle a tangled web of Washington intrigue for...love and honor. (1-933110-10-4)

Honor Bound by Radclyffe. Secret Service Agent Cameron Roberts and Blair Powell face political intrigue, a clandestine threat to Blair's safety, and the seemingly irreconcilable personal differences that force them ever farther apart. (1-933110-20-1)

Above All, Honor by Radclyffe. Secret Service Agent Cameron Roberts fights her desire for the one woman she can't have—Blair Powell, the daughter of the president of the United States. (1-933110-04-X)